OLD ACQUAINTANCES

Richard: middle-aged and increasingly listless, looks back on his life. The brightest spot was a brief teenage affair in Scarborough with Nancy, a girl from a childrens' home. Richard still remembers her with passionate longing.

Helen: abandoned by her mother at the age of twelve, Helen doesn't really know who she is. Her stepfather cannot answer her questions and she yearns to find her real parents. When she discovers an old postcard from Scarborough, Helen goes in search of her past.

Nina: after an eventful life, Nina is settled in leafy Surrey, intent on becoming a writer. But Nina finds she can't shake the past off as easily as she thought.

OLD ACQUAINTANCES

Old Acquaintances

by

Frances Anne Bond

Magna Large Print Books
Long Preston, North Yorkshire,
BD23 4ND, England.

British Library Cataloguing in Publication Data.

Bond, Frances Anne
    Old acquaintances.

    A catalogue record of this book is
    available from the British Library

    ISBN   0-7505-1503-1

First published in Great Britain 1999 by
Severn House Publishers Ltd.

Published in Large Print 2000 by arrangement with
Severn House Publishers Ltd.

Magna Large Print is an imprint of Library Magna Books Ltd.

Printed and bound in Great Britain by
T.J. (International) Ltd., Cornwall, PL28 8RW

Prologue

Should auld aquaintance be forgot
                                    Robert Burns

1956

Richard Argyle, cosy beneath his thick blankets, lay flat on his back in bed and stared at the night sky through the round window above him. The weather was frosty and the stars winked and glittered as they gazed back. He looked for the well-known stars and spotted the Great Bear.

Everyone knew where that was. But he knew the lesser stars, too. He had been nine years old when he first became interested in astronomy and now he was fifteen, almost sixteen. He'd asked his parents for a decent telescope for his birthday. They hadn't actually said yes, but he thought they would probably buy him one. They were good about things like that.

If only they were a bit more ... he stirred restlessly in his bed. If only they were more like the parents of his classmates at the college, but they were too busy with the hotel to be interested in him or to go out socialising and to college events. Just as well, really. They were so old. It was an embarrassment being seen with them.

He pushed away a feeling of guilt. They weren't that bad. If only they didn't treat him like a child. But he'd be grown up soon and then things would get better.

Astrology. He had scorned the very word until two weeks ago. How could the study of stars foretell the future and interpret dreams? But then the girl had come. Richard moved restlessly in his bed as he thought about her. Hell, he thought of little else. She was a torment and a delight. She had turned him from a boy into a man.

She had come into his life from the residential home on the outskirts of the town. Richard had eavesdropped on his mother's telephone conversation so he knew all about her. She was an orphan and had been taken into care when she was nine. Kids in care grew up fast. Everyone knew that. Even his education, since he joined the college, had grown enormously. Now, thinking about the girl, something else was growing enormously and he was both proud and alarmed. He swore under his breath and his right hand slid down beneath the bedclothes and encircled the source of agitation. He sighed gustily and closed his eyes, shutting out the stars. He wanted to think of Nancy.

She knew all about it, he was sure. Those sideward glances beneath heavy eyelids when she passed him in the hallway. The way she swung her hips when he was around. She knew what she was doing to him. But did she really like him or was she making fun of him? If only he could talk about her to his schoolmates but he couldn't. He just couldn't.

He never said much at school, but he listened. His classmates were always talking about sex. Some girls would do it as early as fourteen, they said. Especially the girls at the Home. All those boys and girls living so closely together. Of course they did it.

Oh, God. If only he could do it with Nancy.

Richard's hand moved more quickly.

His parents didn't see a thing. They wouldn't. They were dried up, past it. He bet the last time they did it was when he was conceived. His hand slowed. Not a pretty thought. But Nancy ... she was pretty. She was made to be loved. No, she wasn't pretty. She was beautiful. But what sort of future did she have? She had come to them as a skivvy. She did the rough jobs. She even made up the fires. The guests liked the old-fashioned values so that meant poor Nancy had to lay the fires.

And yet his parents had gone all self-righteous when they employed her, saying they were giving the girl the chance of earning a decent living. That's what they did at the Home, kept the kids until they were fifteen, then they got rid of them. The boys went to be army cadets and the girls into menial jobs.

If only he were older, he would love and take care of Nancy.

The door creaked and opened a crack. Richard's eyes flew open. He yanked the bedding over the lower part of his body. If his mother...

But the shape in the doorway was not his mother.

'Nancy.' He sat up now, totally unaware of the bedclothes falling away.

'In the flesh.' She laughed softly. Her bare feet made no sound as she came towards his bed. She sat down by the side of him, put out her hand and touched his chest. Almost conversationally, she whispered, 'I knew your skin would be nice to touch.'

When he did not speak she gave him her devastating sideways glance and murmured. 'Do you mind me visiting your room?'

'God, no.'

His voice was hoarse. The top of her prim, white cotton nightdress was unbuttoned. He could see the curve of her breasts. They rose and fell in unison with her soft breathing.

She tilted her head and stared up at the

window. 'So, this is where you do your stargazing?'

He nodded, overcome by the soft line of her throat, the whole, inviting whole of her.

'Could I star-watch with you?'

Totally unable to speak, Richard reached for her hand. She curled her fingers around his wrist and, without words, slid into bed beside him. She laid her head upon his pillow and looked up at the sky.

'I wish...' she said. Her voice was a whisper.

She turned so she was facing him. She smiled and it was a smile so unguarded, so moving he wanted to weep. She slipped her arms around his neck and moved closer to him.

'I've seen you watching me. You like me, don't you?'

She read his answer in his eyes and went on, her voice small.

'I like you, too. If you want...' Her voice faded as her lips touched his.

The heavens wheeled round him as he was enveloped in the softness of her. As he fell into paradise his last conscious thought was:

I'll never be more happy than at this moment.

1967
'Come on, Helen. This is supposed to be a treat.'

Helen Morrison waited as her mother flourished the complimentary ticket beneath the nose of the man in the kiosk, then tagged along behind as she swept through the entrance into the zoo.

Nina Morrison looked around. The rain was beginning to fall and most of the animals in the paddocks had huddled together beneath trees or were disappearing into their sleeping quarters.

Determinedly cheerful, she waved her hand to the right.

'Look, over there. It's a reindeer. Makes you think of Christmas, doesn't it?'

Helen studied the animal. 'It's not a reindeer. It's an elk, I think.'

'Well, it's a deer, isn't it? The same family?' Nina's cheerfulness took on a ragged edge. 'Why do you always have to be so...'

'Awkward?' There was a gleam in Helen's eye. 'Maybe I take after my dad?'

Nina stared down at her. Her eyes had narrowed. 'I wouldn't know.'

There was a short, tense silence before Nina's face relaxed. She sighed, bent down and ran a finger round the back of one of her high-heeled shoes.

'I knew I shouldn't have worn these,' she said. The tone of her voice was conciliatory.

Helen responded to her mother's offer of peace. 'No, you shouldn't have, but you look so good in them.'

Nina smiled. 'Look, love. It's starting to rain really hard. Let's go and find Frank and he'll take us round the parrot house.'

Helen's flush of pleasure faded rapidly. 'I hate the parrot house, Mum. It's noisy and smelly and I hate it.' Helen's voice broke on a high note.

Her mother looked at her with some consternation. 'What's up with you, today? Are you feeling ill or something?'

Helen lowered her head. 'No.'

'What is it, then? What's got into you?'

Helen wouldn't look up. She shuffled her feet. Finally, she whispered. 'Are we going to move in with Frank?'

Now it was Nina who took time to answer. 'Well, it's still early days.' Her voice was evasive. 'But he's a nice man. You know that, Helen. I thought you liked him?'

'I liked Michael but you know what happened...'

Nina drew herself up. 'I told you not to mention his name. Not ever.' She looked at Helen's pale face and, somewhat diffidently, put her hand on her shoulder. 'Frank's been good to us, Helen.' She sighed. 'I'm not getting any younger, you know. We can't go racketeering around for ever.'

Helen wiped her nose on the back of her hand. 'I know. But do you have to be with a man. It's better when there's just the two of us.'

'Maybe, for you.' Nina's voice sounded funny. 'But when you grow up, you'll know more about things.' When Helen did not answer, she sighed and put a hand on her shoulder. 'Come on. At least in the parrot house we won't get soaked. That's something, isn't it?'

One

'This comet will change our lives. You mark my words.'

'What?'

Richard Argyle, shrugging into his sports jacket and checking his pockets for the keys, eyed his cleaning lady with a certain amount of irritation. She was a good woman and fond of him. Sometimes, she turned up with a nice piece of steak or a punnet of early strawberries because she knew he enjoyed a treat. He always paid her for her purchases, of course, and he appreciated her kindness, even though her actions made him feel rather like an elderly stray puppy, but he did wish she wouldn't get so enthusiastically involved in his life. Also, she talked too much.

Sensible conversation Richard enjoyed, often pined for, but Amy's conversation was rarely sensible. If she had been born in an earlier century, he often thought, Amy would have been burned for a witch but, since it was the late 1990s, she got away with spreading her wild predictions.

On the days she visited Richard's house, Amy insisted on reading aloud his horoscope from her daily newspaper. Sometimes she asked him about his dreams and interpreted them. But her latest obsession was the recently sighted Hale Bopp comet.

Richard was sick of hearing about the damned thing.

He said. 'Of course our lives will change, Mrs Langton. Last week you told me the end of the world was nigh. I'm still waiting for that.'

'Ah, Mr Argyle. I made a pig's ear of that, didn't I?' She shrugged her heavy shoulders. 'Got my portents mixed up a bit that day. But there's no wonder, there's such a lot happening, up there.' She gestured towards the ceiling. 'Still, it's well proven that this comet signifies change for the better. I've consulted the tarot cards and read lots about it in the newspaper.' She paused. 'A proper newspaper, like the ones you buy, Mr Argyle. Those big pages are devils to control.'

'I don't need change, Mrs Langton. I'm perfectly happy as I am.' Richard moved towards the door. 'I'm going out, now.'

'Usual routine. Lunch about one thirty?'

'Yes. And you don't have to stay. Get yourself off home.'

'I'll set it out in the kitchen, then. All you'll have to do is put a light–'

'Yes, I know.' He nodded to her and hurried from the room.

How did she think he managed on the days she didn't come in?

Closing the front door carefully, Richard paused for a deep breath and then found himself contemplating the view before him. Ah, but it was a bonny day. His gaze ignored the wide road lined with parked vehicles directly in front of him. He focused on the landscaped gardens beyond the road, the masses of flowers bright under the summer sun, the Victorian railings and, beyond, glimpses of the bay below with its blue, blue sea.

On such a perfect day the North Sea resembled a mill pond. It was so calm he could see quite clearly the couple of yachts, busily tacking from side to side, hoping to catch and utilise the slightest puff of wind. Watching their white sails, Richard decided, with a conscious effort, that he would try to make this day a happy one. The dark moods that possessed him from time to time must be banished. There was no reason for him to be depressed. He was solvent and likely to become more so since the work on the flats had finally been completed. The decorators had finished the ground floor ten days ago. He could start advertising for new tenants.

The thought of people in his home again pleased him. The place was much too big for him to rattle around in all on his own. He'd have to be careful to pick the right kind of tenants. When everything was settled he might treat himself to a holiday abroad. He'd thought about it long enough. It was time for action. After all, he was fifty-six years old. Not ancient, by any means, but it didn't do to hang around too long. Deciding where to go would be tricky, though. Hand on heart, he couldn't immediately think of one place that stood out from all the rest.

Amy Langton's nonsense came into his mind. 'This comet will change our lives.' He rubbed his chin and smiled. Maybe he wouldn't have to decide. Maybe fate, alias the comet, would do it for him. He set off to do his shopping.

After collecting an ordered book from the library, Richard called in at the supermarket on the main street. Amy Langton saw to his regular weekly shopping but he wanted some decent cheese and a couple of bottles of wine. The thought of Amy's choice in such matters made him wince. Some things you had to do yourself.

The supermarket was cheerfully lit, not too busy and the background music was bearable. Richard relaxed as he collected his wire basket and headed for the drinks section. After choosing the wine, he picked out stilton and mozzarella, then paused and looked around. A nice-looking woman in a light green overall was walking in his direction. Obviously noting his hesitation, she stopped and enquired whether he needed any help.

'No, thanks.' He coughed. 'Well, now that you asked, perhaps you could tell me where I would find Basmati rice and, possibly, some sun-dried tomatoes in oil?'

The woman, who he guessed to be in her late forties, smiled. 'Of course. I'll take you there. Follow me.'

'Oh, there's no need...'

But she was already striding out whilst making conversation with him. Over her shoulder, she said: 'So you're a gentleman who knows how to cook? That makes a change.'

'No. Not really.' He lowered his head and coughed again. 'I sometimes catch the cookery programmes on the box and very occasionally I have a go at one of the more straightforward recipes, but I have more failures than successes.'

'Well, at least you try.'

She was setting a brisk pace. Richard quickened his step to keep up and found he was watching her trim, overall-covered behind as it swayed slightly from side to side. He felt a flicker of interest which, paradoxically, depressed him. How long had it been since he had even talked to an attractive woman? He frowned, thinking: God, why am I so pathetic? Getting excited at a chance encounter with a shop assistant.

Again, he thought: I'm not old. There are pop stars in leather pants jigging around on stage who are older than I am.

Stopping in front of a display of rice and pasta packets he stared into space and wondered if things would have been different had he stayed on at work. Perhaps retirement had delivered him early into the 'slow' lane? But really, he had been given no option. His parents had needed him.

'The sun-dried tomatoes are further along this aisle.'

'What?' He stared at the assistant. 'Oh, yes. Thank you.'

'That's all right. Good luck with the recipe.' A cheery smile and she was gone.

Richard picked out his purchases and then took himself and his wire basket to the checkout where his depression sneaked back as he stood behind a young female with a shaven head. She wore a tight sweater, denim shorts and what looked like labourers' boots.

He looked at the row of butterfly clips at the back of her ears and decided he needed a drink. His mood improved as he pushed open the door of the Stafford Arms. He had been looking forward to a chinwag with the landlord but there was a stranger behind the bar. The tall young man stepping forward to serve him observed his look of surprise and explained.

'Bill Bretton's away today. I'm standing in for him. Annual Outing, see. That's why we're so quiet.'

Richard didn't see. Mystified, he asked, 'What outing?'

'Trip to Thirsk Races. You know.'

Richard didn't know. Pulling a handful of change from his jacket pocket he tossed it on the counter and ordered a double whisky. When the drink was placed before him, he slopped a little water into the glass from the jug on the bar and retreated to a corner table. Sitting down, he glanced around and concluded the race trip must have been popular with the regulars. Apart from the barman and himself, the only other occupants of the room were a man studying his newspaper at the end of the bar and two old guys playing dominoes at a corner table. Concluding his sweep of the bar Richard's gaze dropped into contemplation of the contents of his glass.

Over the past twelve months it had become a habit to call in at the Stafford after his shopping trips. He enjoyed a lunchtime drink but for the last six or seven months the main attraction at the Stafford had been the burgeoning friendship between himself and Bill Bretton, the Stafford's landlord.

At first there had been the usual pleasant nod of greeting from mine host then, after a couple of visits, an enquiry as to his health or a comment on the weather.

Richard's replies had been non-committal. Easy conversation was hard when one was used to being solitary. But gradually, the slight awkwardness faded as the two men discovered they had opinions in common. Even better, as time went by, they found subjects they could amiably disagree about. Bill's easygoing nature soothed down Richard's self-conscious prickles and soon friendly arguments became enjoyed by both. They progressed to taboo subjects; politics, immigration laws, even the damned silly new traffic system recently forced upon motorists. Richard became so involved in their discussions he went so far as to search out newspaper articles backing his views to present to his friend.

Sometimes he was disappointed to find the pub was just too busy for the landlord to engage in conversation. On those days, Richard would nod, down his two whiskies and take himself off home. On other days, when trade was slow, Bill would see him enter, hand over the care of the bar to one of his staff, pull himself a pint and come and sit with Richard. Within a few minutes they would be winding each other up and laughing and, when that happened, Richard was delighted, although he never allowed his pleasure to show. God forbid.

So why, if Bill was his friend, had the race trip not been mentioned?

Richard gulped down the contents of his glass and clenched his teeth as the liquor hit the back of his throat. Of course, he was hardly a regular at the pub. He only called in once a week. He never played for the darts or dominoes team and he didn't mix too easily with those who did. But, surely, Bill could have mentioned the trip.

Staring down into the empty glass, Richard decided he was being stupid. Bill knew what he was like. He had realised that he had no interest in backing horses. Come to think of it, the idea of a coach trip with people he hardly knew sounded horrendous. Nevertheless, he decided to have another drink. After the third he thought he'd better go home.

Sober enough to know he shouldn't drive he left his car in the pub car park and walked. He walked slowly and carefully. He'd be late in but no one would care. Amy Langton would be long gone, please God. She wouldn't be in until Tuesday so he could get rid of the evidence of wasted food. As for his cooking, that could wait.

A young woman passed him walking in the opposite direction and he smiled at her thinking how pretty she looked. She smiled back. She was wearing a dress, summery and floaty and strappy sandals encased her small feet. The dress was white with a multicoloured pattern on the flowing skirt and he thought that, perhaps, after years of women dressing like commandos, things were changing back to how they used to be.

It was too late for him, of course. His womanising days had been short, and were long over with, but he felt glad for the younger chaps. Head down, he mused on how the world had changed.

It was common knowledge that they 'got their leg over' more now than in previous times but to his mind it was swings and roundabouts. The first kiss, the holding of hands had been sweet. Old-fashioned courtship had bestowed pleasures. After his too-early first sexual encounter, he had avoided women like the plague, but his courtship of Jill had been sweet.

He had been so proud of being seen out with her. She had been taken for a model once; so slim and fine-boned. Nowadays, models sported rings through their navels and worse. Richard sighed, remembering the young woman with the shaven head in the supermarket. Maybe it was just as well he was getting old.

Climbing the four steps to his front door, he searched in his jacket pocket for the door key. The sun was still shining but he did not turn, as he had previously, to admire the view. He squinted to put the key in the lock, opened the door and stepped inside the wide, cool, quiet hallway. He climbed the stairs that led up to his first-floor flat. Once inside, he dumped his shopping bag on the floor of the kitchen, ignored the food laid out and ambled into his bedroom. He drew the curtains, slipped off his shoes and flopped on to the bed where he lay on his back and stared up at the ornate high ceiling above him.

This room had been the master bedroom when the house had been a small but exclusive hotel. Only important people had slept in here. His parents had occupied the bedroom above this one and he, as a boy, had slept in the attic, close to the stars. Lots of people in the house then. Now there was just him. His eyes closed and a moment later, he was snoring.

Two

It was as if the train were tired and knew it was reaching journey's end. It slowed, jerked slightly and then dawdled its way into the station. The brakes sighed as the engine came to a halt.

Helen Stephens was already on her feet. She couldn't contain her impatience. Ever since she had found the crumpled envelope containing her mother's photograph, trapped at the back of a drawer in her step-father's flat, she had been determined to come to this seaside resort. She needed to learn the truth about the past. She needed, even more, to exorcise ghosts and start afresh – but it had taken longer than she had anticipated. Three years of frustration, a broken marriage and a period of painful re-adjustment. But never mind. She was here now.

Her wide, thin mouth tightened and she stared at the group of old ladies twittering ahead of her. They were blocking the exit from the train. They filled the narrow space between the seats, fussing over carrier bags and luggage, fixing the young man standing directly behind them with gimlet glares, defying him to leave without first lifting down their remaining cases from the rack and helping them to get them down on to the platform.

She couldn't cope with this delay. Helen reached up, swung her own case down from the luggage rack and turned towards the alternative exit at the other end of the carriage. Despite the heavy case she walked with long strides, her wide shoulders moving easily.

This exit was less congested. A couple of minutes and Helen was out of the train and standing on the platform. She looked around her. This station was a far cry from the one she had left earlier in the day. King's Cross had been a hive of activity, full of jostling people, the sounds of multinational chattering and tannoyed information. This station was quiet. There were only a couple of uniformed staff on duty watching the travellers alight.

The elderly ladies had finally negotiated the steps. They burst out of the train creating a widening pool of colour as they spread out along the platform. Bright in their summer suits of green, red and blue, their voices sounded loud in quiet air. They reminded Helen of a flock of noisy parrots. She had lived in many places during her youth. One place was Chester and, in-evitably, soon after arriving there, her mother had found a man.

This one had a job at the zoo. In the early stages of their relationship, before the rot set in, in order to ingratiate himself with her mother he was always bringing them free entry tickets. They had visited the place regularly. Helen had never liked zoos, even when she was a small girl. The stupid people poking sweets and bits of sandwiches through the bars of the cages, even when notices everywhere asked them not to. The frantic scampering of the smaller monkeys and their sad eyes when they stilled and watched the gathering crowds outside. Most of all she had hated the bird section and the greedy-eyed, noisy inhabitants of the parrot house.

Once, she had thrown a tantrum outside the gates, hoping her mother would agree to a cancellation of their visit, but her rebellion wasn't strong enough. She knew she would fail. Had her mother ever listened to her when there was a new man on the scene? Her mother, when she was in her prime, had been like a beautiful animal herself sleek, powerful but not tamed, not in a zoo.

Helen sighed. The station was emptying. She watched the last couple of backpackers disappear. She savoured the silence. A porter nodded to her as he trundled away a trolley piled high with mail sacks. Now she was alone. She liked that. She felt like a

31

turn-of-the-century traveller taking a long deep breath before starting to climb his mountain or cross an uncharted desert. She was on a journey of exploration.

She glanced at the sky which was, beginning to darken. She breathed in fresh air and her lips turned up at the corners with pure pleasure. For a long time she had lived in London and she now realised how much she was looking forward to a walk by the sea. The thought calmed her. She grasped her suitcase and strolled through the station exit. No one bothered her. Her ticket had been checked on the train.

On the station forecourt, she spotted three taxis waiting hopefully. The driver of the first cab leaned sidewards and swung open the door.

'Need a ride?'

'Yes.'

Helen put down her case and took a letter from her shoulder bag. She showed it to the taxi driver. 'I want to go to this hotel.'

The taxi driver took the letter from her and studied it. 'Yes, I know the place. About ten minutes' ride.' He handed the piece of paper back to her.

'Fine.' Helen got into the back of the cab, leaving the driver to stow her suitcase in the boot.

He did so. As he got back into the driving seat and started the car, he asked: 'Come from London?'

'Yes.'

'Here on holiday, I suppose?'

She wondered what business it was of his but a glance at his face through the car mirror showed he was simply making polite conversation.

'Yes,' she said.

'Brought good weather with you.'

'Um.'

In truth, Helen was resisting the temptation to shiver. In London the weather had been heavy and humid. The temperature in this north-eastern resort must be at least ten degrees lower, she thought. She was wearing trousers and a short-sleeved blouse. The front windows of the cab were wound down and the breeze blowing into the back of the car felt cold. Surreptitiously, she rubbed the goose bumps appearing on her upper arms and wished she had put on her jacket. She wished, too, that the taxi driver would stop talking, although the Yorkshire accent made a change from the Londoners' twang. She shut out his voice and gazed from the window at the passing scenery.

The cab had turned off what she thought was the main thoroughfare. They were now driving along a narrow road flanked by rows of tall terraced houses, well maintained and in a hotchpotch of designs, but close together. Gardens were tiny or non-existent and cars were parked everywhere.

For the past five years, Helen had lived in a small but comfortable flat close to St James's Park. There had been a long climb up narrow stairs to reach her home but the view from her windows had compensated. Now she felt a sudden wave of nostalgia for her bedroom view of green spaces and the glint of water.

I'm crazy, she thought; I can't possibly be missing London already. But London was familiar to her. She had a routine to her life there. She enjoyed her work and she had a couple of good friends. In this place, everything was unknown. How long would it take, she wondered, how long to fill in the missing spaces in her life?

The taxi driver pulled up outside her destination. The hotel looked expensive, more expensive than she had anticipated. Had she read the terms in the brochure correctly? She'd got her credit cards, of course, but she couldn't afford to go mad. Supposing her search took longer than she anticipated? Maybe she would need to find somewhere less expensive to stay?

The taxi driver was already out of the cab. He collected her case from the boot, but still she sat there, staring up at the hotel. Suppose she couldn't trace the clues hidden in her mother's postcard – or find anyone who recognised her photograph? Suppose

Nina had just spent the day here, not found herself a job as Helen had surmised?

Should she try the Town Hall to see if she could check the census for the time in question, or would the public library be a better bet?

The taxi driver opened the door, giving her a curious look. She forced a smile to her lips, climbed out and searched in her bag for his fare.

'Thank you.'

He grinned, got in his seat and drove away.

Helen picked up her suitcase and walked towards the hotel. The feeling of excitement she'd experienced in the railway station had disappeared.

Maybe, she thought, I *am* crazy.

It was odd, waking up in a strange room, in an unfamiliar bed and in a town where not a soul knew you. Helen had moved around all the time as a child but always, there had been Nina. When her mother was present, other people had been superfluous. Anyway, Nina had the knack of drawing people to her. No matter how many times they moved, before a week had passed, they had acquired a posse of acquaintances. There would be their new landlady; they always lived in rented accommodation. Doorstep conversations with the milkman – Nina was an early riser. The man or woman running the nearest corner shop would be targeted and cultivated so that, after a couple of days, they would slip Helen the cigarettes her mother desired, even putting them on the slate.

Helen stretched out in bed remembering – how her mother had set her stamp of personality on the string of anonymous rented rooms with incredible ease. A trip to the local market and she would return clutching potted plants and a package of richly coloured material to drape around the window. Or, if she couldn't find the material she wanted, she would buy something else – crockery decorated with wild poppies, a huge floor cushion or a fine green glass goblet with a crack running through it.

Once she returned to their one-roomed bedsit with a sentimental Victorian picture of family life. Helen had been too young to realise the picture was idealised but she was old enough to grasp that the smirking golden-haired child seated on her mother's lap enjoyed a more secure life than she did.

Remembering the picture, the grown-up Helen smiled, then frowned and wriggled her toes beneath the quilt. As she had grown, Nina had become increasingly dismayed at her only child's tendency to cling to familiar people and places.

'You're certainly not like me,' she would complain.

'So? Maybe I take after my father's side of the family?'

Helen would smirk as she said the words, and other words like them, but beneath her cheek and surly manners she hid sorrow. Why did Nina never, ever, talk about the man who had fathered her? Was it all too painful or had she simply forgotten? Had her father been a smooth, devious gentleman who had seduced a young girl?

Helen knew her mother had been a month short of her seventeenth birthday when she had given birth – still only a girl herself. Perhaps the man had been married with a family already? Perhaps it was worse. Nina liked a drink. She liked dancing. Perhaps she had been drunk at the time and didn't even know the man's name. No, that wasn't fair. She wouldn't think that of her mother, despite her desertion.

Helen ran her fingers through her tangled hair and sat up in bed. She turned her thoughts to more tranquil matters. The room she occupied was pleasant enough. Decorated in restful colours it was at the back of the hotel and therefore quiet. Reaching for her watch on the bedside table, Helen blinked when she saw the time. Nine thirty. Surely not? She screwed up her face in disbelief. She never slept later than seven thirty. True she had spent time walking round the town yesterday but even so... Maybe the sea air had tired her.

She realised she was hungry. Why had no one tapped on her door, told her breakfast was ready? But then, this isn't London, she reminded herself. She sat up, slung her legs over the bed and tried to locate her slippers with her toes. Finding them she slipped them on to her feet, stood up and walked towards the window. She drew the curtains back and looked out. The road that ran behind the hotel looked tidy, respectable and anonymous.

Arriving in London, Helen had worked for three years at a publishing firm and during that time had spoken to many authors. Writers, she had found, often spoke glowingly of the small towns in which they lived and complained about the drab, anonymous nature of London. She had never agreed with their views. She enjoyed living in London and during the first twelve years, when she had lived alone, she had rarely felt lonely.

Ultimately, she now thought, as she moved over to the shower unit, it didn't matter *where* you lived. You go where the job is, you find a place you can afford to live in. You try and turn the new place into a home, you acquire hobbies and, hopefully, a lover, and you think you're set for life. If it doesn't work out that way, you move and start all over again. The place it all happens in doesn't matter one fig.

Beneath the pleasantly warm water, soaping her arms and neck, she continued her line of thought. We establish patterns for ourselves to make us feel secure. We're like all the other animals, really. We mark out our own territory and our own boundaries. Was Nina brave, or feckless, moving on so often, even leaving her lovers and her daughter behind her?

She grimaced. Where was Nina's present territory and how would she react to a grown-up daughter ringing her doorbell?

The water began to run cold. Helen, shivering, abandoned the shower. She wrapped herself in the bath towel and moved over to the wardrobe. Her keys lay on the table by the bed, the black lettering on the red tag showed up clearly. Following her divorce she had not changed her name. Laziness, she supposed and she had felt so tired. Stephens sounded well enough and it went with her Christian name.

Morrison had never been a name to fire the blood. Actually, she had often wondered if it was really her mother's maiden name but she guessed it was. If Nina had picked out a name for herself it would have been something flamboyant. No, Stephens she would stay. It was a reliable, pleasant name but not as anonymous as being a Smith or Brown.

39

A crease appeared between Helen's forehead. That word again. Never mind, she could stand being anonymous but if she...

A knock at the door. Signs of life other than herself. Helen jumped, snagging a fingernail on the zip of her skirt as she finished dressing. 'Damn.'

A cough and then a timid voice. 'Could I do your room, miss?'

'Just a minute.'

Helen bit the ragged end of her nail then hastily buttoned up her blouse. She unlocked the door.

A young girl dressed in a blue overall smiled at her.

Helen stepped back to let her in. The girl brought a vacuum cleaner into the room before addressing her.

'If you're nippy, you'll just make breakfast. They serve until ten on Sundays.'

'Thanks. I *am* hungry.'

Helen grabbed her purse, left the room and went quickly down the stairs to the ground floor. Hopefully it would be a full English breakfast. She could pig out and then skip lunch. Since she had decided to come on this – she paused – quest, yes, quest was a good description, she felt hungry most of the time. She would have to watch herself. However, she had started from a low base. She was naturally a slim woman and the stress resulting from her divorce had made her almost skinny. She could allow herself a few weeks of excess. Ploughing her way through eggs and bacon she wondered how long it would be before she returned to London.

She would have to find somewhere else to live. The lease had almost expired on the flat. She had wondered if her ex-husband had deliberately delayed the revelation of his betrayal to coincide with the need to move. Had he hated her enough to do that? No, she was being paranoid.

Doggedly, she swallowed a mouthful of toast. A friend who lived in Swiss Cottage had offered to put her up on her return to London. It would mean a different route on the Underground when she went to work. She'd miss her favourite busker. She didn't know his name or anything about him but a certain empathy had developed between them. He was a skinny young man with his hair caught back in a ponytail. He played the violin exquisitely. Dashing through the tunnel, her briefcase thumping against her thigh, she had caught a snatch of his music and had stopped to listen. Why, she had wondered was he not in a dress-suit in the string section of an orchestra. Too much competition, she supposed.

That was the trouble nowadays. Why was she, a slim, not unattractive woman of forty going through a divorce after ten years of marriage? Too many blonde twenty-year-olds seeking a man. Was it that simple?

Helen took a mouthful of stewed tea. After her first encounter with the busker she had started saving loose change in her jacket pocket. When she dropped the coins on to his coat, laid on the floor awaiting donations, she had been absurdly pleased to see him smile. After that, he always nodded to her. The old newspaper seller parked at the exit of the Underground also acknowledged her. Sometimes, he called her 'darling'. If she had five minutes, she stopped and talked to him, about the weather or the state of the country. It didn't matter that his breath whistled through his teeth during their discussion. When you were alone in the world, people like the busker and the newspaper seller gave you ballast. Made you feel real.

Well, now she was proving that she was real. She had taken leave of absence and come to this seaside town in Yorkshire to find... She pushed away her empty plate. What was she hoping to find? A loving mother to soothe away her pain. That was a laugh. But when there was no one in the world who you could relate to, somehow you lost your sense of humour.

Three

After three days of enquiries, Helen reached a dead end. She grimaced as she left the Town Hall and wandered down to the beach. She had known her task would be difficult. How could it not be? From her birth, until the day her mother finally ran out on her, the two of them had moved around. Change had been a way of life and Helen couldn't begin to remember the various towns in which they had lived. No wonder retracing the past was so hard.

What *was* surprising was the affection her mother had retained for Scarborough. She'd had no time for beach holidays but she had told Helen, 'Scarborough was a great place for teenagers. Lots of nice young men on holiday, looking for a girl.' Laughing, she had added: 'I'll take you there, one day.'

She never did, but now Helen was here and she had accomplished nothing. She had thought her mother had been born in the town but there was no mention of her in the records. Helen had contacted the schools with no success. No one could trace a Nina Morrison. She was advised that the upheaval of the change to comprehensive schooling had caused many earlier records to be destroyed.

'You'd have done better if you'd been researching earlier times; Church schools have records going back hundreds of years. And, of course, Morrison is a pretty ordinary name.'

Helen had now reached the bottom of the main street. She crossed the road and turned her face towards the sea, resting her arms on the iron railings fronting the beach. A warm breeze touched her face and lifted the hair on her forehead. As she became aware of the soothing wash of the incoming waves, she tried to let the tension ease from her form. She closed her eyes for a moment.

For a few seconds she relished peace before childish shouts disturbed her. She rubbed her chin, an irritated gesture and glanced round. The tide was encroaching on the sand, the waves advancing in a pincer movement on discarded sandcastles, snatching at the toes of sturdy grandmothers holding up their skirts and attempting a last paddle with chunky toddlers.

Close by, a family was packing up their belongings. The father struggled with deckchairs and his wife or, Helen smiled slightly, his partner, stuffed spades and buckets into Tesco bags. Their two little boys were running wild at the water's edge, their shouts mingling with the shrill barking of their mongrel dog.

Helen watched them. Never one to cluck over babies, she could appreciate the boys' energy and exuberance. There had been a time, short but intense, when she and Phil had tried for a baby. It hadn't happened and neither partner had seriously considered taking the matter further ... perhaps if they had...

Helen frowned. As things turned out, it was a damn good job they didn't.

The mother subdued her boys with a few sharp words and Helen continued to watch them as they toiled up the nearest slipway. The eldest boy had the excitable dog on a lead. Off the beach, the mother dealt with sand-filled sandals and the smallest boy threw an awesome tantrum. Helen decided she was fortunate to be childless. She could never summon the patience to be forever mopping up after children. Then, she thought, perhaps I am beginning to change into Nina.

Not that she could remember playing on a beach. Oh, Nina had taken her places, but they had been adult places. They visited the cinema and, when money was available, went to restaurants. Even picnics, Nina found distasteful, so it was easy to see why she wouldn't venture on to a beach. Sand in the sandwiches!

So why had she returned to this place after

running out on her daughter? Helen blinked her eyes. Had her mother come back here to try and find someone? Who? And how could *she* ever find out anything? The truth was that Nina's whole life had been an enigma to her daughter. She hadn't an earthly as to where to go from here.

The tide had now systematically destroyed the sandcastles and the breeze was chilly. Helen left the almost empty beach to the raucous seagulls and headed back up the street towards town.

What, she wondered, should she do this evening? In a seaside town, or any town in which you were a stranger, the evenings were not easy to handle. And then, as she continued to walk up the main street, she spotted a large building almost opposite the railway station. *The Stephen Joseph Theatre.*

Of course. She stopped. Remembering. A theatregoer, she had read with interest of Alan Ayckbourn's quest to find a new venue for his 'Theatre in the Round' in Scarborough. She remembered he had attempted to buy, through various fundraisings, a closed-down Odeon cinema he hoped to transform into a playhouse. He had obviously been successful, for there it was, in front of her.

Not exactly beautiful, was her first thought. She surveyed the construction, the stark black and white tiling. But then, she frowned, didn't the article she remembered say this building, now before her, had been one of the first luxurious cinemas to be built in the art-deco style in the mid-thirties? Ayckbourn's intention had been to restore the original ambience of the thirties and he had done just that. Good luck to him. His success had solved her problem as to what to do this evening.

She crossed the road to study the billboards. Yes, a new Ayckbourn play was being performed at the moment. Now, if there were tickets available... She pushed open the swing doors and walked over to the ticket booking area.

'Any seats left for this evening?'

She crossed her fingers. Please, not another night of television!

'We're just about fully booked, I'm afraid. New play, you see.'

'Oh.' Helen was surprised at the level of her disappointment.

'Well, I suppose I could book a seat for another night?'

'Just the one?'

'Yes.' She caught the faint sigh of apology in her voice and frowned.

The young man looked up from his computer. 'If it's just the one, there may be a chance... Yes.' He smiled as he studied his screen. 'I think we can accommodate you.'

'Really.' Helen suppressed a wry smile.

For once, being single meant a plus. In many ways, she reflected, her married years had been lonely. The sex had been good at first but that soon faded and there had been precious little else they agreed on. They had both enjoyed the theatre, however. And now, on her own again in a darkened theatre or cinema, she would have to stop herself from turning in her seat to make a comment to some stranger. She would forget there was no one there to listen to her.

'Sorry?' She jumped when the booking clerk spoke.

'Yep. There is a single. Look, there.' He tapped his biro pen on the screen. 'And it's a good seat.'

'Then I'll take it. Thanks.' She smiled and was gratified when she saw him blush.

'My pleasure.'

Long afterwards, feeling a cold sweat break out beneath his shirt, Richard occasionally remembered he had almost opted out of that particular theatre outing. Had Amy Langton's comet been looking after him? Or maybe, it was because he had met Alan Ayckbourn and he liked the man. He liked his down to earth attitude and what he was attempting to do. On the other hand, he wasn't all that keen on his plays. The fault, Richard acknowledged, was his. Ayckbourn's plays were famous around the world but his comedy was a bit grim. Richard liked plays like *The Deep, Blue Sea* and he adored Noel Coward's stuff. Just old fashioned, he supposed.

He was a supporter of the theatre, though. He had joined the fund-raising organisation called 'Friends of the Theatre' in the early days and he went to most of the plays because he had a season ticket; and even if he found some of the 'comedies' rather depressing, he felt as though he was doing his bit. He had dithered about the present offering but it had received wonderful reviews and he thought he needed to get out, so he put on his second-best suit and took himself off to the theatre.

He was late arriving which brought him out in a sweat. He finally found a parking spot, rushed off to the theatre, trotted through the empty foyer and galloped up the steps, praying he could get to his seat before the house lights dimmed. This theatre in the round set-up could lead to embarrassing moments if you didn't watch out. Once the lights dimmed, the actors often made their entries down the same stairs which a latecomer might be dashing up. Nasty!

Of course, the house lights and suchlike were timed, but mishaps did happen. Three years ago Richard had come face to face with an actor descending the stairs and declaiming the opening line as he scurried upwards after finding himself in the wrong aisle. It had been the most embarrassing moment of his life, or almost.

Fortunately, this time things went smoothly. As a matter of fact, the person sitting next to him was just settling in her seat. Obviously she had been in a rush, too. The lights dimmed and Richard, with a sigh of relief, stretched out his legs. His right foot banged against a woman's shoe and she muffled an involuntary exclamation.

'Oh! I'm so sorry.'

The woman's darkened profile turned towards him and she whispered it was probably her fault... 'Encroaching on his space'.

'Oh, no.'

Richard admired her voice, He caught the trace of perfume in the air and of this, too, he approved. He glanced again at her profile and looked forward to the lights going up so he could see her properly.

Richard liked women and, without false pride, knew that they liked him ... initially. On first acquaintance, he had no trouble conversing with them so long as the topics were superficial. Women, he knew, enjoyed small courtesies, particularly if they were of a certain age. He had no ulterior motives when he first engaged them in conversations. If too much interest showed in their faces, he ran a mile. But he loved to see a not-so-young but still pretty face light up at a genuinely meant compliment.

Richard liked the way women's thoughts jumped about as they talked. He liked the way they used their hands to emphasise an important point. As long as the rapport stayed tenuous he enjoyed their company very much. So when the first act finished, he took a cautious sidewards glance. She was younger than he had thought and she was pretty. She was also looking at him so he looked away but said: 'Are you sure your foot's all right?'

She nodded. 'It's fine. Anyway, it *was* my fault. I encroached on your space. I'm tall, you see.'

'Ah. Yes.'

A moment's silence as they assessed each other.

She was middle thirties, he guessed. Slim, with broad shoulders, she was attractive rather than pretty. Her suit was plain and smart so she was probably in Scarborough on business. Not a tourist, then. Perhaps she was involved in the world of the theatre? He debated whether or not to ask her. Her expression was friendly, so he did.

She laughed. 'Oh, no. Nothing so interesting. I work as a clerk in an insurance brokers.'

'In Scarborough?'

'No. In London. I'm here...' She paused. 'On a personal matter.'

'Oh.' He was intrigued.

There was a short silence.

She looked around the audience and then back at his face.

'Are you enjoying the play?'

He hesitated. 'I think so.'

He saw her eyebrows rise. Her eyes were quite striking. There was something about them... He realised he was staring and he blushed.

'What about you?'

'Oh, I'm hooked. I'm a great fan of Ayckbourn.'

Richard rubbed his nose. 'I am too, I suppose.'

'You don't sound too sure?'

'Well, I think it depends on my mood when I come here. Sometimes I find his work funny and profound, at other times I find him depressing. I suppose that's part of his skill.'

A little crease appeared between her eyebrows as she considered his words. 'Yes, I can agree with what you said. His plays can be unsettling.'

'Oh, I don't know. Probably talking rubbish.' Richard eased his collar with a finger. Why on earth had he spoken out like that. To a complete stranger? He cleared his throat. 'You mustn't mind me. It's just, I find them somewhat intimidating. My life has been so simple. Dull, almost. Maybe that's why I feel a little uncomfortable with his plays.'

'Why uncomfortable?'

She was looking straight at him. Why did he find her gaze so unsettling? Where had he seen eyes like that?

Richard's cheeks grew warm and with growing horror, he heard himself say:

'I'm not sure. Only, sometimes. I have an uneasy feeling I'm a real-life counterpart for one of his stranger characters. You know the sort of thing; the boring chap who's completely oblivious of what's going on around him. The comic figure, but he isn't comic, is he? He's more tragic.'

The memory of his exclusion from the pub's racing trip bit into his consciousness. He'd never gone back to the pub. Bill probably hadn't even missed him.

'You know the scenes we remember the most.' Richard spoke rapidly. 'When someone comes visiting and people hide behind their curtains rather than entertain them.'

Her soft chuckle shocked him into silence. He thought: What the hell am I going on about? He forced himself to look into her disturbing hazel eyes. A twinkle lurked within their depths and he felt better – foolish but less tense.

She shook her head, a puzzled expression

on her face. 'How can you possibly equate yourself with characters like that.'

'Oh, I didn't mean...'

'You did, and it's ridiculous.' Her face sobered. 'The mere fact that you can articulate such thoughts and say them to me, a stranger, shows how far away you are from being such a character. Can't you see that?'

'I've never done or said aloud anything like that before.' Richard studied his hands so he didn't have to look at her. He would have liked to have said she did not seem to be a stranger to him, but he could not.

The colour rose in his face as he struggled to understand his uncharacteristic outburst. 'Please,' he said. 'Do forgive me for talking total rubbish.'

'It was interesting.' Her face was serious now but her look was not unfriendly. 'I'd like to talk some more but,' she lowered her voice, 'the lights are going down. Maybe we can continue this discussion later, in the bar?'

Without waiting for his reply she settled herself back into her seat and stared down at the stage set, the entering actors.

Richard's glance also took in the stage set but he couldn't concentrate on the play. In the bar? Surely, she'd be off like a shot at the end of the performance. If she didn't, he must. He had behaved like an idiot. But she

54

had suggested a drink and he was loath to part with her. Just why? He didn't know.

One of the actors gave a sharp cry and the audience laughed. Richard forced his attention back to the play. If they were to continue their conversation later he wanted his part in any discussion to be considerably more coherent and sensible.

Four

Hurrying round the supermarket, Richard failed to notice the friendly smile bestowed on him by the woman who had helped him on his last visit. He was busy concentrating. He was keeping his mind focused. He added a pack of assorted biscuits to the items already in his wire basket but decided against buying wine or cheese. Helen was coming round to see him for a specific reason. Coffee, biscuits and a possible plan of campaign, that was their itinerary. Pity, really. He suppressed a sigh. Still, she *was* coming. That was a bonus.

Last night, leaving the theatre, he had, naturally enough, asked if he could escort her back to her hotel. No ulterior motive, of course. That's what a man of his generation did as a matter of course. Unfortunately, she, just as naturally, refused.

'Absolutely not.' She had smiled at him, kindly. 'There's no need. I live on my own in London, remember? I'm perfectly capable of looking after myself in Scarborough.'

'Perhaps.' He remembered he had felt embarrassed but unaccountedly had insisted. 'But, as you may have realised – thinking of our conversation in the bar – I gladly admit to being a little old fashioned in my ways. It would make me feel much happier if you allowed me to escort you to where you are staying.'

She had studied his face and then acquiesced.

'OK.' She had grinned. 'But only because it's only a ten-minute walk from here. I don't want to take you out of your way.'

The streets had been quiet. There was music and noise from a pub they passed but only a few pedestrians about. There had been a recent shower of rain and the pavements were damp. The sound of their footsteps echoed.

'We keep in step well.' After some moments' silence, Richard felt he ought to break the silence. 'I suppose that's because we're almost the same height.'

'Yes.' She glanced sideways at him. 'I think you're about an inch taller.'

She smiled then paused to look into a lighted-up shop-window selling porcelain. Richard took the chance to study her profile. A straight, well-shaped nose, broad forehead and generous mouth. He wondered why he felt such a rapport with this young woman. It wasn't a sexual feeling. He'd given up all that stuff long ago and even in the past, when he had indulged in a few romantic daydreams – he grimaced

– he had always been attracted to soft, rounded blondes; the kind of woman who needed looking after. Helen was nothing like that.

Helen turned her head and glanced at him. 'Penny for them?' She enquired.

He cleared his throat.

'I was thinking about what you said, about coming here to try and trace a long-lost relative?'

'Yes.'

Her voice warned him off. She probably regretted confiding in him. He could understand that but he wanted to make her realise he was pleased she had done so. If he dared, he would like to offer to help her.

'I've been thinking. Could you tell me a little more about the person you're looking for? Of course, if you don't want to, I'll understand.'

He stopped. God. His voice was going squeaky. He cursed himself. 'The thing is, I think I could help you. I was born in Scarborough. I've lived here all my life. I know an awful lot about the place and the people who live here. Local stuff. Stuff you might not find in the library.'

Her footsteps slowed then stopped. As she turned towards him, he saw the frown lines on her forehead. He knew her answer before she spoke.

'Oh, no. It's kind of you to offer, but it's a

personal matter. Anyway, it would be an imposition. I couldn't encroach on your time.'

He sighed, an irritable sigh.

'Time, my dear, is one thing I have in abundance. Please reconsider. I would really like to help.'

She started to walk again. 'It's good of you, but I think not. You see,' her voice lowered. 'I'm trying to trace my mother. I last saw her when I was thirteen. We were living in Chester then. Before that, we'd moved around a lot. I can't remember half the places we lived in but I do know she had spent time in Scarborough when she was young and she had an affection for the place. It seemed a good place to start looking.

'I've also got a couple of clues which link her to this town.'

'You're looking for your mother?' Richard's face had creased with concern. 'Oh, I'm so sorry. I didn't realise...' He stopped. Started again. 'Somehow, I imagined a more distant relative, a long-lost cousin or aunt; even an ex-boyfriend ... but your mother?'

She frowned. A look of impatience made her face look hard.

'Not everyone has a life as settled as yours has obviously been. Things happen in some families. It doesn't mean...' She broke off and stared across the street.

'We're here. That's my hotel.' She gestured to a building across the road, looked back at Richard. 'Thanks for seeing me home.'

'My pleasure.' Richard, caught a note of dismissal in her voice but was loath to accept it.

'I'd still like you to consider my offer of assistance.'

'I think not.' She took a step away from him. 'It's my search and my business.' She smiled a tight smile, as if apologising for the harshness of her words. 'After all,' she added, in a milder tone of voice. 'You have your own life to lead.'

'Yes, that's true.' Richard nodded. 'You're also right about my life being settled. I'm lucky.' He shrugged his shoulders. 'I've always had a good job. A bit boring, but then, I managed to retire early. I looked after my parents, but lots of people do that. My ex-wife's re-married. Lives abroad, so there no hassle there.'

Without realising, his voice had risen, not a shout but louder than he naturally spoke.

Helen, watching his face, took a step backwards.

'I live on the Esplanade,' he continued. 'In a house I grew up in. I occupy a delightful flat overlooking a wonderful view of the sea. I even have a cleaning lady. Trouble is,' he raised his voice. 'I'm bored to tears with my settled life.'

He was silent.

They looked at each other.

In a slightly abstracted way, she said: 'I'm sorry.'

He felt the tide of colour rise from beneath his collar. He hung his head. 'No. I am. I'm behaving completely out of character tonight. I can't understand it.' He grinned, shamefaced. 'Maybe I'm getting flu.'

She nodded but she seemed to be miles away.

'I'd better go.' Richard turned away, hesitated, then turned back.

'I've recently been feeling I should involve myself more in something worthwhile.' He shrugged. 'I'm not the type of man to start driving trucks to Africa, stuff like that.' A self-disparaging smile tilted his mouth. 'But I could help you. However, you don't know me. It was a stupid proposition. I understand your reservations. So I'll just say good luck and goodbye.'

As he turned away, she made a small noise and put out her hand. He looked back at her. Somehow, something had changed. He didn't know how or why.

'You're a good man, Richard.' She smiled at him. 'Maybe I *should* let you help me?' She paused. 'You say you live on the Esplanade?'

He nodded.

She thought for a moment, then nodded her head. 'OK. I accept your offer.'

As he struggled to understand her change of heart, she went on. 'If you have the time, can we meet tomorrow?'

Richard blinked. 'You're sure?'

'Yes. I'd like your help. As you say, you know Scarborough inside-out. I'll fill in the details about the circumstances and it's up to you whether or not you want to be involved. If you decide against it, there'll be no hard feelings. So, shall I come and see you tomorrow?'

'Yes. Yes, of course.' Richard felt in his pocket for a pen and something to write on. 'But wouldn't it be better if I take you out for lunch? Neutral ground, so to speak.'

A gleam of amusement appeared in her hazel eyes and softened her tense expression.

'I'm not Little Red Riding Hood and I'm positive you're not the Wolf. I'd rather speak to you in private, actually. I'd ask you to come to the hotel but the place is full of visitors. Your place would be best. What time would suit you?'

'Oh, let me see. Anytime, really. How about eleven. Come for coffee.' Amy would have gone by then, he thought.

'Fine.' She smiled and held her hand out for the address.

She arrived exactly at eleven, five minutes after the departure of Amy Langton.

Richard thanked God for small mercies and stood back from the front door to allow her to enter. She was in no hurry. After greeting him, she had retreated back from the short flight of steps and stood on the pavement looking up at the house. She studied the frontage for a minute and then, catching Richard's eye, hurried back up to him, a half-smile on her face.

'Imposing residence.' She glanced past him, into the hallway. 'Which flat is yours?'

'First floor. It's the best one.' Richard ushered her across the hallway towards the graceful, arching stairs.

She was taking her time. She stopped to admire the stained glass landing-window which flooded the hallway with light and projected rainbow glints on to the black and white tiles on the floor of the hallway.

'There's one thing I don't understand,' she said, as she followed him up the stairs.

'What's that?'

'Didn't you say you grew up in this house?'

'Yes, I did.'

'But it's divided into flats?'

'It wasn't when I was young.' He glanced over his shoulder. 'I'll tell you about it.'

Richard flung open the door to his flat with justifiable pride. Surely, Helen would respond positively to the subtle colours, the comfortable yet elegant furniture. Then there was his glorious view.

She disappointed him. She walked straight through the flat without comment. Studied the view briefly, then sat down in a comfortable chair and stared at him.

'Tell me,' she said.

Suppressing his disappointment, Richard sat down opposite and obliged.

'My father grew up in the hotel trade. This house was a hotel, originally. Not a large one, of course, but it was high quality and well thought of in the thirties. A lot of wealthy people came to Scarborough at the time. Dad worked at the Grand before he came here as Manager and worked for the owners of the property. He'd just married my mother then. It was 1937, if I remember rightly. I was born in 1941.' He smiled. 'Bit of a surprise, I was. They hadn't reckoned on children.'

Helen nodded. 'Go on.'

'Because of the war, my father was working in an aircraft factory when I was born. He was in Hull. This place had been requisitioned by the Army. Later, when peace was declared, my parents came back and took up their old jobs. They saved hard and finally bought the hotel from the original owners.

'It was a big step up for them, of course,

but dreadfully hard work. They got the place cheap because it hadn't been treated too well by the Army personnel. A lot of cleaning up to be done and then they had to rebuild the trade. They worked so hard, there wasn't room for anything else. I don't remember it as a happy time.'

'But you stayed here?'

'Oh, yes. I was their only child. When I was young I had been rather delicate. I gave them a lot of worry. I couldn't leave them when they needed my support. But I had a good job, too. I worked in the Borough Treasurers' Department at the Town Hall.'

Richard shrugged. 'It wouldn't have been my first choice for a career but it was a safe job and I was good at figures.'

She nodded. 'So, how long was this place a hotel?'

His brow creased. 'Well, let me see. When my father died, I took early retirement to help my mother. We struggled on until—' he did some mental calculations '—1980. That's when we converted to flats. My mother lived until she was a very old lady but she was never reconciled to the change-over. Still, it had to happen.'

Helen nodded. 'This is certainly a beautiful flat.'

He smiled. 'Yes, I am pleased with it. As you'll realise, I've just had the whole place refurbished. I couldn't do it until mother passed on. It's taken a lot of money but it's been worth it. I'm still getting used to the changes. The decorators only moved out ten days ago.' He paused. 'I should start looking for new tenants.'

'Yes.' Helen agreed, but from her face he thought she looked miles away.

He apologised. 'I'll stop talking now. We must think about your plan of campaign.'

She was quiet for a moment, then asked: 'Was this place a hotel in 1969?'

'Oh, yes. The late sixties were a busy time for us.'

She nodded but remained in deep thought.

Richard stood up. 'I'll go and make the coffee.'

When he came back with the tray, she was more animated. She accepted her coffee and biscuits and began to talk. She sketched in her early life. Richard learned about the constant travelling; the long, or sometimes short stays in boarding houses, flats and bedsits. Her mother's jobs included being a barmaid, waitress, shop assistant, cleaner. Helen's experiences were of always being the new girl, starting halfway through the school term. Briefly, she sketched in the difficulty of making friends and later, the hard experience of leaving them behind when another move occurred.

Richard's kind heart was touched. 'I can't

help wondering why you *want* to find her?' he ventured.

'Oh, no.' She was shocked. 'I loved her. She was fun. She was bright, too, but she had no qualifications so she couldn't get a decent job. She always looked after me OK. She knew all kinds of games and, if she had money, she spent it. We went to some really good restaurants and she took me to see all the latest films.'

'But then she left you.'

Helen examined her hands. 'Mum had to have her own space. There was something almost *fey* about her. Even the men,' she sighed. 'Nina wasn't really promiscuous, not really.'

When Richard remained silent, she gave him a cool glance.

'You don't understand. How can you? You see, when Nina had a boyfriend, she stayed with him quite a long time but there always came a time when ... she got restless, you see. When she met Frank, I thought she would settle down. He was quite a lot older than her and he was kind. He was the only one she married.'

'Oh, she did marry him?'

'Yes. I wasn't happy about it at the time but, when I got to know him better, I grew to respect him.'

'Is that why you stayed with him, when your mother left?'

She nodded. 'It was an unusual situation. There was no one else, you see. Social Services talked about a foster home for me but none of the ones available were really suitable and I said I wanted to stay with him. We both thought Nina would come back.

'Finally, after a lot of meetings and reports, it was agreed. They kept their eyes on us, of course. We had to be careful. It was sort of him and me against them, so we joined forces.'

Richard, seeing how tightly Helen clutched her empty coffee mug, stood up.

'More coffee?'

She shook her head.

'May I ask, after all these years, why it is now you've decided to try and find your mother?'

'Oh, different reasons.' Avoiding his gaze, Helen opened her handbag and searched for something.

'I stayed with Frank until I was seventeen and finally gave up on the idea that I would ever see Nina again. I moved to London to work. I had secretarial skills and Frank helped me financially for the first year. After a couple of jobs, I settled into what I do now.'

'Which is?'

'I work for a company of insurance brokers in the City. Started small, but I've a good job now.'

She had found what she was looking for. She took an envelope from her handbag.

'Frank died of cancer four years ago,' She bowed her head. 'I was surprised how much I missed him. We were never demonstrative with each other. Anyway, I went back to his place to sort things out. While I was there, I found this envelope. It was wedged behind a drawer full of old bills, renewal policies, things like that. I'd never seen it before.'

She opened the envelope and handed to Richard an old, faded, postcard and a crumpled photograph.

Richard studied the postcard first. It was a view of Scarborough taken from the South Cliff. He realised the picture must have been taken very close to his property. The datemark had been obliterated. He began to realise why Helen had been interested to learn he lived on the Esplanade.

He read the scrawled message on the back.

Sorry about the row. I had to come here, where it all started but I'll contact you. See you, soon. Nina. xxx

He looked back at Helen. 'Surely, you don't think your mother may have stayed here?'

'It's a possibility.' Her voice was defensive.

He shook his head. 'I don't know, Helen. It seems a very slim chance.'

'Well, there's a possibility she stayed in this area. She must have liked the South Cliff, otherwise, why would she have picked this postcard?'

'Half of the postcards of Scarborough are taken from the South Cliff, there's such fantastic views. Anyway,' he paused, 'I gather your mother never had a lot of money. I doubt she would have been able to afford to stay here.'

'I thought about that, but if Nina had money, she spent it. She would rather have stayed two days in a good hotel rather than a week in a B & B. I thought, perhaps you could look through your old registers, if you still have them. It's a long shot, but worth a try.'

Richard sighed. 'It's more than a long shot. It would be a miracle if...' he broke off. 'It wouldn't even help you. Even if I turned something up, we'd have no records as to where she went from here.'

'I know, but it would be a start. It would give me hope and then, with the photograph ... there are a few details on that which might be a clue.' Helen leaned forward in her chair. 'If you look in the left-hand corner, you'll see part of a billboard.'

'I suppose I could turn up the old registers. They're in the attics, I think...' His voice faded.

'Richard?'

He continued to stare at the snapshot.

The silence in the room grew and spread like a bottle of spilt red wine.

'What's wrong?'

'Nothing.'

'Something's the matter.'

'No, really.' He blinked and passed his hand over his face. 'Your mother...' He tried again. 'Your mother looks very young.'

Helen's face was puzzled. 'Yes, I suppose she did. She was only just seventeen when I was born.'

Richard stood up, dropping the snapshot which fell on the floor. 'Would you excuse me for a moment?'

'Yes, but...' Helen started to get up. 'You're very pale. Are you sure you're all right?'

'Oh, yes.' He tried to smile. 'I take pills for a minor complaint. Nothing serious, but if I miss one I feel a little woozy. I'll just go and get...'

Hurriedly, he left the room.

Helen went and picked up the photo. Richard's behaviour was a little peculiar but if he would go and get the registers, she could put up with a certain degree of strangeness.

Richard sat on the side of his bed, his head in his hands. One glance at the photograph had been enough. He had recognised her at once. He was positive it was her. Nina, Helen's mother, was the girl who had haunted him for years. Only he had known her as Nancy.

Nancy! He rubbed his burning eyes until they hurt. He had carried the memory of her in his heart ever since that awful day his parents had caught them together and thrown her out. It had changed his life and his relationship with his parents.

'Corrupting our son!' his mother had screamed, her face distorted with fury.

But it hadn't been like that. He had tried to make them see. It had been a wonderful, magical experience. Nothing else that had happened to him had been half as good. Perhaps that's why his marriage had failed? No one could be like Nancy.

Tears were steaming down his face. He had to get a hold of himself. He had to go downstairs. Nancy's daughter was downstairs and he had to face her.

He hauled himself from the bed and went over to the washbasin, ran the cold tap and splashed water on to his face. Grabbing the towel he faced his image in the mirror. Anguished, hazel eyes gazed back at him. His dark hair lay damp on his broad forehead. He leaned closer. Another shock hit him. He realised why he had found Helen's face familiar.

Five

The next day, there was a tap on the door of Helen's bedroom. It was the young girl in the blue overall. During her stay, Helen had become friendly with her. Whatever time of day, she always seemed to be on duty. Helen hoped she was getting a fair wage.

'I've got a message for you.' The girl spoke in a conspiratorial whisper.

'Have you?'

'Yes. There's someone downstairs asking for you.'

The girl waited and then, apparently disappointed at Helen's lack of reaction, she said: 'It's a fella. Quite old, but nice-looking.'

'I see.' Helen chewed her lip, considering her best line of action.

The messenger frowned. In a voice that brooked no nonsense, she asked. 'Well then, what shall I tell him?'

'Tell him...' Helen dithered. She didn't want to be rude. Richard had been so nice at first but then, after hearing her story, he had suddenly changed. He had rushed her out of the room. He couldn't wait to get rid of her. Of course, he did say something about feeling unwell and he had looked pale, but people didn't get ill that quickly. On the other hand, he had been the only person she had met who was interested in her search and there was no doubt about it: she needed help.

'Tell him ... tell him I'll be down directly,' she said.

The young girl smiled.

'We might as well go in here.'

Greeting Richard with a composure she did not feel, Helen led the way into the hotel lounge which was fortunately empty.

'Thank you for seeing me.'

She gave him a cool look. 'Would you like to sit down?'

He nodded but she noticed he remained on his feet until she was seated.

There's nothing wrong with his manners, she thought, with a softening of mood. She also noted the dark shadows beneath his eyes and the exhausted look on his face. She felt obliged to ask him about his health.

'You look so tired.'

'I'll be all right.' Richard sat in a chair next to her. He passed his hand over his hair. 'Unfortunately, I suffer from migraine attacks. They come on very quickly but after a night's sleep I start feeling better. By tomorrow, I'll be fine.' He shifted in the chair so that he could see her better. 'I apologise for my behaviour yesterday, but the thing is,' he paused, 'when the migraine hits me, the only thing I can do is go straight to bed.'

'I see.' At a loss to think of something to say, Helen studied her hands.

Richard leaned towards her.

'I must have seemed very rude. But now you see there was a reason for it, I hope you haven't changed your mind about my helping to search for your mother?'

'It's kind of you,' Helen swallowed. 'But I think I have.'

She spread her hands out. 'I keep thinking, there's nothing at all to involve you in all this...'

She was too intent on picking the right words to see a spasm of pain flicker across his face.

'And now you tell me you suffer from migraine attacks. Surely, it would be stupid to involve you in such–'

'The headaches are very infrequent.' He interrupted her. 'And there is no obvious reason for them. Stress, isn't a factor. Indeed, it's quite the opposite. If I'm absorbed in something, I rarely experience them.' Richard's face grew tense. 'Please reconsider.'

'I don't...'

'Before you finally decide, may I look at the photograph of your mother again?'

'What's the point?'

He managed a smile. 'Something caught my eye. In the background. A poster, I think. Maybe it offers a clue?'

Helen gazed at him with suspicion for a moment and then relented. 'All right. You might as well have another look.' She took the photograph from her bag and handed it to him, saying: 'It *is* a poster, but you can only see part of it.' She watched his face. 'It's advertising a pop concert. There's what appears to be a list of groups but you can't read the details properly. I suppose the concert was held in Scarborough but,' she frowned, 'if you look there,' she pointed, 'you can make out the word Liverpool.'

'Yes.' Richard nodded and looked at her. 'Why is this a clue to your mother's whereabouts?'

Colour flowed into Helen's face. 'If the concert was on in Scarborough while my mother was here, she would *definitely* have gone to it. Nina was absolutely crazy about the Mersey Sound; she loved the Beatles. Alternatively, if the concert was taking place in Liverpool – if that's why the word is on the poster – then she might have decided to stop off there on her way back to Chester. They are not so far apart, after all.

'Mind you, if you think about it, the word is unlikely to indicate the location because Scarborough seems a long way away to advertise a Liverpool gig.'

A flush had appeared on Helen's face as she was talking but as she stopped to consider, it faded. She shrugged. 'Whatever. The poster is still a clue. I'm convinced of that.'

Richard studied the photo. 'Hard to see much.'

'I know.' She sighed. 'I'm weaving a plot round this faded photo because I don't know what to do next. Maybe I should go back to London and get on with my life.'

'It's a thought.' Richard ignored the photograph to look at her. 'Is it a happy life?'

'That's hardly your business.'

She spoke sharply, reminding him he was a stranger.

He winced. 'Sorry.'

He tapped his finger on the snapshot.

'I've still a few contacts at the Town Hall. There's a machine there, rather special. It enlarges and cleans up the most blurred and decrepit documents.'

He lifted the photograph up in the air to maximise the light from the window. 'There's something written at the bottom of this poster but it's impossible to read.'

He stood up. 'I think you and I should visit the Town Hall. I'll ask a favour.' A smile appeared on his face. 'Are you game?'

She frowned. 'I don't know.'

'It could be a clue, Helen. Maybe an important one?'

He was walking out of the room.

She found herself following.

'McNulties Associates.' Richard muttered the words to himself as they walked down the steps of the Town Hall. He permitted himself a quiet smile. 'I *knew* that machine would do the trick. Now, if we can only trace the firm. They must have been the people setting up the concert.'

'We can't be sure.' Helen walking a step behind him had a mulish expression on her face.

Richard refused to be depressed. 'Of course we can. Who else could they be?'

'I don't know. Maybe you're right, but it was years ago. How can it help us now?'

Noting the word 'us', Richard's spirits rose. He tried to reassure her.

'They might still be in business. They probably are. After all, there's still plenty of artists about, plenty of pop groups. Not a patch on the sixties' groups, of course.' He pulled a face trying to make Helen, *his daughter*, lighten up. He chattered on. 'The modern, stuff isn't a patch on the sixties' and seventies' music. Even I know that.'

Helen managed a small smile. 'How do you know? I can't imagine you ever watching or listening to them?'

He nodded. 'That's right, but sometimes I switch on the TV a few minutes early.'

He glanced at her again and suggested they go for a coffee.

Without actually touching her, he steered Helen towards a popular cafe close by the Town Hall and, fortunately, someone had just vacated a prime table close by the window.

'Grab that table, Helen. I'll get the drinks.'

Helen sat down and turned her face to look out of the window. Her expression had turned bleak again.

Trying to ignore his growing sense of foreboding, Richard joined the queue at the counter. He returned to their table and placed a coffee in front of her. 'Here you are.' He cursed the false buoyancy in his voice. 'Sugar?'

She shook her head.

He sat down, hesitated, then asked. 'What's the matter?'

She sighed. 'I'm not sure I can explain.'

'Is it me?'

'Not exactly. It's lots of things.'

He looked across at her and felt an ache in his heart. She looked lonely and unhappy. He wondered why she was on this search. Had she no husband, no children? She was his daughter. How he wanted to comfort her. Find out about her – but he couldn't. Not yet. He sighed and then began talking, slowly at first and then faster.

'Did I tell you I once had a daughter?'

His abrupt words reclaimed her attention. She started. 'No, you didn't.'

'I think I mentioned to you that I had been married.'

When she nodded he transferred his gaze to a point behind her head.

'I rarely talk about it. It was a long time ago.'

She did not speak but she was listening.

'Our marriage didn't last very long. Mostly my fault, I fear. Not cut out for marriage. But I've always liked children.'

He could feel the tension building inside him. He concentrated on the space above her head.

'Not long after I married Jane she became pregnant. There were difficulties and she lost the child at six and a half months. It was a little girl. Stillborn. Jane was all right, at least, as much as she could be.' He swallowed. 'I saw the child. She was so beautiful. Perfect.' His voice thickened. He paused, coughed.

'We had a proper funeral for her. Not particularly religious but it was something to focus on. They never really told her why it happened. That was hard.' He dropped his gaze to Helen's face. 'We just never knew why.'

She reached across and touched his hand

with the tip of her fingers.

'I'm so sorry.'

He took a deep breath. 'It happens. But it messed up a rather imperfect marriage. Nine months after she lost the child, Jane ran off with someone else. Eventually, they married. They live abroad now. She wrote to me to tell me and asked for my forgiveness. There was no need. Poor Jane. It wasn't her fault.'

'It must have been hard for you.'

'No worse than for anyone else.' He blinked and roused himself. 'I didn't tell you this to get your sympathy, Helen. I just wanted you...' He paused and started again. 'I know you're wondering why I am so intent in getting involved in your life, aren't you?'

'Not really.'

He felt her draw back from him.

'Be truthful.'

She bit her lip.

'I'm grateful for your help. But I find your interest rather uncomfortable. Nina is nothing to you. She's *my* mother.' She stopped. 'I know that sounds rude.'

'It sounds sensible.' He felt the ache in his heart.

I knew Nina as Nancy, a magical sixteen-year-old who taught me to love. A girl who took away part of me with her. A girl I never really recovered from. If I could have forgotten her then my marriage might have survived, but no one could match her. And now I've found you.

He cleared his throat. 'I like my own company but one can get sick of a solitary existence. If it doesn't embarrass you, I'd admit to being shy. I *am* shy, but now and again I come across someone I can relate to.

'When I talked to you at the theatre, that's what happened. I felt at ease with you.' He shrugged. 'Then you confided in me and I was honoured *and* interested. I thought: Maybe I could help her.'

He sighed. 'Basically, that's it. I guess I'm finding my own life boring and I'm snatching at the chance of livening it up. So, you see, I'm being totally selfish. It's not a very good argument for you to trust me, but it's the truth.'

Beneath the cafe table, he crossed his fingers.

'Say the word and I'll get up, walk out of here and that's the last you will see of me.'

He waited.

'I don't know.' She frowned. Then she smiled. 'I suppose we could at least find out if this firm still exists?'

He nodded.

She drained her coffee cup. 'We could find a directory of agencies at the library.'

'We might, but I've a better idea.' He stood up. 'Are you game for a small adventure?'

'I suppose.'

She looked up at him.

'Right.' He held out his hand. 'Let's go to Liverpool and see for ourselves.'

Six

They arrived in Liverpool late that afternoon. They had travelled by rail; seated opposite each other and speaking only occasionally. An observant onlooker might have noticed their careful conversation and wondered at their relationship but the day was humid; the heating, for some reason, turned on, and the travellers, for the most part, half asleep. They yawned as the train slowed and the guard announced the imminent arrival at Lime Street Station. They blinked their eyes and stretched before stumbling to their feet – the men began to swing down suitcases from the overhead racks as the women marshalled their offspring into a neat line in preparation for leaving the train.

Only Helen, seated in the corner seat opposite Richard, did not move. She stared out of the window and he stared at her pale profile. He wondered again at her likeness to him and also wondered why she had not realised the similarity. But there again ... why should she? To her, he was just a strange old codger who had, by some whim, offered to help her.

He bit back a sigh, leaned forward and touched her arm.

'Are you all right? You look tired. Perhaps I should have used the car?'

'No. I'm fine.' She smiled. 'As you said, it would have been murder trying to find parking spaces.'

He had pushed for travelling by train. A good service from York; car-parking difficulties.

In truth, the idea of driving to Liverpool had unsettled him. For the past ten years he had never gone out of Yorkshire in his car. He was pathetic, he knew, but the occasion had never arisen and he had lost his nerve for long journeys. Always play safe was his philosophy ... until now. He felt a lump in his throat as he swung Helen's case down from the rack. He had a daughter and some miracle had allowed him to meet her. He'd do everything in his power to help her and if another miracle happened and they managed to contact Nancy...

He drew a deep breath and said, his voice too loud:

'I suppose, living in Chester, you often came to Liverpool?'

'When I'd grown up a bit.'

Helen followed him towards the exit. 'It only takes about forty minutes now but when I travelled as a teenager it took much longer. Not that I minded. I used to love coming here. There was always a bustle and something going on.' She stepped from the train and looked around, smiling at her memories. 'The music scene had changed a bit since the Beatles of course, but there were still a lot of good groups. The clubs were swinging. I used to come with a couple of girlfriends. We'd shop and hang out. We had a whale of a time.'

With Richard carrying their cases they moved through the crowds of people working their way to the exit.

'Doing what?' He wanted her to keep talking. He was greedy to hear about her earlier life.

She creased her brows into a querying glance at his interest.

'Oh, we didn't do anything mad. My step-father, Frank, was strict about behaviour. He'd have skinned me if I'd stepped far over the mark.'

'I didn't mean...'

'You're puffing.' Ignoring his protest, she retrieved her suitcase and strode out next to him. 'I remember going to the first ever McDonald's when it had just opened. We thought we were so cool. The papers sent a photographer and he snapped us and we thought we'd be famous but they never used the photo. We dared each other to go and buy girlie magazines. They were always on the very top shelf then. We raised eyebrows a few times.' She grinned. 'And we went to a few clubs but we always had to leave early to catch the train home. Goodness,' she laughed. 'I'd forgotten.'

They came out of the station and Richard nodded towards a waiting line of taxis. 'Grab one of those.' He raised his hand and the taxi driver got out of his seat to take their cases from them.

Richard asked. 'Do you know of a decent hotel, Helen?'

'Good grief, no.' She dimpled. 'It's years since I've been here and we never, ever stayed in hotels.'

'Ah, well. I'm sure the taxi driver can recommend one.'

He did. They took his advice and he drove them to a pleasant-looking building in the Sefton Park area. They booked in and were shown up to the second floor. Richard had just stowed away his meagre belongings when he heard a tap on the door.

'Yes.'

The door opened and Helen's face appeared. 'Can I come in?'

'Yes, please do.'

She entered the room and glanced around. 'Absolute duplicate of mine but my wallpaper's lemon.'

She plumped down on a small easy chair. 'Pretty good, eh?'

He nodded, rejoicing in her relaxed

manner. Since her arrival in Liverpool she seemed to have discarded her defensive caution.

'We'll go down for afternoon tea, shall we, Helen? Then we can plan what to do first.'

'Yes, OK.' She hesitated, obviously considering her next words. 'Now, we've arrived Richard, we have to get certain things straight. For starters, any expenses incurred are my affair.'

'I was thinking fifty-fifty.' Richard's voice was purposely bland.

She frowned. 'No way. It's *my* search and I can afford–'

'I can afford it more.' He watched her open her mouth to speak and he jumped in, giving her no chance to argue. 'Coming here was my idea. I invited myself along. I have busied myself in your concerns and–' he held up his hand to forestall her '–I've got more money than you and not much to spend it on.'

Danger flags flew in her cheeks. 'I absolutely refuse and I think it's despicable of you to–'

'What's despicable?'

'You know. You're taking charge by flaunting your wealth. This is none of your business and...'

His face paled. 'You're quite right, but look at it this way; I've told you there are no strings attached to any help I give you. I'm interested and intrigued by your story. I've plenty of money and I am willing to spend a little on a good cause. I can help you and stop myself dying of boredom. Anyway, we haven't spent any money yet. Let's argue when we do.'

He managed a smile. 'Turn down my offer later, if you feel you must but let's see what happens first, shall we? And just think for a moment ... if I'm so awful, you would be a fool *not* to take advantage of me.'

She stared at him, then began to laugh. 'You're not awful, I'm beginning to realise that, but you are a very strange man.'

'I told you I was.' A smile of relief stretched his mouth. 'Remember when we met... I told you I was out of an Ayckbourn play.'

After talking throughout their afternoon tea and learning how to relax in each other's company, their growing spirit of camaraderie encouraged them to take a stroll together and get their bearings. Helen was leader but she soon got lost, admitting the place had changed a lot since her last visit. They wandered around, hopped on a bus and arrived outside the Merseyside Maritime Museum. They decided to go in, but only had time to inspect two of the five floors of permanent displays before the building closed.

Then Richard acquired a tourist map and studied it, exclaiming at the variety of places to go to and things to be seen.

'I told you there's always plenty going on around here.' Helen's eyes were sparkling. Momentarily, she seemed to have forgotten the reason for their journey. It was as if being in Liverpool had recalled happier times, when she was a teenager.

Richard was pleased. Her animated expression made her look years younger. He wondered about her more recent life. If only he had been there to help her. He thought: How can I have a daughter of thirty-nine? Then he looked down at the footpath. He would never be able to tell her he was her father. How could he? He knew how it would sound. Helen had been conceived during a one-off coupling between a fifteen-year-old boy and a girl slightly older. Not a thing to tell anyone, and yet he sighed. It hadn't been a sordid act, it had been wonderful. It was the one thing in his life he could think about without a taint of bitterness or regret. He regretted the aftermath. Oh, God, yes. But not the time with Nancy. There had been nothing sordid about that.

His eyes misted over and he passed his hand over his face. Helen must never know. All he could be for her was a friend to rely on, and even achieving that status would be difficult.

'Penny for them?'

He started. 'Sorry.'

'Penny for them?'

'Not enough.' He sighed, roused himself. 'Just working out a plan of campaign.'

'You look a bit tired.'

'I'm fine.' He ran his hand over his immaculate haircut. 'Now's the time to go to work. What do you know about the pubs and clubs?'

'Not so much. They knocked down half of the city during the sixties. From what I remember of the seventies, the place was a patchwork quilt. New developments of spick-and-span maisonettes next to waste ground.' She smiled. 'Often you'd see a complete bombsite and in the middle of it a pub still operating, full of boozy customers.'

She glanced at Richard and explained. 'The breweries were rich and powerful. They opposed certain developments. When the dockers were in work they spent a fortune in the pubs. They were more interested in keeping their local open than moving to a flat with an indoor toilet.'

'That's good.' Richard nodded. 'But we need to think about the younger people. The ones that lived for club life and the music.' He shrugged. 'They'll be in the pubs now, I suppose, but we must try and find some and tap their memories.'

'But will they know anything about theatrical agents?'

'It's our only hope. The library didn't help us, did it? And loads of kids must have tried to get into groups during the magic years. Perhaps they're still around. So, what else do you remember?'

She pursed her mouth. 'There was a Yates Wine Lodge opposite Lewis's. One of the first in the country, I think. That was popular with everyone.'

Seeing Richard's look of scepticism, she hurried to explain. 'It wasn't anything like the Yates Wine Bars nowadays. Most customers drank pints of Porter.' Her face brightening as she remembered more, she continued: 'That's where we should start. There was the Bold Hotel and the main shopping area. Lots of eating and drinking places. Oh, yes. There was a local landmark, a sculpture of a standing man. That was where you met people. There were always groups of youngsters hanging around – "See you under The Man".' She nodded her head. 'We should start there.'

Nearly three hours later, they decided to take a break. They had hung out in various places. They had consumed a reasonable meal. Richard had drunk one pint of beer and two whiskies with water. Helen, after two glasses of wine, was on orange juice.

They were tired.

They had struck up a few conversations. People were friendly but they were more interested in modern Liverpool rather than dwelling on the past.

One man, an old docker, remembered the sixties' Liverpool vividly, but spoke about weeks standing beneath 'The Docker's Umbrella' – an overhead railway – hoping and praying a 'gaffer' would pick him out for a few hours work. Talk of the Beatles annoyed him.

'Bloody row, if you ask me. Do you know something...' He paused for a huge swallow of beer. 'One newspaper called them the greatest composers since Beethoven.' His face screwed into a mask of comic despair. 'Which would you prefer. Beethoven's Septet or 'Yellow Submarine'?'

Richard, whose taste in music was definitely classical, nodded sympathetically and bought the old guy another pint before leaving the pub. Outside, he said to Helen. 'We might as well call it a day.'

She nodded.

They walked along in silence until Helen, trying to lower the gloom factor announced: 'Tomorrow, I'd like to take a trip on the ferry. I used to love doing that when I came here with my friends.'

'Good idea.' Richard glanced at her. She hadn't mentioned her mother all evening.

Was she realising how difficult their task was? Was she beginning to see their search would probably end in failure? Maybe she was coming to realise that failure might be for the best? If they did find Nancy, what would Helen say to her? What would *he* say!

'If you go on the river, I'll go along to the Planetarium for a couple of hours.'

'The Planetarium? You're interested in astronomy? I never would have guessed.'

'Why? What do you think would interest me? Cricket? Stamp-collecting?' Richard felt grumpy.

She smiled. 'No. I never meant ... it's just ... astronomy?'

'You'd be surprised by the enthusiasm for the subject. There always has been.' Richard's voice became more animated. 'Do you know that the stars looked much the same to the Ancient Greeks as they do now and that the birth and death of a star takes thousands of millions of years? Think about that for a minute. It gives you a new slant on life. Puts your preoccupations into another perspective.'

'Oh, thanks!' Helen frowned. 'Is that supposed to make me feel better?'

'No.' Richard stopped walking. 'I didn't mean anything. It's just I'm inclined to get carried away with my hobby. I was just trying to explain the fascination of the subject.'

They started walking again – in silence – until Helen asked: 'How is a star formed?'

'From vast clouds of dust and hydrogen gas in space.' Richard glanced at her. 'You don't really want to know, do you?'

'It sounds complicated.' She walked a little further and then, unexpectedly: 'If you do go tomorrow – can I come with you?'

This time he halted. 'You really want to?'

'I wouldn't ask if I didn't mean it.'

He studied her profile. She was cast in his image yet he imagined he saw a flash of Nancy's expression as she turned her face towards him. He caught his breath. What if he told her she had been conceived beneath a canopy of stars?

For a split second he was transported to the past; to a boy in his attic bedroom, looking at the stars and dreaming about Nancy – and she had come to him. He recollected the soft pad of her bare feet, her light breathing. The way she had sat down next to him and how the starshine had picked up the sparkle in her eyes.

How had she felt when she knew she was pregnant? She must have been frightened. She was only a kid and she was on her own. How had she managed to keep the child? Why hadn't she come to him?

Richard's face hardened into stone. Maybe she had come. His parents would never have told him. They would have

98

turned her away. To them, Nancy was a slut. 'A depraved trollop', his mother had called her. She had corrupted their innocent boy.

He closed his eyes.

'Richard, are you all right?'

He blinked. 'Sorry, I was miles away.'

'Up there with the stars?'

'Not exactly.'

'I thought not.'

Bless her, there was concern on her face. He forced himself to relax.

'I was remembering something.'

'Good or bad?'

'Like life, a mixture of both.'

She was silent.

He sighed. 'Let's go back to the hotel.'

Seven

The next day the sun shone. Richard encouraged Helen to go on her ferry trip while he acquired a local directory and sat by the telephone in his hotel room trying to contact someone who might remember McNulty. He worked his way through the listed agencies. It wasn't easy, mostly he didn't get further than the reception desk, but a few agents agreed to speak to him. However, when he mentioned the man he was seeking had been active in the late sixties and early seventies they lost interest.

'Music's what's happening now, mister. If you're going back thirty years go out and buy the books.'

'No, it's not like that...'

He would begin to explain, but usually the phone went down before his sentence was completed. Only one man spared time to explain.

'Too much going on to remember, see? The whole music scene was shifting and moving. There were reputable agents and managers but loads of wheelers and dealers, too. They'd burst on the scene then just as quickly vanish again.'

The speaker paused, considered his words. 'It was a media revolution. Not just music. Everything was changing. Started with theatre. I remember the impact *Look Back in Anger* caused. Came out in the mid-fifties, that's when it started. All about the working class finding their own voice.' He laughed. 'My dad was disgusted with the language in it but I was a kid and I thought it was a great play. It certainly influenced me. Do you remember the pirate radio stations?'

Carried away with his own memories, he went on. 'I worked for a pirate radio station. I remember I was hooked on the black American artists in the early sixties. Didn't play their kind of music on the radio here but I'd tune into the American Forces' stations broadcasting from Europe and sometimes American sailors passing through Liverpool would sell us their records.'

'Yes, that's interesting but...' Richard tried to distract his informant's attention and bring him back to the question in hand.

'Right.' The man coughed. 'You're trying to track down this McNulty character?' He paused for thought. 'During the late sixties, younger and newer agents and managers took over from a lot of the established guys. They dared to push the new sounds. Some lasted and some disappeared. I don't personally recall the man you're looking for but I'll make a few enquiries, if you like.'

Richard told him he would like that very much and the man laughed and told him to ring back tomorrow afternoon.

When Helen returned to the hotel he told her of this one useful contact.

She pursed her lips. 'Not promising, is it? But one person is better than none.'

'Yes.' Richard glanced at his watch. 'Let's have lunch. I'm hungry.'

'OK. But let's go out. The hotel's too quiet. Let's go somewhere cheerful.'

After a fish-and-chips lunch at Harry Ramsden's Helen reminded Richard of his plan to visit the Planetarium.

Privately delighted, Richard ushered Helen to her seat just as the lights dimmed. A forest of heads tilted backwards to gaze at the panorama above and around them, and Richard, unable to resist showing off his knowledge, added bits to the recorded commentary.

'Over there, that's Jupiter. Jupiter's a good starting point for a first time stargazer.'

'Why?' Helen whispered.

'Because Jupiter spins so rapidly its disc is flattened at the pole. Can you see?' He pointed. 'And you can also spot it because it has four bright satellites.'

'Shush.'

They exchanged grins. Richard sank lower in his chair and watched the show. From time to time he glanced towards Helen's profile and was delighted to see, from her absorbed interest, she was genuinely enjoying the spectacle.

She confirmed as much when they left the building. 'I enjoyed that.'

He nodded. 'I'm glad.'

They smiled at each other.

In unspoken but relaxing harmony they temporarily gave up their search for Nina and drifted through the rest of the day. They took the Two Cathedrals Tour, had a pre-dinner drink and visited a Russian club and restaurant for their evening meal. Richard couldn't remember spending such a busy and enjoyable day.

Whenever they found themselves in an area that might reveal something to help their search, they instigated casual talk with the locals. They became ruefully resigned at their lack of success. They both realised they were beginning to admit defeat. Richard wasn't too downcast. He'd never really thought they would find Nina. It was sad, but for him it didn't matter so much, because he had found his daughter. Most of his thoughts were concentrated on ways to keep her in his life and how, perhaps, he would one day be able to tell her the truth.

The following day, when Richard contacted his helpful agent, Helen was there with him, curled up on the end of his bed, tension showing in her tight face and clenched hands.

'Yes, he's expecting my call. I'll hold...' Richard mouthed the word 'secretary' to Helen and then straightened his back as a man's voice was heard.

'I see. Yes, that's good.'

'Has he found out something?'

He waved his hand to silence her.

'Yes. Just a moment, I'll write that down.'

He gestured to Helen who almost fell off the bed in her eagerness to pass a notepad and pen.

'Daltry Hotel, you say? Yes, I've got it.' He listened for a moment. 'I can't tell you how much we're obliged to you. Yes, of course I'll let you know if anything comes of your information. Thank you.'

He replaced the receiver.

Helen clasped her hands. 'He's found something?'

'Yes, he's given me a contact.' Richard held up a warning hand. 'It's only tenuous.'

'I don't care. But tell me more.'

'Parke's a decent bloke. He's obviously gone to a lot of trouble...'

Seeing the thunder clouds on Helen's face, Richard stopped rambling.

He took a deep breath and said slowly and

distinctly: 'Parke's secretary rang round and managed to trace a guy called Terry Warden. Warden worked for McNulty for about three or four years. He started with him in the mid-sixties, which makes it the right time for our enquiry. He's a bit of a drifter, now. A bit of this. A bit of that. Had lots of jobs but he's managing a small hotel now, just off Chaloner Street. Parke contacted him early this morning and Warden's agreed to meet us. Mind you, he did say he didn't think he would be much help.'

'Oh.' Helen's face lit up. 'That's wonderful. He *might* remember something, when he sees the photograph. When can we go to see him?'

'This afternoon. Three p.m.'

'I can't wait.'

Terry Warden, a burly man with thinning hair, entered the bar of the Daltry Hotel carrying a tray on which stood a full glass of beer and a plate of food He nodded to Richard and Helen and came to join them.

'Sorry about the grub.' He put down his tray on the bar table. 'We're really busy, see. Haven't had time for a bite since seven o'clock this morning.'

'It's good of you to see us.'

Warden nodded at Richard. He picked up a sandwich stuffed with cheese and ham and took a bite. Thickly, he replied, 'Well,

106

when McNulty's name was mentioned, I was curious.'

'You were friends?'

He considered. 'Well, I worked for him, but yes, I suppose we were friends. Do you know where the old bastard is?'

Richard winced. 'No.'

Helen leaned forward. 'It's not Mr McNulty we're trying to trace, but we think there's a connection to the person we're looking for.' She looked across at Richard for help.

He picked up her threads. 'It's actually a woman we're trying to trace. There's only a slim chance of a link with your former employer but it's the only one we have, so we're here talking to you.'

Warden wiped his mouth with his hand and laughed. 'Find the lady? Doesn't surprise me there's a woman involved. Alex was always one for the ladies. He handled some good groups when I was with him, and where there's young lads, you get the groupies. They're after the performers, of course, but Alex was a good-looking guy and he did all right.'

'The woman we're trying to find was no groupie. She was about thirty years old; she had a child.' Richard refrained from looking at Helen.

'But she loved the Mersey Beat. We've a snapshot of her taken when she was in

Scarborough just before she went missing. On the photo you can just make out a billboard with a poster advertising McNulty Promotions.'

'Don't remember Alex operating in Scarborough.' Warden shoved the remains of his sandwich into his mouth and washed it down with beer. 'Too far away. He wasn't interested in seaside resorts.'

'We appreciate that but we think she might have seen the poster and decided to come to the show when she was returning home. She lived in Chester. No distance at all, but she never returned home.'

'Well, a lot of people go missing.' Warden finished his beer. 'Still, I don't mind looking at the photo. Can't say I hold out much hope though.'

He took the photograph from Helen, laid it on the bar table and pulled a pair of spectacles from the breast pocket of his shirt. He placed the spectacles on his nose. 'Hundreds of people packed into gigs. Not like nowadays. Fans would queue outside for hours, regardless of the weather. If the woman did come, there isn't a cat in hell's chance I'll recognise her.'

He picked up the photograph and held it close to his face. 'You'd best...' His voice faded.

Richard, who was watching him closely saw his eyebrows shoot up behind the frames of his spectacles.

'My God.'

Warden took off his glasses and rubbed his hand over his face. He stared across at them. 'It's Nina.'

'Alex McNulty was a fighter. A tough kid from Glasgow. He tried his hand at a lot of things but it was when he got into the music business, at just the right time, that things worked out for him.' Terry Warden laughed.

'Alex didn't know a damn thing about music when he started, but he knew people. When I got pally with him he was just beginning to pull in the cash. I'd worked for him for three years when Nina came into his life.'

'Do you want more coffee?' He waved his hand at Helen.

'No.' She shook her head. 'No thanks.'

It was twenty minutes after the bombshell. Warden's beer glass and sandwich had been replaced with a coffee pot and three mugs. Also on the bar table stood a whisky bottle and three glasses.

'You ought to have a slug of this.' Warden picked up the bottle and refilled his own glass and that of Richard's.

'I don't want a drink.' Helen's voice was terse. 'I just want to hear everything you know about Nina.'

'Well, let's see.' Warden paused for

reflection. 'I wasn't around the day he met her, but a couple of days later he brought her backstage with him when the gig finished and I knew straight away she was different. This one, I thought, might be here to stay.'

He shrugged his shoulders. 'Usually, women chased Alex but with Nina, Alex made all the running. Not that she didn't fancy him. It was there for all to see. You could practically see the air vibrating between them but she was cool. Maybe that's why she got him.' He shook his head admiringly.

'Within a month of their meeting each other, she was making suggestions to improve the business, mostly presentation stuff and, by God, most of her ideas worked. Alex became more besotted. Not only was the woman good-looking and sexy, she had a brain like a man.'

Warden paused and shot an apologetic look towards Helen. 'No disrespect meant. Nowadays we all appreciate that women are the equal of men in the brainbox area but in those days, it was different.'

Richard hardly dared think what Helen was going through. At last she was hearing about her mother's life after deserting her but what was it doing to her? He looked across at her pale face and willed her to meet his eyes but she did not look at him.

She stared at Warden, waiting for him to continue.

As if impelled by her force of will, he obliged. 'They became inseparable and so no one was surprised when they married.'

At the sound of Helen's involuntary soft cry, Warden stopped speaking. He stared at Helen, who had put her hand up to her mouth, and then he looked at Richard.

'Is something wrong? Something I've said?'

'No, but perhaps we ought...'

Richard stopped as Helen interrupted him.

'Go on, Mr Warden. Tell us the rest.'

'Well,' Warden shuffled his feet and downed the remainder of his whisky before continuing. Obviously uncomfortable, he said, 'Not a lot to tell, in truth. The firm did OK. Alex organised some fantastic gigs. Not the very tops, I suppose, but we did all right. We thought we'd got the Rolling Stones at one time but the deal fell through. Then, as always, things began to change. Recording studios in London scooped the pool. Nina, as always, was the first to see which way the wind was blowing. She told Alex they ought to move to London.'

'London? When was this?'

Warden thought before answering Helen's question.

'It would be about three years after their

111

marriage. Yeah, that was it. She talked Alex round. She always did, but I didn't go with them. I'm a Liverpool lad and I was married and my wife was expecting our first kid. Mary wouldn't leave her mother so we stayed put.'

Richard asked the next question as Helen had become silent.

'Did you keep in touch?'

'For a couple of years. They did OK. Then the phone calls tapered off. You know how it is.'

'And you don't know their present whereabouts?'

'Christ, no. They moved around all the time. Haven't a clue where they are now.'

'That's a shame.' Richard glanced across to Helen. 'But we do thank you for all your help.'

'That's all right. Brought back old times, talking about it.' Warden glanced at Helen who was staring into space. Leaning forward, he said quietly, 'She all right?'

Richard nodded. 'She will be.'

'Right then.' Warden stood up.

'What if I make myself scarce for ten minutes, then I'll come back to see you before you go?'

'That would be fine.' Inwardly blessing the man for his unexpected sensitivity, Richard rose to his feet. When the hotel manager had lumbered away, Richard took the chair closest to Helen. He leaned forward and rested his hand on hers.

'All right, Helen?'

'No, I'm bloody well not!'

She raised her head and he saw the sheen of unshed tears in her eyes.

'She was in Liverpool all that time and she never came to see me, never contacted me. How could she do that?'

'I don't know.' Richard felt a lump form in his own throat. 'I really don't know, Helen.'

'And she *married* that man – when she was already married to Frank. She's a bigamist.' Helen pulled her hand away from Richard's grasp and wrapped her arms about her slim body. 'I hope she burns in hell.'

'Don't say that!' Richard was shocked. 'We don't know all the circumstances.'

'No. And we never will.' Helen stood up and rubbed violently at the tears which started to pour down her face. 'I'm finished. I'm sick of Nina. I hope I never see her again.' She gasped on the last words.

'Helen...' Richard put his hands on her arms and felt the shudders vibrating through her body. 'Without all the facts, we really shouldn't judge,' he said, gently.

'Shouldn't we?' She glared at him and he realised it was only her anger that was holding her together. She pulled away from him: rejected his support.

'I'm going to the ladies, to sort myself out.

When I come out we'll return to the hotel and check out. Please don't mention Nina's name ever again.'

'But...'

She had already left him.

A cough from behind told Richard that Warden had returned. He sighed and turned to face him.

'Upset, isn't she?'

The banality of his words made Richard unable to answer. He shrugged.

'Sorry it hit her so hard, but you did come to me. You did ask me.'

'Yes, we did.' Richard forced a smile. The man was right. They had asked for information and he had told them.

'It's difficult for her. She's not seen Nina since she was twelve. She lived in Chester for years so the thought that...'

Richard shut his mouth. It was not his place to tell Warden about Helen's problems. But again, the hotel manager surprised him with his sensitivity.

'She's Nina's daughter, I bet?' He waited, and reluctantly, Richard nodded.

'Poor lady. No wonder she's upset. You expect your mother to stand by you, don't you.' He paused. 'You're related, aren't you?'

'What?' Richard started.

'You and the lady. I can see the family resemblance. Cousin, or something?'

Richard saw Helen come out of the ladies

and head towards them. He stammered. 'Yes, that's it.'

'Oh, well. You'll help her through, won't you?'

'Yes, I will.' Richard hurriedly shook Warden's hand. 'Thanks for your help.'

'You're welcome. Wish it could have been better news.'

'That wasn't your fault. And at least, we know more than we did.'

'That's true.' Warden picked up his whisky bottle. 'If you ever find them, give Alex my best wishes.'

Giving a clumsy wave to Helen he shuffled away.

She ignored his wave. Her attention was on Richard and her control was awesome. She said: 'Let's get out of here.'

He nodded and followed her to the exit.

Outside the hotel, he asked. 'What shall we do now?'

She stopped walking. 'Do? Why nothing. At least, nothing that has anything to do with Nina. I'm sick of her, Richard. I was a fool to try and find her. If I've learned anything by coming here I've learned I must not continue to be a fool.'

'You're not a fool, Helen.'

'I'm packing my case and I'm catching the first train to London. It's time I picked up on my own life and stopped chasing memories.'

Seeing Richard's expression change, her lips began to tremble. 'And you must go back to Scarborough and do the same. After all, none of this is your concern.'

Eight

The village lay close enough to Guildford for Nina McNulty to go there for shopping. After one such trip, travelling back after buying new winter clothes she realised, with a small shock of surprise, that she felt happy. For the past twelve months she had felt, what was the word? Content, yes, that was it, but now, this very minute, by some inexplicable change of focus, she realised she was happy. She slowed down the car and with a grin widening her face, she admired the countryside through which she was passing.

She was taking the scenic route home. The narrow road she was travelling passed through woodland and autumnal tints were colouring the leaves on the trees and the bracken beneath them. She calculated that it was two years and one month since Alex had died. Then she had thought she would never feel happy again but, today, time and nature had proved her wrong.

Keeping part of her attention on the winding road – she was a good driver and confident – she also allowed her mind to dwell on her husband. She re-wound their first meeting. How he had been standing by the entrance to the auditorium watching the crowd swarm in and how, as she had walked passed him, he had put out his hand and caught hold of her elbow.

'What's a class lady like you doing amongst this lot?' He had grinned at her and she had thought how attractive he was. A tall, good-looking man with dark blond hair and deep blue eyes.

Still smiling, he had nodded at the groups of chattering teenagers thronging past them.

'Not exactly your style, are they, lady? They'll be screaming, fainting and crying when the group gets going, you know.'

She had laughed. 'That's OK. I won't do any of those things but I do love the music they make.'

'That so?' He still had hold of her arm. His grasp was light though, not intrusive. She could feel the warmth from his fingers.

He'd hesitated, then said. 'If you're such a fan, maybe you'd like to meet the boys, after the show?'

She frowned. 'I'm not sure, actually.' She looked at him full in the face. 'Sounds good, but sometimes it's wiser to keep things you admire at a distance.'

'Ouch.' He relinquished his hold on her. 'Sorry, I didn't mean to be pushy.'

'That's all right. No offence taken.' She

took a step back to study him. 'Who are you exactly?'

'I'm their manager.'

'Oh, I see.' She tilted her head back and narrowed her eyes. 'Well, in that case...'

And that's how it started.

Nina braked as she negotiated a particularly sharp bend and, as she did so, her face clouded over.

She had behaved badly. So badly that even after all these years, she still couldn't believe it. A decent woman would have pulled back right then. A decent woman would have taken herself back home, even though she was unhappy there. A decent woman wouldn't have slept with a handsome stranger but she had and in doing so forged a commitment that would never be broken. There had been no doubt in her mind; not then, not ever, even at her lowest ebb of self-loathing. Alex was the one she had been searching for all her life.

Afterwards, she might have told him the truth, but she didn't. She couldn't bear to lose him. Soon, she had thought, I'll tell him and I'll go back to Chester – sort things out. Oh, she was a bitch there was no denying it.

Later she went back – when it was too late, much too late.

Frank was much as she had expected; livid with anger but controlled and hard as iron.

'You've forfeited all claims to your

daughter, you bitch.'

She had bowed her head. 'Just tell me, is she all right?'

'I won't tell you anything. You don't deserve to know. Keep out of our lives, now and for ever.'

He had every right. She had none. She had forfeited her rights. She had chosen Alex and must live with the consequences. She had done so and her love for Alex had stopped her from going under. God, how she had loved him. After his death she had thought herself destroyed but, here she was, feeling happy again.

Why, today? What had triggered the magic switch? Her successful shopping trip had nothing to do with her positive feelings, neither did the beautiful weather. Maybe it was just the right time for her to start living again. Impatiently, she switched on the car radio. Why *did* she have to analyse everything? Enough that she was driving back to a house she loved and that she was happy. Thank you, God, she thought. She didn't really believe in God but someone deserved thanks for the miracle. Was it God, she thought, that had prompted her to change her lifestyle, pull up roots and move out of the city into the country?

How Alex would have laughed. His Nina transported out of the city office and on her hands and knees grubbing away in her large garden. Nina wearing sensible shoes and going on five-mile walks. What would he have made of her? But maybe, deep down, he would have understood and applauded.

Nina had always believed action could help you out of the doldrums. She had made several major changes in her life and always she had looked forward, not back and each time she had embraced her new surroundings and new role in life wholeheartedly. She was getting on a bit now, however, so perhaps there would be no more changes in the future.

Nina allowed herself a faint sigh as she left the wood behind her and headed the car towards the village. She wound down the window, thinking: It really is a bonny day. There was no other vehicle in sight and her Peugeot was a quiet runner. It was as if she were the only person in the world, she thought and the world was holding its breath.

She grinned. It was not like her to be fanciful. First happy and then fanciful ... it must be the perfect weather.

Above, the sky was becoming faintly veiled in mist and suffused sunlight imparted a silvery tone to the foliage in the hedges she passed. She sniffed and guessed someone was having a bonfire. A pungent smell crept into the car through the open window mixed with another scent, probably the fresh bracken.

She passed through the outskirts of the rambling village and drove through the centre, passing the post-office-cum-grocery store and the chemist's shop. She slowed to turn right and a passer-by waved her hand.

'All right, Mrs McNulty?"

Nina nodded. 'Fine, thanks.'

'Pick up any bargains?'

She laughed. 'Not really.'

'Shame.'

She drove on. How did Ellen Bray know she had been shopping for clothes? How indeed. But the villagers were kind as well as curious and they didn't know everything. Thank God. She drove by the garage and spotted two strangers standing on the forecourt, discussing the car before them. Two men with a strong family resemblance; obviously father and son. Unconsciously, Nina slowed the car. She may be getting old but she still admired good-looking men and good-looking cars, and both men and car deserved an admiring glance.

The older chap was tall, grey haired and strong featured; the younger man likewise was lean-jawed but he was dark haired. He laughed at something his father said and his head went back, showing off the clean brown line of his throat.

Nina felt disturbed and then angry with herself. It was too bad if her feeling of happiness meant that baser feelings were creeping back. At her age she could do without such disturbance. Oh, it wasn't fair, particularly as she had just been congratulating herself on her tranquillity.

Frowning, she transferred her gaze to the car. Nina knew about cars as well as men and this one was a beauty. A Saab 9-3 Turbo Sport. She looked at the scalloped side-sill extensions and the three-spoke alloy wheels and reckoned its top speed would be over 140 miles per hour.

An irate blast from behind her made her start. She glanced in the mirror. A fat woman wearing a lurid flowered top scowled at her from behind the wheels of her Volvo. Nina realised she was blocking the way to the pumps. She flushed, raised her hand in apology and drove on. Ten minutes later she turned into the drive of her property.

She stopped in front of the house, low, white, unpretentious but possessing ample charm, where she unloaded her purchases and carried them indoors. The central heating had switched on automatically and she welcomed the warmth, realising that during the last fifteen minutes the heat had drained from the day.

She dumped the bags on the hall carpet, kicked off her shoes and wandered into the sitting-room where she poured out a gin and tonic. Seated in her favourite armchair she switched on a table lamp and glanced round appreciatively before blowing a kiss to Alex's photograph which took pride of place on a nearby coffee table.

'I'm back, my love.'

She liked to talk to his picture, it was the next best thing to talking to him. That's one thing they had always shared, the ability to talk to each other. What a blessing that had been. After all the years struggling on her own, the pure luxury of curling up on the sofa next to him, his arm around her, her head on his shoulder; to talk and listen to each other, why that had been as wonderful to her as their love-making. God – she sipped her drink – she had been so lucky.

The couple of good friends she had made in the village knew how fortunate she had been in her life with Alex. They loved hearing about her brushes with show-business characters too and she was pretty sure they envied her exciting life. Of course, they didn't know her earlier history. Nina took another sip of gin and imagined how their faces would look if she told them everything. They would be shocked to their sensible M&S underwear. Their lives had followed pleasant but dull paths. Jill, in particular, had married her childhood sweetheart who was well placed financially but the most boring man Nina had ever met. During their wine and cheese evenings or coffee mornings Nina couldn't resist winding Jill up, hoping to light a spark in her friend so that she would go home and give her spouse hell.

Nina emptied her glass and gave a twisted little smile. Maybe she was mischievous but in her opinion far too many women settled for much too little. Jill was a sweet woman with an impish turn of humour but when she was with her husband she was a mere appendage, an audience for his stupid jokes. Still, that was her affair. As for Alex, he had been a man in every sense of the word and she only embroidered one or two things about him. Things like his instinctive flair for forward planning and knowing when to change tack.

For instance, she'd allowed her friends to think Alex had been the prime wheeler-dealer in their management business. The truth was that Alex had been an energetic and competent agent but it was only after she became involved in his business that things had really taken off. The move to London had been her idea and during their years there most of the better ideas had come from her.

Fortunately, Alex had never been jealous of her innate skills. He had encouraged her and backed her all the way and then, despite her horrendous grief at his sudden death, she had somehow managed to keep her head together to negotiate an excellent price for their company. She could have stayed on but she didn't want to, not without Alex. Ah, well. It was all over now, the world of schemes and deals and jetting about the country. Now, smaller things occupied her attention.

Nina roused herself from her thoughts, finished her drink then went to unpack her purchases. She hung up her new clothes tidily in the wall-length mirrored wardrobe in her bedroom then she made herself a snack of scrambled eggs and toast which she washed down with a glass of dry white wine. Nina's figure was excellent for her age and she was determined to keep it; tonight it was not diet that restricted the size of her evening meal but the shortage of time.

At seven thirty, the village writers' group was reconvening after the summer's break. Nina had joined the group towards the end of the spring session. A mixture of people attended, some merely turning up for social reasons but there was a core of members who genuinely wanted to break into print and Nina was one of them. Her life in the music world had been varied and eventful and she thought a book about her experiences could stand a good chance of being published. Once started, she found she was enjoying the experience of learning to write more and more and now she was hell-bent on achieving publication, even though she knew the chances of this happening were slim.

Tonight, she was looking forward to reading her latest attempts at writing to her fellow enthusiasts. The group was meeting at Mrs Springfield's house, about twenty minutes' walk from Nina's home. After finishing her meal, therefore, she popped the few dishes in the dishwasher before going into her bedroom and taking a large brown envelope from a drawer in her dressing table. She took out a few type-written pages and scanned them. Yes, they would do.

Mrs Springfield's house was cosy and welcoming. Alice had lighted a log fire. Sitting down in an easy chair, one of several arranged in a semicircle around the fireplace, Nina gave a sigh of pleasure. She nodded at the would-be writers already assembled. The doorbell rang again and Alice stopped her chatting and left the room, returning soon after followed by a stranger – a tall, spare man dressed in sports jacket, checked shirt and corduroy trousers. Nina immediately recognised him as being the older man she had noticed standing on the garage forecourt.

'We have a new member.' Alice beamed

round the assembled company. 'And a man, too!'

The group of four ladies smiled and the two gentlemen present nodded stiffly towards the newcomer.

'This is Stuart Urquart who moved to the village five weeks ago. If you'd like to take the remaining chair, Stuart.' Alice waved her hand. 'You don't mind me using your Christian name, do you? We're an informal bunch.'

There was a murmur of assent, again notably from the ladies and Nina hid a grin behind her hand.

An interested collection of eyes followed the movement of Mr Urquart as he stepped around feet and sat down in a vacant easy chair with a certain. easy degree of grace.

Well, thought Nina. What an interesting development. Through lowered lids she inspected Mr Urquart senior. She had admired the younger Urquart but on closer inspection it was easy to see from where he had inherited his assets. The writing group was looking up.

'We'll start by refreshing our memories, shall we?' Alice, producing a dining-room chair squeezed herself into the group. 'For the benefit of Stuart we'll just say our names and what sort of writing we are engaged upon.'

'That's fine but...' The newcomer leaned

forward. 'Please, Alice. I would much prefer for you to take my chair.'

'Oh, no.' Alice blushed delicately. 'I am perfectly happy here. This is much better for one's posture.'

'If you're sure...' He shrugged his broad shoulders.

'I am. Now...' As hostess for the evening, Alice Springwater assumed the position of chairperson. 'Would you start the ball rolling, Nina?'

'What? Oh, yes. If you like.' Nina cleared her throat, annoyed that the presence of the newcomer had unsettled her. 'Well, as most of you know, I am writing a novel using a factual background based on my knowledge of the music scene during the sixties and the seventies. I suppose I'm about halfway through but at this stage, I'm not sure.'

'Is it a romantic novel?' Stuart Urquart looked directly at her.

He had a nerve, asking questions when he'd only been in the room for five minutes.

'No.' Her voice sounded so sharp, she modified her second 'No'. 'Relationships are important, of course, but it's more of a...' She hesitated. 'More of a *rites of passage* novel.'

'Of course.' His voice was serious but he smiled at her.

She frowned down at her manuscript. 'I'll read the beginning of chapter fourteen.'

The group settled down.

'Fancy a nightcap?'

It was nine forty-five and the writing group was dispersing. Nina had lingered to talk for a few moments to Alice whose grandson had been ill. She'd pulled on her jacket and walked down the garden path where she found Stuart Urquart waiting for her.

She looked up at him and there was a moment of silence before she asked. 'Where?'

'At the pub, of course.' A lop-sided smile split his lean face. 'Wouldn't compromise you by inviting you back to my empty house.'

'You better believe it.' Nina laughed and relaxed. 'But even the pub's suspect, you know. If we're seen together in there more than twice, the underground intelligence group will be forecasting our engagement by Christmas.'

'Maybe, but that doesn't bother you, does it?' Very casually, Stuart touched her hand. 'You're not bothered about what people say, surely? Anyway, there's no ulterior motive. I just want to talk. I'd like to know more about your writing.'

'You would?' Nina felt her face flush with pleasure.

'Really. I thought your stuff was the best of

130

the bunch, and I mean that. Mind you, I could also do with a drink.' He glanced at his watch. 'The bitter at the Snooty Fox is excellent. Too good to gulp down, so let's go, shall we?' He smiled again and put his hand beneath her elbow. Nina found herself being steered along the pavement in the direction of the pub.

She felt a flicker of annoyance at Stuart's high-handed attitude but beneath her annoyance was another emotion, a certain warmth which she wasn't, as yet, prepared to analyse.

Nine

The lights from the pub shone cheerily through the darkness as they approached. Inside, a glowing log-fire welcomed them, and the landlord, leaning on his bar and chatting to a local, raised his arm and gave them a cheery wave.

'Welcome. What's it to be?'

Stuart looked at Nina.

'Dry white wine, please.'

'You heard the lady. I'll have a pint of your best bitter.' Stuart searched in his pocket for change and muttered from the side of his mouth. 'Any shocked faces? Anyone taking notes?'

She laughed. 'Not that I can see.'

'Good.' He grinned, paid for their drinks and picked them up. He nodded towards two empty seats at a small table near the fireplace. 'That all right for you?'

'Yes, fine.'

Nina led the way to the table. They sat down and studied each other's face. There was a haze of tobacco smoke drifting towards them from a man smoking a pipe nearby. Stuart jerked his head towards the trail of smoke. 'We're in the line of fire. Do you object?'

Nina shook her head. 'Not here, in the pub, although I draw the line at anyone smoking in my own house. The smell clings for ever.' She paused. 'Do you smoke?'

'Used to. I was a ship's engineer for many years; it was practically obligatory to smoke in those days. I enjoyed my pipe and cigarettes but when I transferred to passenger liners and smoking began to be socially unacceptable I weaned myself off the dreaded weed. I saw a few of those educational shorts on the box and I decided I wanted to live to a good old age. Nowadays, I wouldn't thank anyone for a cigarette, but the scent of pipe tobacco gets me going.'

Nina's lips quirked into a smile. She asked: 'Been retired long?'

'A few years.'

'Do you miss the life?'

'I miss the sea.' Stuart ran his hand over his hair. 'Much as I like talking about myself, we came in here to discuss other things. What about your writing?'

'Yes, that's right.' Nina drank from her glass. He really was interested in her work. She felt flattered yet a little bit disappointed. He was the most attractive man she had met for quite a long time. She looked down at his long elegant but workworn fingers and then tuned into his words again.

'Have you tried a publisher? Asked for an opinion?'

'Oh, no. Not yet.'

'Maybe you should?'

She began to feel irritated. Typical man ... taking over and making suggestions about something he knew nothing about.

'I considered it,' she replied, keeping her voice low and calm. It took some effort. 'I made a few enquires but I understand that unless you are an established, published author, no one will look at half-finished work. They prefer to see the completed book.' She shrugged. 'And who can blame them. They must get some terrible stuff submitted.'

'Yes, but—'

She interrupted him, feeling sure of her ground. 'I was told the odds of a first book being accepted is about one thousand to one, unless you're a celebrity, of course.'

He gave a soft whistle. 'That's really long odds. I didn't realise.' He grinned. 'Thank God, I'm not interested in writing for publication. All I want to do is put down my experiences of life at sea for my own enjoyment and, hopefully, for the enjoyment of my grandchildren.'

'You have grandchildren?'

He drew his thick eyebrows together and his grey eyes twinkled. 'Not yet, but I'm counting on it. I've only one child, my son, but he's a personable chap. Gets on well with the ladies. It can only be a matter of time.'

Nina lowered her eyes. 'Yes, I think I spotted him, earlier today.'

'I rather thought you did. If so, you'll see what I mean.' His eyes crinkled most attractively when he smiled Nina sipped her wine as Stuart continued. 'I recognised you when Alice Springfield introduced us. You drive a Peugeot.'

'Yes.' Nina's eyebrows arched. 'You're most observant.'

His smiled widened. 'Tell me, was it Ian who caught your attention, or the Saab?'

She blushed, laughed and came clean. 'I admired both of them.'

He looked away from her pink cheeks and glanced at his watch. 'Don't mind my teasing you.' He squinted a little. 'Would you like another drink? There's just time.'

'No. I'm fine.'

'So am I.' Stuart picked up his drink and swirled the remaining beer round his glass. 'We'll get kicked out soon and we still haven't discussed writing. I want you to know that I was honestly impressed by the piece of work you read out. The main character was very strong. Tell me, is she a composite of different people you've met or does she spring wholly from your imagination?'

Nina propped her chin on her hand surprised by the seriousness of his gaze.

'That's hard to say. There's something of me in Stella, that goes without saying, but there's lots of other things. Bits and pieces from people I have met and been interested in, I suppose, and then facets of her which have come into being as I've been writing.' Nina shrugged her shoulders. 'Your question takes some thinking about.'

'Sorry.' He sat back in his chair. 'I've always been an avid reader and I love probing beneath the surface of what I read. Most sailors read, you know. There's time to fill when you're on a long haul and reading is a wonderful way of escaping the confines of the ship.'

He shook his head. 'It must be marvellous to envisage a time and place and people it with your own creations.'

She gave a short laugh. 'I wouldn't know. I'm not a proper writer. This stuff is my first attempt at a book and most of the situations I describe are based on fact. I worked in the music business during the sixties and seventies, when everything was changing, so I have plenty of material. I also met some very strange characters which I've adapted and used shamelessly. I don't know if I can call what I'm writing a *novel*. It's more of a hybrid with names changed, of course.'

'Well, whatever it is, it works. I'd like to

read it when it's finished, Nina McNulty.'

He leaned forward and stared into her eyes until she felt her cheeks glow.

'Thank you,' she said. She heard her voice sound uncertain which annoyed her. The guy was experienced in ways of charm, she thought. How much of what he was saying was genuine. She sat up straight and frowned. 'But no one will read the whole manuscript until I feel it is ready.'

'OK.' The amused note was back in his voice. 'But we can meet up again, can't we? You seem to know a bit about cars, the way Ian's car caught your attention.' He grinned again. 'What did you think of it. A beauty, I'm sure you will agree.'

Nina cleared her throat. 'Yes, it's a beautiful car.'

'A funny one, my son. He has a first-class degree in mechanical engineering, could have taken his pick of a number of highly paid jobs, but he insisted in specialising in automobile engineering and now he's decided that all he wants to do is 'hands-on' work. Nine months ago he packed in a brilliant job with masses of prospects and bought his own garage. It's not far from here. I was dubious, but it's his life and he's doing OK. Happier than he's ever been. That's why, when I decided it was time I put down some roots, I came to this place. I wanted a property that was easily accessible to other places but not in a big town. I also wanted to be fairly near to Ian, but not too near. That would never do.'

'So you've found the ideal place.' Nina had regained her composure. She placed her empty wine glass on the bar table. 'So, you have just the one child. Is there a Mrs Urquart?'

'Not now.' Stuart drained his glass. 'Ian's mother died when he was fifteen.'

Nina looked down at her hands. 'I'm sorry.'

'No need. It was a long time ago.' Stuart gave her a keen look. 'What about you?'

'I also made a change in my life when I came here. After my husband died suddenly I decided to sell up our property in London and adopt a quieter lifestyle.'

'Any children?'

'No.' Her voice was even and her eyes did not blink as she met his gaze.

'That's a shame, but there again,' he paused, 'that's not quite true now, is it?'

'What?' Her shoulders tightened.

'In a sense, you do have children.'

She stared at him, uncomprehending.

'*Your characters.*' His eyes seemed to her to be extra sharp as he looked at her. 'They're your children.'

'Oh, yes. I see what you mean.' She looked down at her hands. They were quiet, folded on her lap. 'I suppose you could say that.'

She surprised herself by giving a huge yawn. 'I'm sorry, but suddenly I feel very tired.'

'That's all right.' He was already on his feet. 'I'll get you home.' The grin up-tilted his mouth again. 'As quickly as possible. It does my image no good at all to have a beautiful lady yawning all over me.'

She had to smile and he added, approvingly, 'That's much better.'

She explained. 'I've had a busy day shopping, which is always tiring, I find.'

'Never do it myself. Can't understand females' enchantment with shopping.' He moved his chair out of her way and courteously extended his arm. 'Mind that peculiar iron bit sticking out from the base of the table.'

Observing his shabby but well-cut slacks and sports jacket, Nina thought he was the kind of man who didn't need the adornment of sharp clothes. Then she remembered that Alex had always prided himself on his snappy dressing and she felt a curious wave of guilt.

'I'll see you home, of course.'

'No need,' she protested.

But he had already taken a firm hold on her elbow.

As they walked towards the door the buzz of convivial talk was interrupted when the landlord took from beneath the bar a large brass bell and rang it vigorously.

'Time, gentlemen, please.'

The noise made them jump and both were smiling as they stepped into the quiet, starlit street.

'He was quick off the mark,' Stuart said, cheerfully.

'I think it depends on the night and the company present. Rumour has it certain colleagues are sometimes locked in until two or three in the morning on certain occasions.'

'When the local bobby's away, I bet?'

Nina smiled. 'How did you know?'

Stuart laughed. 'It's the same all the world over.'

They fell silent as they walked. After the smoky atmosphere in the pub the wonderful freshness of the night air was sweet.

Stuart looked up at the sky. 'The stars seem so low here,' he whispered. 'In the city you don't even notice them.'

'Yes.' Nina turned up the collar on her jacket. She stared upwards. 'I once knew someone who studied the stars.' Her voice was low and something, a certain timbre in her voice, made her companion look at her.

Perhaps she felt his gaze for she added, her voice brisker, 'It's quite frosty, perhaps that's why they twinkle so much.' She glanced at him. 'Please don't come any further. Look, there's my house.'

He shook his head. 'As befits my age, I

stick to the old-fashioned courtesies. Allow me.' He cupped her elbow with his hand and escorted Nina to her gate.

She thought how little he resembled a senior citizen. She liked him. She liked him a lot.

He broke the short silence. 'The writing group meets in a fortnight's time, is that right?'

'Yes.'

'That's too long.' He looked down at her. 'Will you come round for coffee one morning, or maybe you can come to tea.' As she began to speak, he added. 'Please, I'd like to show someone my new home and I'd like it to be you.'

As she still hesitated, he continued, 'Ian's coming over on Friday. Why don't you come then? You can meet him, and his new car...' His eyes twinkled. 'Also, I need a woman's advice. The sitting-room needs new curtains. By the way, I bake a damn good cake. What do you say?'

What could she say but yes.

Ian Urquart, arriving at his father's house after an early pub lunch at the Poachers' Pocket, was not unduly surprised to find a personable female reposing on the sofa in his father's sitting-room. The old man hadn't been long in the village but it didn't take him long to find and charm the best looking mature woman in a radius of forty miles. Ian had observed his father closely over the years and had often wondered at his success rate – he wasn't that good looking – but it wasn't until he himself had turned thirty that he began to understand. His dad was a romantic at heart. He meant what he said to his lady-friends. He genuinely enjoyed their company. He admired and respected females. They, apparently, in their turn, sensed his genuine warmth and accordingly reciprocated his emotions, blossoming and flourishing in his company.

Of course, Stuart being decidedly male, painful hiccups occurred. From time to time a lady would misinterpret his intentions, begin to mention words like rings, commitment. When that happened, the old man became a little perturbed – he hated hurting people – but usually, with inordinate grace, he extracted himself without too much difficulty.

Not that he confided to his son, of course. Stuart never boasted of his conquests. But Ian had seen him in action. The troubled pensive air Stuart adopted when a lady became a little too insistent; his suggestion that despite a strong feeling of attachment, no one could ever occupy the position of his dear, departed wife.

There was truth in that, too.

Anyway, this particular attractive lady ensconced on his father's sofa didn't look like a clinging violet. She looked more like a rather full-blown but exotic prize-winning chrysanthemum.

Ian, who had taken a short cut through the garden, opened the patio door and breezed in.

'Hello. Is my aged old man around. I'm Ian Urquart, by the way.' He extended his hand.

She put out a well-shaped capable hand, long fingers ending in buffed, oval nails, and shook his. Very much his father's son, Ian studied without seeming to her twopiece suit, semi-classic in style, her good quality leather shoes and particularly her slim legs. Well aware of his scrutiny, although it was discreet, she met his gaze with a cool, appraising glance of her own.

'Hello, Ian. I'm Nina. Nina McNulty. I'm a neighbour of your father and a friend, albeit a new one. He'll be through in a couple of minutes. He muttered something about concocting your favourite cake.'

Ian pressed her hand and released it, moving to an easy chair facing the sofa. 'I can guess what. I've always been a sucker for chocolate cake.'

'Is that right?' She smiled, disclosing strong, white teeth. 'I'm a chocolate lover, too. That's two things we have in common.'

144

Two things? Oh, yes. Ian smiled to himself.

'Actually,' Nina smiled back at him. 'When I first saw your father, you were with him, but it was the Saab Turbo that caught my eye.'

Ian sat up straight in his chair. 'You know about cars?'

'A little. My late husband taught me something about them. I certainly coveted the Saab. Are you keeping it for yourself or selling it?'

'Haven't decided yet. I'll probably keep it for a little while.'

'Well, if you change your mind, you might get in touch. Although–' Nina gave a mock scowl '–I doubt I could raise the price you'd ask. It's a wonderful car but above my lifestyle.'

'I'll remember.' Ian's voice was non-committal but his mind was working overtime. Maybe she couldn't afford the Saab but she looked expensive and if she lived in the village, she must have paid out a lot of money for her home. His father, he knew, was basically uninterested in money, so long as he had enough to get by on; but, in Ian's book, there was never such a thing as too much money. This new lady intrigued him. He looked forward to learning more about her. Who knows ... on the next visit, he might do better than a couple of slices of his father's chocolate cake.

Ten

Richard Argyle, absentmindedly jingling the loose change in his trouser pocket, glanced out of the window and caught sight of his new tenants walking up the path to the front door. They had moved into the second-floor flat two weeks ago and, as his agent said, they were tenants from heaven.

'Excellent couple, first-rate references, extremely polite and childless. You won't have hooligan grandchildren rampaging around above your head on weekends. They also seem a quiet couple.'

They were that all right. Richard wouldn't have believed two people could be so quiet. Did they ever raise their voices? The only sounds he ever heard was water gurgling in their cistern and occasionally, the sound of an alarm clock trilling. Mr and Mrs Shapley could have been ghosts. He knew they had a television. Amy Langton, conveniently dusting the hallway when they moved in, informed him she had seen their set carried in.

'Just a little portable.' Her tone of voice was dismissive. 'Couldn't have been more than fourteen or fifteen inches across.'

Well, apparently they had excellent hearing as well as good sight because he had never heard a whisper from their viewing. Perhaps they wore earphones?

When the Shapleys began to mount the steps leading to the front door, Richard dodged back behind his curtains. He mustn't be caught spying on them. He felt guilty enough because he did not appreciate them as he should. He *didn't* dislike them. It was just ... they were just so damn quiet.

He sighed heavily. No, it wasn't even that. He was using the Shapleys as scapegoats. It was *his* life that was too damn quiet. And he was missing Helen. Missing her so damn much. Since her return to London she had phoned him twice but for the last fourteen days he had heard nothing from her. During her last call she had mentioned she was moving to another flat but she had assured him she would let him have her new address. He was still waiting but, he told himself, she would be busy getting settled.

His eyes felt sore. He blinked and looked up at the sky. A large cloud out to sea threatened rain to come but he still decided to go out. Walking helped, he found. Also, on a more mundane level, if he went out now he would miss the arrival of his cleaner. He really couldn't face up to Amy today, particularly as she had a new obsession. She had decided to take up the cudgels on behalf of Scarborough pensioners.

'Do you realise, Mr Argyle, that there are *no* concessions whatsoever on the buses for pensioners?'

When she first broached the subject he had murmured that he wasn't aware of the fact.

Neither had she been until her recent trip to visit a cousin who had moved to Leeds.

'I couldn't believe it, Mr Argyle, I really couldn't. I got the bus from outside the railway station and I went miles and miles for only forty pence. Why, it costs you more than I paid to go from Queen Street to Northway. That's not fair, is it? Especially for the older people. Why do people in Leeds get a better deal?'

'Leeds have a Labour Council.' Richard ventured to reply.

'What's that got to do with anything?'

'Well...' He had edged away from her. 'It's a bit complicated.'

She had fixed him with a withering glance. 'You worked for the council. You know about these things.'

'I did, but times have changed.'

'But you still *know* people who could do things. Can't they have a meeting. Pensioners are pensioners whether they're in Scarborough or Leeds. They should be treated the same.' She had crossed her arms – an ominous sign.

'You should get *involved*, Mr Argyle. I've noticed you mooning about lately, although it's not for me to say. Maybe if you took something on, like helping the pensioners, it would be good for you.'

She had gone too far and so Richard had terminated the conversation. Determinedly but not harshly because, although aggrieved, he was not really offended by Amy. He sometimes wished he had her clear-cut outlook on life. However, he did not relish a repeat conversation and so he intended absenting himself before her arrival. His timing was out. They met on the stairs.

'Mr Argyle. I'm glad I caught you.'

'Yes, what is it, Amy? I'm in a hurry.'

'Won't take more than a minute.'

He bit back a sigh and waited.

She surprised him. 'It's about the comet.'

She hadn't mentioned it for weeks. He wondered what had triggered off her interest again.

She enlightened him. 'Don't know if you saw last night's local newspaper?'

He shook his head.

She ploughed on. 'They said we'll see it real clear tonight. I thought you'd want to know in case your telescope needed shifting.'

Bless her! Richard hadn't bothered with the local paper for some time and since finding and then losing his daughter, he had forgotten about the comet. He was therefore grateful for Amy's information and said so.

Her cheeks went pink. 'That's all right.' She smiled and then sighed. 'Remember what I read about it in the paper a while back? It said it would bring us good fortune but it hasn't happened yet, has it?'

'No.' Unconsciously, Richard echoed her sigh.

'Well, we'll have to be patient, I suppose. We can't know everything, can we? If that comet's travelled millions of miles to whizz over our coastline on this particular evening then it stands to reason something's going to happen. There must be a plan somewhere.'

'I hope you're right.' He managed a tight smile and thought: the human race have a way to go yet. How can anyone expect a happier future simply because they spot something different in the sky? If I explained to Amy that her magical comet consisted of crumbly dust and water ice, that it originated about 50,000 AU from the Sun, and that it was going to be visible to us for a few minutes purely by chance, would it destroy her faith in the miraculous? Probably not. Ah, well – if it kept her happy and ... his mouth relaxed into a more natural smile ... stopped her from thinking about concessionary rates for pensioners, it was a good thing.

His mood continued to change for the better. Because the tide had recently gone out, the sand was firm, good for walking on. Richard strode out at a good pace. He passed the usual little family groups clustered round rock pools looking for crabs and, inevitably, the regular dog-walkers. Dogs were barred from the busy area of the beach during the season and their owners tended to congregate on the rocky area below the spa.

Richard had no firm thoughts on dogs. He didn't dislike them but he had never felt the need to own one. However, the little brindle cairn, chasing a ball, catching it and now cavorting around his feet was quite a charmer and hard to ignore. His long, pink tongue lolled out of a triangular shaped face, festooned with greyish-black whiskers. His eyes were large black raisins twinkling good-humouredly up at him through a veritable forest of coarse, wildly sprouting hair. His ears, pricked and quivering like TV antennas on a windy day, were obviously great sound detectors but his most appealing feature was his grin.

Richard had never seen a dog laugh. He stared down, fascinated.

'Sorry.' A fair-haired woman in trousers and a brown, zipped up jacket came panting up to him. 'Hope Reg hasn't jumped up at you. He's very wet, been in the sea.'

'No, he's all right.' Richard transferred his gaze to the woman. 'I was just studying his mouth. It's odd, but...'

'He's laughing.' She nodded. 'It's because of his teeth. They're overshot or undershot, I never can remember which.' The woman pushed her hair back from her forehead. 'Looks as though he's grinning at you, doesn't it? We were told he could have been a champion at Crufts but for them. Everything else is perfect, that's what the breeder said.'

'He certainly looks happy.'

'He is. I guess he enjoys the beach a lot more than he would have enjoyed dog shows. I like him like he is. He makes everyone smile.'

'I...' Richard looked directly at the woman and forgot what he was about to say. 'Don't I know you?'

Her face, already pink from fresh air and exercise, turned pinker.

'Yes. You know me a little bit. I wondered if you would remember. I've helped you out at the supermarket a couple of times. I remember you because you said you liked to cook.'

'Of course.' Richard blushed. 'Although I

153

don't, really. Cook, I mean. Just now and again I attempt something slightly more exotic than bangers and mash but I usually make a mess of it.'

The pause after his words became a little uncomfortable and the woman looked away and then made a grab for her dog. Reg immediately bounced out of reach and headed straight for the nearest rock pool.

'Oh, damn.' His owner rolled her eyes upwards. 'He always plays up when it's time to go home.'

'Maybe I can get him?'

Her doubtful look made Richard determined. Keeping his eyes on the cairn who was now occupied in shaking to death a large piece of seaweed, he ventured into the area where the waves were encroaching and balanced himself on a piece of driftwood. He crouched down and made a grab for Reg's collar. The piece of wood tipped sidewards, Richard fell on his knees and his right hand plunged into the pool, drenching his jacket sleeve up to his elbow. Reg, distracted by the splash, dropped his seaweed, rushed over and caught the cuff of Richard's wet sleeve in his mouth and tugged.

Richard's earlier empathy with the dog abruptly disappeared. He tapped Reg on the nose. Obviously offended, the cairn's smile disappeared. His teeth still showed, however. Intent on each other, neither saw Reg's owner creep up on him from behind and make a grab of his collar. She kept a firm grip on the wet, twisting dog and clicked on his lead. Then she slapped his rear end. Reg let go of Richard's jacket.

She turned to Richard. 'I'm so sorry. Let me help you up. Oh, you are wet. Has he torn your jacket?'

'No. I don't think so.' Upright again, Richard felt a complete fool. He could feel his face had reddened and the glance he sent towards the cairn was less than kindly.

'Let me see.'

'There's no need.' He actually snapped. His colour went even higher. He was not behaving like a gentleman. She hadn't asked him to catch the dog. He'd been a damned fool. He turned to go.

'I insist.' The woman's voice was low but determined. She rested her left hand on his dry arm. He looked down. Her nails looked good, not painted but buffed and well cared for. She wore a wedding ring.

She bent her head and examined the wet sleeve. She was wearing a flowery perfume, very faint, not cloying. 'Thank goodness, no real damage. I didn't think Reg would...' She shrugged then looked up at him. 'However, I must insist on paying for cleaning.'

'Oh, no...'

'But it was my dog...'

'You didn't ask me to try and catch him.'

They both looked down at Reg who was sitting with his back turned towards them, watching a group of seagulls riding the waves. Only a faint twitching of the tip of his tail showed he was alive.

They looked back at each other.

'Nevertheless–' a faint smile showed on her face '–if you knew me better, Mr–?'

'Argyle. Richard Argyle.'

'Mr Argyle. You would know how stubborn I am. Also, if you continue to use the supermarket I work in I shall feel awkward every time I see you.' She tilted her head. 'And so would you.'

Richard remained silent. He was examining the idea of seeing her again and finding the thought very pleasant.

'Well, I suppose...'

She interrupted him. 'In fact, you can use the dry-cleaning department in the store. Take your jacket there and mention my name and I'll settle the bill. Do you agree?'

He nodded and was rewarded by the sight of a fleeting dimple in her right cheek as she smiled.'

He asked. 'What is your name?'

'Greening. Mrs June Greening.'

He bit back a sigh. Of course, the wedding ring.

She turned to go and he hunted for something to say to keep her with him.

'Mrs Greening.'

'Yes.'

'Do you mind telling me, why Reg? It's a strange name for a dog.'

'I suppose it is.' She bent to pat her pet. 'My husband started it. When my son and I came back from the kennels, Chris was so excited. He had wanted a puppy for ages. My husband kept teasing him, suggesting the most ridiculous names. You know what fathers can be like.'

Richard nodded, but he didn't know. His father had never teased him and he had never had the opportunity. The thought of Helen came into his mind. She was never far away nowadays.

'Reginald was one of the names John suggested. Chris was really cross but then...' She fell silent, pressing her lips together; but after a moment she continued, looking away from Richard and out to sea. 'Two weeks later John was killed in a car crash so Chris decided on Reginald, Reg for short.'

'Oh, Lord.' Richard put out his hand and then dropped it to his side. 'I'm so sorry. I never...'

'Of course you didn't.' She smiled. 'It was a long time ago. Reg is nine years old now, although he doesn't act it.' She bent down and patted the dog.

There was a short silence which Richard broke. 'And your son?'

'Chris is eighteen now. Almost nineteen.' She paused. 'He left for Australia eight months ago. We have relatives over there and he fancied a bit of adventure. He's working in a garden centre just outside Sydney at the moment. He's hoping to come home to visit next year but I don't think he'll come back to stay.'

'It must be lonely for you?'

She shook her head and smiled. 'What? With this little tyke to look after?' Then, glancing at her watch she frowned. 'I really must dash. You'll remember to bill me for the cleaning?'

'I will.'

He watched her walk away from him and thought: I'll remember you. How comfortable he had felt with her. He wasn't too sure about what to do next but he did know he would be doing more shopping at the supermarket in the future. He turned to walk home, forgetting about his wet sleeve and putting his right hand in his jacket pocket. As the wet fabric stuck to his wrist he grimaced and then smiled again.

Returning home, he changed his clothes then climbed up to the attic room, the one room in the house he had kept the same since his childhood. He positioned the telescope for the viewing of the comet. Then he took a few minutes to browse through the Yearbook of Astronomy. The word luminosity caught his eye. Mrs J. Greening had beautiful skin, he thought. He went down to his flat and forgot to check his phone to see if Helen had called.

Eleven

The flat was pretty good, considering. The carpets were not Helen's choice but she could live with them. The seller had generously thrown them in with the price. He was going to work abroad so they were of no use to him. Helen wondered what it must be like, going to live and work in a foreign country. It depended on the country, she supposed. An opportunity had once opened up for someone in her department to go and work in Paris for a year but she had never even considered it. She had just become engaged to Phil and had other things on her mind. She might have been successful, too. She was good at languages and could speak French well and had an A-level in German. The chance had come when she was working for the publishing company where she was often called upon to deal with telephone calls from overseas. Now, she couldn't help wondering what her life would be now if she had applied for the post. On the other hand she had a job which paid more than publishing and now she had her very own home.

Moving to the window and relishing the

fact that she had finished all the outstanding tasks of moving, she parted the nets and looked out. Not a bad outlook. Built up, of course, but there were a couple of trees outside. Her flat was on the first floor and looking down upon the leaves, stirring in the breeze, reminded her of the view she and Phil had shared when they were living in the vicinity of St James's Park. Directly facing her were private houses with front gardens and next to them a shop but, fortunately, it was a florist.

She pulled a face. Oh God! She was turning into a snob. No. She shook her head. She wasn't, but she didn't want friends to come and visit and think, 'Poor Helen. She's come down in the world since her divorce.' The flat was fine, for a single person. She moved away from the window and went to sit in her most comfortable chair. Gazing at the blank screen of the television she debated what she should do. After a lot of hard work her new home was as organised as a new home could be. It was now, she glanced at her watch, almost twelve noon. If she wished, she could be totally lazy for the rest of the day.

There was one snag. Ian Milton, the manager of the section of the insurance company for which she worked had telephoned her a couple of hours earlier. The company had recently acquired two offices in the next-door property to their premises. The offices were going to be used mostly for storage and for the last month staff had been busily bundling up documents and records ready for transfer. The proposed re-organisation of the office layout had been delayed because of a rush of claims following flooding in the region of the Severn Valley. Nevertheless, Ian Milton had allowed Helen time off to deal with her flat move. She was grateful but she had not been surprised to hear from him last night.

'How's things going, Helen?'

'Pretty good. Still things to do.' She had crossed her fingers. It was Friday evening but that meant nothing to Ian. Work was his life.

'But the essentials are sorted out? You've got gas, electricity, stuff like that?'

'Yes.' There was a note of caution in her reply.

'That's good.'

A pause. Helen waited.

'I was wondering, if you're more or less settled in, might you be able to spare me a few hours?' Barely pausing for breath, Ian hurried on. 'We've worked wonders since Wednesday. John Porter, Alan White and myself have moved the old stuff next door and reorganised the space we've made in the main office. You've benefitted, Helen. Your desk is by the large window now. Anyway, John and Alan have left but I've decided to work on, it's so much easier when it's quiet. I'd like to tackle the files to be stored. They're everywhere at the moment; on chairs, on the floor.' He paused. 'It would be much quicker if two people worked on them.'

Helen bit back a sigh. 'I see your point, Ian, but I've been pushing furniture around for the last two days and I don't...'

'Oh, no. You don't have to do any *heavy* work. I thought you could run through the boxes relating to commercial enterprises. They're old so most of them we can destroy but we still have to check each one. You know the insurance world. Still–' he sighed '–if you really can't spare the time...'

She dithered, then compromised. 'Let me ring you back.'

Ian had given her time off for her move. They had a good working relationship, and with her higher mortgage it paid her to be co-operative. She sighed and picked up the phone.

Going through to the bedroom to collect her jacket, she paused in the doorway and took another look at her sitting-room. It was a decent size, well decorated and she had arranged her furniture to the best advantage – but it wasn't *quite* right. It lacked something. Helen studied the mirror and the curtains. They were OK. Did it need a picture or two?

Nina would have known what was needed. Helen had a sudden memory from the past. Her mother dashing out of a gloomy, depressing, newly rented room and returning, clutching in her hand a huge bunch of ruby-red paper flowers. She had rifled in their battered suitcase and found a dark blue pillow case which she promptly tacked over a plastic waste bin standing in a corner. Filled with the flowers and standing in the empty hearth the whole room had been transformed.

Helen sighed and shook her head. She grabbed her jacket and shoulder bag and ran down the stairs and into the street. She shouldn't be thinking of Nina. The flat was part of her plan for a new future. No ghosts were allowed there.

The nearest tube station was only five minutes' walk away. Hurrying down the stairs Helen chalked up another advantage of her house move. Finding a seat on the tube she stared through the window into the blackness, but in blocking her mother from her mind she began to think of Richard. She wondered yet again whether she had done the right thing leaving her new phone number on his answering machine.

It was an odd relationship that had sprung up between them. Why *had* he been so interested in her search for Nina? When she was on her own, she always ended up thinking their relationship was peculiar, or he was; but recollecting his immaculate behaviour towards her, her opinion softened. He had been supportive and kind at a time when she needed someone to be on her side. Oh dear! She sighed. She had dithered for days before contacting him. Well, perhaps she would never hear from him again and she could forget all that had happened, just like one day she might be able to forget her mother's disappearance.

'Hi. Thanks for coming.' Ian's dust-streaked face lit up as he opened the entrance door. 'I'm working in the outer office. I've shifted the files I want you to check over in here.'

Helen followed him into the adjoining room. The boxes of files were thick with dust and she was glad she was in her old jeans and sweatshirt. Ian, dirt streaks on his Oxford blue shirt and jeans, picked up a large box and placed it on to one of the desks. He waved his hand. 'There you go.'

She looked at the piles of faded brown files tied with red tape. 'Do we have to check them all?' She picked one up and opened it. 'My God, the second copies have been done with blue carbon paper.'

'Be thankful you're not working for a solicitor, my girl.' Ian ran his hand through his hair. 'You'd be deciphering eighteenth-century handwriting. People and businesses fade away but files go on for ever. You know that.'

'I suppose so.'

'Anyway, you don't have to study them all.' He handed her a three-page computerised list of names.

'Here's the people we're no longer in contact with but with whom we've done constant business in our past recent history. I reckon we need to keep their files where we can easily find them. And these–' he dumped another cardboard box beside the desk '–are files of previous lucrative customers going back twenty or thirty years. Some of the people will be dead and gone but there'll be a note on the cover of the file. Get rid of those but save the rest.'

Helen sighed, pushed up her sleeves and plunged in. After half an hour she realised she was finding the files interesting. The commercial language used twenty, thirty, forty years ago was not so different from today, but the premiums and pay-outs were laughably small. By three o'clock she had worked through one box and started on the other. Ian had sent out for sandwiches and coffee earlier so she was not hungry but she relished the thought of a hot bath when she returned home. Her hands were grubby and her nose and mouth felt dry from the amount of dust swirling around her.

Time passed. It was a quarter to four. Helen took out yet another file which had been thrust down the side of the second box. She turned it the right way round to read the label on the cover and then her breath caught in her throat as she read:

McNULTYS' MUSIC AGENCY
Jazz, Blues, Duo's, Trio's, etc.
Waldour Street
Soho
London
(Comprehensive Insurance)

The memory of the conversation with Terry Warden came flooding back. *She told Alex they ought to move to London.*

'Hi, how you doing?'

The door swung back as Ian strode in.

Instinctively, Helen grabbed another file, opened it and fanned it over the desk.

'Fine.'

'That's good. How about working another hour and then calling it a day?'

'Yes. OK.'

He glanced at her. 'Are you sure?'

'Yes.' She swallowed. 'Why do you ask?'

'You look a bit pale.'

'I'm all right.' She managed a smile. 'Maybe the dust's getting to me.'

He grinned. 'Could be. Another hour, then.'

He left the room.

Blessing the fact she had brought her large shoulder bag, Helen took the McNulty file and slipped it inside.

Back at the flat, she put off investigating the contents of the file she had appropriated. She had a bath – badly needed – made a sandwich and ate it. Then she sat down in her favourite chair, took a deep breath and opened the cover. The first reading was not a success. She raced too quickly through the legal jargon, the 'whereas and wherefores', trying to read between the lines. She read it again, this time more carefully. She realised the McNultys' business had been successful. The floorspace and staff proved that. Also the premiums. But as her professional mind assessed the business facts the child within her was struggling for attention. The child won.

Why had her mother abandoned her for a man who managed pop bands? Where had she met him? Had she known him before the trip to Liverpool? She must have done. Nina was headstrong but she would never have run away with a total stranger. Would she? It wasn't as if there had been trouble with Frank. He bored her mother, Helen knew that, but he was tolerant with Nina and let her have her own way. Whatever the circumstances, why had Nina never got in touch again? What the hell had happened?

Helen ran her hand through her hair. Her eyes misted as she remembered how she had laid in bed for months wondering if Nina had been murdered. It happened. It happened all the time.

And while she had been suffering, Nina had been in a club somewhere or booking a group for a tour. *Jesus.* Helen rocked herself backwards and forwards in her chair. All her early life, her mother's boyfriends had come and gone, but there had always been the two of them. Two against the world.

Her eyes flooded with tears. She stood up and walked around the room. Her mind scrabbled frantically, trying to find another explanation. Maybe there was something, a strange quirk, an abnormal gene in Nina's physiology? She stopped dead. The scientists nowadays were discovering all sorts of peculiarities in the human psyche. She ran her fingers through her hair. If that was so, maybe she had it, too? She wasn't particularly maternal, was she? She hadn't been enthusiastic about having a baby. And with regards to her mother, she was becoming obsessive about being deserted by her. Why couldn't she let it be; move on and concentrate on the future? She sighed, walked over to the chair and picked up the file.

The telephone rang. She jumped so violently the sheaf of papers fell to the floor. She stared down at them as the phone kept on ringing. After a couple of minutes she moved slowly towards the phone. She picked up the receiver just in time to hear the line go dead. She replaced the receiver. Just as well. She didn't want to talk to anyone. Returning to the file, she knelt down and began to pick up the papers from the floor. Part of her didn't want any new, hurtful, revelations but, automatically, her eyes began to scan the copies of accounts and letters.

Eventually, she sat cross-legged on the carpet and arranged the scattered correspondence into the correct order. Then she read through it. She read that Alex McNulty died of a heart failure. Helen's mouth set in a hard, thin line as she read this. She put down the notification of death and picked up the next note of agreement. Nina, Mrs McNulty – in name, anyway – carried on the business for some years. Successfully, it seemed. But then the last piece of correspondence dealt with termination of the contract. Mrs McNulty had decided it was time to retire. She sold the company and the new owners had their own insurance brokers. However, Mrs McNulty had furnished her new address in case they needed to contact her.

Helen, crouched on the carpet, stayed in the same position until her feet suffered from pins and needles.

Twelve

The morning after his meeting with June Greening, Richard was up early planning his strategy. He didn't admit it; he didn't even formulate what he was planning. Strategy was a *cold* word; more to do with war than... He shied away from yet another word, leaning forward towards the bathroom mirror and wiping away the remnants of shaving foam from his chin. That was better. No, the thing was, he felt *confident* about the action he had planned. He was going to take his jacket to the supermarket's dry-cleaning department and, if conditions were right, he would leave it there. If the conditions were wrong – in other words, if he didn't spot June – he would bring the jacket back home and keep trying until he saw her and managed to speak to her again. He was being devious, but what was wrong with that? For the first time in years he had felt at ease with a woman and attracted to her. And, if he was not mistaken, she quite liked the look of him.

He vacated the bathroom and as he crossed to his kitchen he saw the telephone in the hallway and thought of Helen. He had rung her on Saturday night but there had been no reply. He had been disappointed and then pleased, because it meant she was out somewhere, dining with friends or on a trip to a theatre. God, he hoped so. She needed to relax and enjoy herself after their abortive trip to Liverpool. The trouble was, she had his temperament. She thought too much and found it hard to let go.

But she was making a good effort. She had moved to her new flat and different surroundings would help her cope with her loss. Not for the first time, Richard thought about her relationship with her ex-husband. Poor, prickly Helen. He wanted so much to help her but she wasn't a child and the best thing he could do was leave her in peace. Wait for her to ring him.

He went to make his breakfast.

Richard took his jacket to the supermarket on Monday and drew a blank. He went back home, glum-faced and carrying a portion of a peculiar green vegetable called kohlrabi which he had spotted and bought to impress June if he saw her. He looked through his two cookery books without finding any reference to the exotic vegetable, which looked like a feathery cross between a golf ball and a tennis ball, so he threw it away and told himself he was behaving like an idiot. However, he went back next day.

June was among the freezer cabinets, holding a clipboard and checking items of frozen food. Richard faded behind a tall container of plastic milk bottles then dashed off to the dry-cleaning counter. Five minutes later, unencumbered by his sea-stained jacket, he sauntered in June's direction. She glanced up – and he'd swear she blushed – while acknowledging him.

'Why hello, Mr Argyle. How are you? No ill effects from the soaking sleeve, I hope?'

'No, no. I'm fine.'

He was, now she was in front of him, but the confidence he had nurtured in the bathroom had disappeared. He tried to think of something to say.

'I've dropped the jacket off at the cleaners, as you suggested.'

Curse it. He sounded like an old skinflint demanding his money's worth.

She nodded 'Good. You gave my name?'

'Yes.'

There was a short pause. Jane looked back at her clipboard.

He hesitated, then said: 'Well, I guess I'll go and get my shopping.'

She nodded.

Richard turned and walked away from her. Then he paused. Something good had happened when they met on the beach. Why was it so awkward now? He glanced around him. Shoppers hurried by. A young woman in an overall was on her knees stacking cans of beans on a shelf nearby. She was obviously watching them with interest for she smirked and waved when she saw him looking at her. The jingles from the loudspeaker continued. Richard pulled a face. Muzak – wasn't it called? He looked back at June. She was studying her clipboard and her cheeks were pale. Damn it, he thought. It's the place that's wrong, not us. He strode back to her.

'Do you get a lunch break?'

She looked up, startled. 'Yes, in about–' she glanced at her watch '–twenty-five minutes.'

'I'll wait for you in the cafe just across the road. Will you come?'

She hesitated. 'I usually eat in the store canteen.'

'The food's good at the Copper Kettle.'

Her face relaxed. She nodded. 'All right.'

He stole glances at her when it was safe to do so, when she wasn't looking. Her eyebrows were darker than her hair. Maybe she used a rinse or something. Her face was pale. The colour in her cheeks on Sunday had been due to the elements. She was speaking.

'Sorry if I kept you waiting.'

Richard shook his head. 'You didn't. Do

you want the menu?'

She didn't reply. He realised she was nervous.

'I've just recently been made up to supervisor,' she said. 'I'm pleased, of course. There's more money for me but there's such a lot to learn.' She shrugged her shoulders. 'Today was my first experience of stock-taking the contents of the freezer cabinets. I know it sounds silly but I really had to concentrate. There's all these different barcodes...'

'Don't worry.' Richard handed her a menu. 'What would you like to eat?'

'I don't have much at lunchtime.' June studied the card.

'They do wonderful cinnamon and sultana muffins. Let's have them, shall we?' Richard waited until she nodded then raised his hand for the waitress. He enjoyed ordering for her.

'They won't be long, will they? I only have three quarters of an hour.'

Richard kept that in mind.

Halfway through her muffin, June looked round and enquired: 'Where's your shopping?'

'Oh,' he thought rapidly. 'Since we were coming here I thought I would do it later. There's not a lot of space in here for bags.'

'I see.' She grinned at him. 'This muffin is delicious.'

They had both relaxed. They talked, finding mutual interests in several topics, their conversation became animated and enjoyable. Watching the colour come and go in her cheeks as she waxed enthusiastic or dismissive of certain aspects he put forth, Richard was dismayed when he glanced at his watch and saw how quickly the time had raced by. Seeing his gesture, June also looked down at her wristwatch.

'Oh, Lord.' She jumped up. 'I'll have to go.'

'Yes.' Richard sighed.

As they hurried out of the cafe, June enquired: 'Doing your shopping now?'

'Yes.' He shrugged. 'I need quite a lot of stuff.'

She looked sidewards at him.

'I think it's time I had another go at cooking,' he blurted out.

'Good idea.'

They were approaching her place of work.

'We've just had some lovely plump free-range chickens delivered. There's hundreds of recipes for chicken, most of them easy enough to follow.'

She would leave him in a minute. He asked: 'Fresh or frozen?'

She laughed. 'Fresh, of course.' She nodded to a girl on the cheese counter.

'Do you like chicken?'

'Yes, I do.'

She glanced at her watch again, frowned and looked at him. 'Well, thank–'

He interrupted. 'Would you have dinner with me?'

She looked grave. 'Do you think it would be wise?'

'Why not?' He waited for her answer and when she did not reply, he pressed on. 'We enjoyed our snack, didn't we? And it's no use me cooking when I have no one to dine with me.'

'Is that true?'

He nodded his head vehemently. 'Cross my heart.' He saw the beginning of a smile and pressed on. 'Bring Reg with you, if you like. And I'll furnish references as to my character. I'll introduce you to my upstairs tenants.' He gave an inward shudder at the thought of Mr and Mrs Shapley.

'Oh, well. All right.' She smiled and the colour rushed into her face.

'Would tomorrow be all right. About seven thirty?'

'That would be fine.'

'I'll see you then. Or I could come and collect you?'

'Better not, if you're doing the cooking. But,' she paused, 'there's just one thing.'

'What?'

'I don't know where you live.'

'Oh Lord.' He fumbled in his pocket and produced a card. 'I'm so sorry.'

'Thank you.' She took it and pushed it into her pocket. 'Now I have to fly.'

She hurried away from him but he caught her up.

'Now what?'

He grinned, which made him look much younger. 'I'm going to buy a chicken, of course.'

That night, after a wakeful hour, June Greening fell asleep and dreamed about David Randall. When she awoke, suddenly, in the early dawn light, she put her hands behind her head and gazed up at the ceiling. She hadn't consciously thought of David for years but she had known for a long time that he was the man she should have married. They had met at school and he had been her first boyfriend. She and David always had things to talk about. He looked out for her. They had walked hand-in-hand, laughed easily together about other people but with no malice. Later, when the time had come, David had made her appreciate parts of her body she had never even thought of. Not that there had been full scale love-making. She was only sixteen and naturally cautious.

That was the trouble. They had met too early. They both became restless and aware of the big wide world outside. They decided, with much heartbreak, that they were too young to be 'tied down' so David went to work in the South and she enrolled in a course at the local technical college. After a year of writing to each other the letters became fewer and eventually stopped. June banged her pillow and wondered why David had come into her mind. She tried to sleep again but the dawn chorus wouldn't allow her the luxury. She linked her hands behind her head and stared at the ceiling.

Seven years since her husband died. How much did she miss him? Not so much during the daytime but at night, she missed the reassuring bulk of him beside her in the bed. She missed him sitting in his recliner chair and reading the newspaper, looking across to tease her about her addiction to a certain TV programme.

'How can you bear to watch such rubbish?'

'How can you bear to read the Financial Times?' she had replied, often snappily.

June sighed. She had turned into a somewhat waspish wife and yet their marriage had started so well. They met when she went to work at the local building society when she was twenty-two. John was Chief Clerk, an excellent post for a man of thirty-four.

She remembered his appearance had impressed her. He was a tall man, well built and always wore a dark suit which emphasised his blond good looks. His hands and nails were immaculate and all the female employees fancied him. When he asked her out she said yes without any hesitation. In part, because he was a 'catch' and in part because all her girlfriends – young women she had grown up with – were either planning white weddings or, after a year of marriage, were expecting their first baby.

She grew to like him. He was courteous, often brought her flowers, took her out for meals. Her parents were dubious when she finally took him home. Her dad and his dad before him had been blue-collar workers and a man of thirty-four with soft white hands was suspicious, but after a couple of encounters things smoothed out.

'He's a gentleman,' June's mother announced and June's dad had nodded approvingly.

June still had certain reservations. Remembering the fun she'd had with David, she thought that laughter in this relationship was in rather short supply. But, after four months' courtship, John began to show a different side to his personality. He became passionate. His kisses grew more intimate, his trembling fingers unbuttoned buttons and disengaged zips and June's blood began to run more quickly through her veins. Aroused by his actions June indicated through her reactions her willingness to lose her virginity but, to her astonishment, John demurred.

'Better wait,' he whispered, caressing her breasts. 'Your mum and dad would be upset if they found out.'

Taken aback, June wondered who would tell them? She also wasn't so sure of their possible reaction. She hadn't a clue what her parents thought about sex before marriage. Still, she wrapped her arms around his neck. They didn't have long to wait.

The marriage took place the day after her twenty-third birthday and was consummated in a bedroom on the Isle of Wight where they spent their honeymoon. Everything went satisfactorily, if a bit too quickly. A pattern which continued throughout their marriage.

They returned from honeymoon to live in a modern three-bedroomed house with a garden, thanks to a special deal with the building society. Unfortunately, due to the society's rules, June had to give up her job. Married couples could not work together. It was a blow quickly forgotten when June became pregnant. Everyone was delighted when Christopher was born.

'A little lad.' Her father had given her a bear-hug, causing her to wince in her hospital bed. 'Just what we all wanted, pet.'

Actually, she had wanted a girl, but it

didn't matter. Once she had held her child, studied his fingers and toes and his gummy mouth when he bellowed for his feed, she fell in love with him.

Now another man had entered her life. How would he turn out? She sighed, pulled up the quilt and went back to sleep.

Thirteen

June got out of the taxi and looked up at the house. First-floor flat, he'd said. Communication buzzer in the hallway. She took a deep breath, wishing she had stuck to her first choice of outfit, a navy-blue suit with a white lace blouse. At home, she'd decided it looked too businesslike so she had changed into her only alternative, a shirt-style jacket in red worn over a slim black skirt. She was still dissatisfied but there was nothing else she could wear. The only other clothes she possessed were casual tops and trousers. Said a lot about her social life, didn't it? Walking unsteadily, she climbed the flight of steps leading up to the house. God, she hated high heels.

Another thought struck her. What if the flat was too warm? Maybe Richard liked a hot-house atmosphere. She didn't – but no matter how hot she felt she wouldn't be able to do a thing about it. Oh, Lord, why hadn't she thought of that? She was a complete idiot. She bit her lip. This evening was going to be a complete disaster. Could she sneak off, go home and ring him, tell him she was starting a cold? No. That wouldn't be fair.

Richard was cooking a meal.

She stared at the door, opened it, took another deep breath and stepped into the hallway. She approached the row of buttons on the wall facing her and pressed the intercom to Richard's flat.

'Hi. It's me.' Was that her voice? She sounded squeaky, for God's sakes. She cleared her throat. 'Richard?'

'Yes. Come on up.'

She started up the staircase, trying to walk regally. It was that kind of staircase – gracious, curving. When Richard had told her the building he owned had been an hotel she had assumed that, in its heyday, his parents had catered for the lower-middle classes. The building was on the Esplanade and not too large. Her assumption was natural. The phrase 'lower-middle class' was almost comical nowadays, but it had been appropriate during the years just after the war and it stayed appropriate until the end of the sixties. Years ago, June reflected, people and buildings knew their places. When she was growing up a holiday in Scarborough had meant different things to different people.

The Wakes weeks, for instance. The annual holiday for the mill workers; a time when trains and buses poured into Scarborough packed with people determined to enjoy themselves. They did, too. Booked in the same B&B year after year, Scarborough was home from home to them. Cockles and whelks from the stalls and fish and chips eaten from the paper, the men might stroll along the pier and try their hand at fishing before packing into the pubs. The south beach was populated with mothers and children. Come after ten in the morning and it was hard to find a patch of clear sand to park your belongings. Once established, grandmas and mums didn't move. They watched the kiddies splashing in the sea with eagle eyes but even so, loud wails arose from the lost children depot. Food was no problem. You brought your own or sent the kids up the slipways to fetch jugs of tea, crisps and sandwiches from the kiosks.

The Scotch fortnight was different again. Edinburgh week brought money to the town. It was possible such families stayed at Richard's parents' hotel. The usually soft accents of the Scots would be heard as they came down the staircase for a nip of whisky before going along to the spa to listen to the orchestra – always with a guest singer – or perhaps going to a theatre. Yes, the Edinburgh lot were tolerated.

It was doubtful whether the Glasgow visitors would have ventured up to the South Cliff. They preferred the noise, colour and excitement of the Foreshore area. Overlooked by the Norman Castle the 'old town' was full of curio shops, bingo halls and, of course, pubs and bookies. When the pubs chucked out the absence of residents was noticeable.

'Heathens, the lot of them. You can't understand a word they say!'

But the traders and the publicans smiled all the way to the bank.

Why, thought June. Why am I woolgathering like this? Just because Richard's home is more elegant than I anticipated I have no reason to feel intimidated. But she remembered how her husband had teased her, just a little bit too long, when she mispronounced certain words and his comments on her choice of television programmes.

How can you watch such rubbish?

She moistened her lips with her tongue and went on.

She didn't have to ring his doorbell. The door was already open and Richard was waiting for her, a teacloth clutched in his right hand.

'Come in. Did you find the house OK?' He stepped back. 'Goodness, you look very smart.'

Richard wasn't very smart. He wore grey slacks and an open-neck shirt in two shades of blue.

She hurried passed him into the flat.

'I came in a taxi, Richard. I could hardly get lost.'

His smile vanished. 'Sorry?'

'No, no. I'm sorry.' She was blushing now, the heat in her face was burning. 'I didn't mean to be rude.'

He followed into his home. There was a short silence and then he touched the back of her right hand with his fingertips. It was a gentle, fleeting movement.

'It's OK. Forget it.'

She thought, not for the first time: he's a gentleman.

'Dinner's almost ready.' He stepped back and smiled at her. 'You look warm, June. Shall I take your jacket?'

'No.' Her voice was so vehement his eyes widened. She put her hand up to her face. 'Oh, I knew I shouldn't have come.'

'Why? What have I done?'

She gazed at his red face. '*You've* done nothing. It's me.'

'I don't understand. You've only just arrived. What's upset you.'

She bit her lip. 'I can't take my jacket off.'

Richard frowned. 'Well keep it on.'

June detected a certain coolness in his voice, a hardening of attitude. He was losing his patience and she didn't blame him. She twisted her hands together and blurted out:

'I sound stupid, don't I, but,' she paused, 'I can't take my jacket off because I've

189

nothing on beneath it. At least, well ... I'm wearing a bra.'

She snapped her eyes shut as well as her mouth. She didn't want to see his reaction.

He'll think I'm mad. Or, even worse, he'll think I'm here for... Her mind retreated from that line of thought. He's a gentleman. He'll be disgusted or else ... God forbid. What if I'm wrong. He might be ... interested. I might have to fight him off. She took a step backwards.

Richard made a muffled sound. He put his hand over his mouth.

He was shocked.

She turned round and blundered her way back towards the door.

'No, wait.' He put his hand down.

She looked at him. He was grinning. She felt her face go crimson.

'For God's sake, June. Relax.' He pressed his lips together, before continuing. 'I've been married, my dear. I guessed, just a moment before you spoke, what the problem was. But why all the angst? I thought we were good friends. Friends are easy with each other, aren't they? Anyway, think of *me*. I'm *cooking*, for God's sake! Don't you think I'm nervous?'

The tension inside her eased away. She knew she had been a fool but she managed to smile. 'I'm sorry. I'm an idiot.'

'No, you're not. Neither am I.' Richard

took hold of her hand. 'We're two people who have lived alone for a long time and it's difficult to break out of our shells. Would you agree?'

She nodded.

He squeezed her fingers and released them. 'Let's start again.'

He took a step back. 'Can I get you a glass of wine? Oh ... and I'll adjust the heating system, if necessary. Just give me a wink?' His lips quivered as he hurried on: 'The meal's almost ready. It's straightforward cooking – roast chicken and vegetables, but I've made a blue cheese salad and there's a lemon pudding or cheese and biscuits for afters. Will that suit?'

'Oh, Richard, that sounds wonderful.' For the first time that evening, June gave him a natural smile.

'Good. Come on through to the sitting-room and choose your wine.'

'Richard, just a minute.'

He turned back to her. 'Yes?'

'Nothing much. Just...' She stepped closer to him, put her arms around his neck and kissed him. 'Thank you.'

About the same time June kissed Richard and, despite the noise from London traffic on a busy road a mile away from where she lived, Helen Stephens had fallen asleep. Helen had recently discovered that falling asleep was the easiest thing in the world. All you had to do was sit down, close your eyes and there you were ... or not, as the case may be. On one of her few better days, when she could look at life with a wry smile, Helen thought that if she could bottle whatever was happening to her, she could make herself a fortune. Insomniacs from miles around would besiege her flat demanding to know her secret. But on the other days, and nights, she didn't find her attempt at irony remotely amusing. Her usual reaction, when she woke up shivering with cold and suffering pins and needles in her feet and hands due to dozing on her two-seater sofa instead of taking herself to bed, was fury. She was furious with herself; furious with her stupid behaviour.

The trouble was, there was no *time*. Life was hectic at work. Despite the efforts of Ian Milton and the care taken by his staff during the transfer, various hiccups were causing problems. Some important files had gone missing. Also, the volatile weather over the last month was bringing in a higher level of insurance claims. Dealing with these problems had meant staff working longer hours. Helen's nerves were suffering. During the last week she could have sworn she had heard the name McNulty mentioned several times. She had been wrong, of course. She was exhibiting irrational behaviour. The McNulty connection with the firm had been severed years ago.

Helen knew she must take herself in hand. For example, nothing was stopping her replacing the original McNulty file she had taken home with her. She could go into work early, take a photocopy for her own use then put the original back where it belonged and no one would be the wiser. But she didn't. Every two or three days she would take the papers out of her bedroom drawer and pore over her mother's signature. Her *original* signature. In particular, she studied the way Nina looped the letters 'y' and 'l'. *She* did exactly the same. She had finally found one thing she and Nina had in common, and staring down at her mother's signature, Helen began to remember other things about her mother. Things she had forgotten.

Her mother once developed a passion for a perfume called Blue Mimosa. When they were constantly on the move from town to town and when Nina felt down she would treat herself. She would make what she could of their new abode, in Warrington, Northwich or wherever they landed up, and then after 'tarting up', as she called it, she would go out to buy groceries. Inevitably, after putting away the potatoes, bread, tins of baked beans and so forth, she would produce a small, square scent bottle.

Unscrewing the top she would tilt the bottle until a drop of the fragrance fell on to her forefinger and then stroke the perfume at the base of her throat. Her chatter would cease and she would say, dreamily: 'Always allow yourself a little bit of luxury, Helen. Even when you can't afford it. Remember what I'm saying, my girl. We need our dreams.' Then she would laugh, dab another drop of perfume on her finger and touch Helen's earlobes.

'You've got pretty earlobes. Wear your hair short when you're grown up. Show them off.' She would replace the top on the scent bottle. '"Blue Mimosa", my pet. Smell that scent. You'll have wonderful dreams tonight.' And then, tapping Helen's cheek. 'What a serious expression. Cheer up. We'll be all right. We'll have some laughs.'

And Helen had to admit, they did.

Although she drudged through her days at work she knew it was good she wasn't in her flat all the time. At the office, little things happened to stop her from slipping too deeply into the pool of the past. A new member of staff began to show an interest in her. Martin Horton was around thirty-five years old and good looking. Marilyn, the girl on the switchboard, said he was divorced. Helen wondered how she knew but, as Marilyn seemed to know everything, she took her at her word. She glanced at Martin from time to time and wondered why on earth he was targeting her. She wasn't the slightest bit interested in him. Perhaps her attitude intrigued Martin because, a couple of weeks after starting his new job, he asked Helen to go out with him.

'We could have a meal, perhaps? Do you like Thai food?'

She had stared at him with such surprise he was disconcerted. She noticed, with detached interest, the blush spread to his high cheekbones.

'I mean, if you want to?'

She thanked him politely but refused.

The same night Helen went back to her flat, ate cheese on toast, bathed and sat down to watch the television. One of her favourite actors was in a new drama. She watched for half an hour before falling asleep. At two in the morning she woke up and went to bed. Next day she was pleased to see Martin chatting up a woman who worked in the accounts department.

In between work and sleep, Helen tried to make plans. Why not get into her car and go and see Nina? It wouldn't take so long. Should she contact her first? Better not. What if her mother refused to see her? Surely she wouldn't do that? Helen played at different scenarios. She imagined walking up a path, ringing a door bell. The door opening and Nina looking out. Nina would be very much like the last time Helen had seen her, just a little older, of course, and she would fling open the door and say: 'Helen. Oh my God! I've yearned for this moment.'

And there'd be the smell of her perfume and the feeling of her arms around her.

Or ... after a bad time.

'Oh my God. How did you find me? No, sorry, darling. Can't see you today. Bit awkward, see. Someone coming to see me. Look, give me your phone number and I'll get in touch.'

Stupid. Ridiculous scenarios. Grow up, Helen.

The worst thing to happen was the dream she had a few days after finding the McNulty file. In the dream she walked through a neglected garden towards a once handsome house which was now dingy, neglected.

Paint was peeling off the front door. The sound of the doorbell jangled far away, in the depths of the house. She waited, her heartbeat quickening as she heard slow footsteps. The door opened a crack. The fingers curling round the door were swollen and clumsy, the nails bitten down. The door opened wider. Too dark to make out the interior of the house but Helen saw the shapeless figure confronting her. A flat, moon-shaped face on a level with her own.

It was a dough face; it belonged to the dough figures she and Nina made, in one flat or another, when she was small, and the weather lousy and there was nothing else to do. This grotesque figure turned expressionless, deep-pressed currant eyes upon her.

'Helen. Is that you?'

It was Nina's voice.

'You're not my mother.'

If she pushed her finger into the creature's cheek it would go right through the dough and make holes.

'You're not my mother. You're not Nina.'

Helen had shouted the words out loud and woken herself up and, when she touched her own cheek, it was wet with tears.

Drinking coffee kept her going. During the weekends she kept to herself. She paid the milkman every Saturday and that was about it. She lost the desire to invite friends around to view her new home and she kept her answer-machine on all the time. There were few messages. Her growing malaise seemed to affect others. Her friendly neighbour went down with flu and her much-loved elderly car, usually so reliable, began to behave like a disagreeable teenager; demanding much coaxing to start, making rude noises while moving and leaving numerous small splashes of oil wherever she went.

Helen found she was thinking more and more about Richard. He had been so kind to her and she had felt at ease with him, but was it fair to involve him further? He was probably forgetting all about her and their trip to Liverpool. He had never rung her after she had left him her new phone number. Why should he? He'd be getting on with his own life, forgetting about the adventure they'd shared. Oh, God. She felt so lonely.

Stuart was calling for her in half an hour. Nina eyed her sidewards image through the long mirror. Yes, she'd pass muster. Her figure had filled out during the past five years but she still had a trim waist and neat bottom. Her trousers were well cut and her dark green silk shirt and three-quarter length jacket would, she hoped, be appropriate for wherever they were going. One of Stuart's less appealing habits was his insistence on surprises.

Today, they might end up lunching in a smart town restaurant or, seeing as it was a fine day, tracking through an area of forestry before ending up in a pub, drinking beer and eating a sandwich. Ah, well! She slipped her feet into a pair of low-heeled shoes. She had mentioned, on their second excursion, that she liked to plan for things and he had exploded.

'For goodness' sakes, woman, get a sense of adventure. Don't be so cut and dried.'

Nina smiled. If only he knew. She heard the toot of his car horn outside and she picked up her shoulder bag and went to meet him.

Outside the house, the sunshine made her blink. As she approached the car, Stuart leaned across and opened the door for her. She got in.

He adjusted one of the side mirrors. 'Everything OK?'

The tone of his voice sounded, to her, a little off-hand. She glanced sideways at him. He was wearing sunglasses and she couldn't see his eyes. His mouth, so often curving into a smile, was set in a straight line. Nina felt a sudden quiver of apprehension. Their friendship was growing rapidly, but what did she really know about him?

Stuart was charming and he was fun. He made her feel like a desirable woman again and, God knows, she appreciated that but... But what? She was becoming too fond of him, that was what.

She cleared her throat and said: 'You look like the Hanging Judge with those glasses on.'

'Jeffries, you mean? I thought he had a beard.'

'You know what I mean.'

'I don't actually.' He glanced sideways at

her. 'Got out of bed the wrong side, this morning?'

'No.' She folded her lips, put her head back and closed her eyes.

Without warning, a huge need for Alex rushed over her. She had known everything about Alex and he had known everything about her – except for one thing. They had been true partners and so lucky. She knew she would never be able to replace the love she had for him and part of her didn't want to. She missed him so much. Oh, why, why did he have to die?

We were never ill, were we? We thought we would grow old together. She addressed him in her mind. We planned so many things, things we never got to do. We were always busy. You, travelling round the country seeking new and better groups and me in the office, making deals, chasing up contracts. We enjoyed our life but we should have done more with it, Alex. We should have given ourselves some leisure time. It should have been *you* and me driving through this autumn countryside. It should have been you slowing down the car so we could appreciate the flocks of migrating birds scattering across the high blue sky like torn paper.

She blinked away tears.

A couple of miles down the road the car drove at some speed over a traffic-calming hump in the road and jolted Nina. It must have been missed by Stuart for he swore under his breath. She half opened her eyes and looked down at his long legs, clad in corduroy slacks. He's too thin, she thought. He should eat more.

As if reading her thoughts, he turned his head towards her and this time he smiled.

'Getting hungry?'

'No, not really.'

'Well, we won't be long.'

'Tell me where we're heading.'

He shook his head. 'It's a surprise; pleasant, I hope.'

'Oh! You and your surprises.'

But she felt better as she settled more comfortably in her seat and looked out of the window. They passed an extremely handsome property set back from the road with beautiful gardens either side ablaze with autumnal shrubs and she commented on it to Stuart.

'I wonder who lives there?'

He gave a sidewards glance. 'Haven't a clue but you can bet he doesn't do his own gardening.'

She smiled. 'Did you ever hanker after being seriously rich?'

He considered before answering. 'No. I loved the life I led. Wouldn't have swapped it. Now I'm enjoying my retirement. Seriously rich usually equates with heavy commitment to corporate bodies. Wouldn't do for me.'

'You preferred being the "roving vagabond"?'

His lips quirked. 'Got it in for me today, haven't you?'

'No. I...'

She paused. He was right. She was feeling scratchy and taking it out on Stuart. There was no reason for it, this contrary mood. She couldn't even plead an impending storm. From a young age she had always been able to sense thunderstorms. She didn't become headachy as many people claimed to, it was just a heightened awareness of something changing, something ominous. She thought she was rather like the birds she had seen in her garden, birds who stopped their song, ruffled their feathers and prepared for whatever was on the way.

She pulled herself up in her seat. 'I'm sorry. I'll behave from now on.'

The car sped on. She gazed out of the window.

There was no impending storm. The sky was clear. The trees still bore their beautifully coloured leaves. They hung almost motionless apart from stirring in a faint ripple as cars passed beneath them. A stray memory dropped into Nina's mind of the place she had lived in when a child. In that place the trees would already be stripped of foliage. Their bare branches were, most probably, waving wildly in a north-easterly gale. My God, she thought, I've travelled a long way, into a green and pleasant land.

And yet ... she felt a tiny ache beneath her ribcage, remembering the pounding of the waves on the shore, and the scream of the gulls diving and swooping over the old castle.

Stuart glanced across at her. 'Not too long now.'

'That's all right.'

'I guarantee you'll like the place.'

She reached across and touched his hand. 'I'm sure I will.'

Fourteen

The signpost said *Chawton*. Nina turned to Stuart. 'Now that rings a bell.'

'It should. Especially for a writer.'

She thought for a moment. 'I've got it. Jane Austen lived here.'

'Five out of ten.' Stuart slowed the car as he passed a cyclist. 'She died here, too. I thought you might enjoy a look around, but tell me truthfully, have you already visited the house?'

'No, I haven't. I've thought about it but...' She shrugged.

'And you a writer! Shame on you.' There was a chuckle in his voice but Nina was not amused.

'I'm an *aspiring* writer and I know my place. What possible connection could there be between Jane Austen and me?'

'Quite a lot. According to contemporaries, Jane didn't miss much and had a mind of her own.' Stuart sneaked a glance at Nina's profile and began to smile. 'It's been said that as she grew older she acquired an extremely sharp tongue and frightened young men.'

Nina digested his words, determined not

to rise to his teasing. Mildly, she replied, 'I don't know any young men, so I can't frighten them. Anyway, it's impossible to compare Jane Austen with modern-day women. She led such a sheltered life.'

'Oh, no.' Stuart checked the car and gave her an earnest look. 'I can't let you get away with that. *No* one had an easy life in her time.'

'Rubbish! Jane Austen lived with her parents, never married, went to parties and wrote about her neighbours. What did she know about the real world?'

'She knew about never having enough money. She saw her much-loved brother go off to serve in the Navy at the age of fourteen – and remember, England was at war with France at the time. And there was the incident of her aunt being accused of shoplifting.'

Nina's eyes widened. 'A relative of Jane Austen's pinched stuff out of shops?'

'She was accused of doing so. And in those days it wasn't a matter of a month's probation. If found guilty of the crime, the woman could have been hanged at worst, or transported at best. In the event, she was found not guilty but I guess the stress levels in her family circle were astronomical. Respectability was everything to Jane's parents and circle of friends and yet she was tough enough to finish *Northanger Abbey* while all that drama was happening.'

Nina twisted round in her seat to study his face.

'How come you know so much about her?'

His lips twitched. 'Let's say I'm a fan.'

'I would never have believed it.'

'Why not?'

'Well, it's just...'

'Only elderly ladies read Jane Austen nowadays. Is that what you think? Not strictly true, Nina. You want to try one of her books sometime. Anyway, I read all kind of books, factual, adventure – loved the Ian Fleming books when they came out in the sixties. At the moment I'm reading Louis de Bernières.'

He signalled left. 'We'll be there in a few minutes.'

'You've been here before, haven't you?'

'Oh, yes. This will be my third visit.'

Nina was silenced. She stared out of the window. She had never been a great reader. There had never been enough time. Her husband had occasionally dipped into a paperback, usually a war story or a thriller, but only late at night and when he complained there was nothing on the telly. Now, re-running through her mind the conversation with Stuart, she felt ignorant and stupid. What the hell was she doing, trying to write a book! She knew nothing about writing. She actually knew precious little about anything.

Stuart was speaking. She tuned back in, listening to his voice.

'We needn't stay long, Nina. If you're bored just tell me and we'll move on. Go somewhere else.'

'No. Now we're here, I'd like to look round the place.'

Surprisingly, she enjoyed her visit. There were few visitors and walking round the quiet rooms it was possible to imagine how it had been when the Austen family lived there. With Stuart by her side, she had no need of a guide. Nina thought she knew everything there was to know about men but Stuart didn't fit easily into a specific category. On their first meeting she had been intrigued but wary. She had pegged him as the 'self-assured charmer'. He was confident, had easy conversation and a ready smile and the way he swept her off to the pub after their first meeting pleased her. She had been, she admitted it, ready for a light flirtation.

Seeing him at his home and with his son had made her warm to him because it was so obvious he loved and was proud of Ian. Mind you, she did wonder if he would have been so delighted if his only child had been a daughter. Hints of male superiority showed up occasionally in his conversation. It didn't bother her. *If* their relationship continued to prosper – and she hoped it would – she reckoned she could cut him down to size occasionally. Then she discovered he could cook, he knew lots of interesting things and he was good humoured. The plus list was growing.

Stuart was obviously adroit at avoiding commitment, because he had stayed single for many years. That was fine by Nina. She enjoyed single life, too. They were now establishing a pattern which suited them both. After a few days apart, they met up again, chatted non-stop and often argued. Stuart often laughed at her fiercely held opinions but he also considered her point of view. Nina realised that the tentatively entered flirtation was turning into a deep, mutually felt friendship. That was all she asked for and whether anything else developed, she was content to wait and see.

Today, wandering around the house at Chawton, Stuart was definitely in an unusually reflective mood.

'It's said that during the last few weeks before she died, Jane always came downstairs and rested in this room on an arrangement of three chairs while her mother, an invalid in mind only, stuck firmly on the comfortable sofa.' He stopped to stare at the sofa. 'Can you imagine it?'

He gave her a brief smile but Nina caught a look of sadness in his eyes and felt a corresponding lump in her throat. She thrust her arm through his.

'Let's go outside, shall we?'

The fine weather held. They drove back through the sunlit Hampshire and Surrey countryside, stopping off for afternoon tea at Selborne. The cream cakes were delicious and Stuart, back to his usual cheerful self, urged Nina to take a second one.

Smiling, she refused. 'I shouldn't have eaten the first one.'

'Well, I'm having another.' He reached across and picked up a chocolate cream eclair and dumped it on his plate.

Nina eyed it wistfully. 'It's all right for you. I bet, whatever you eat, you never put on a pound in weight.'

'Correct.' He grinned. 'But what is this "pound" you're talking about? We're European now.'

'I'll stay British, if you don't mind.'

'Really, you surprise me, Nina.' He took a bite of the cake.

'Why?'

'From what you've told me, you ran a successful music agency.' He swallowed and dabbed his mouth with his napkin. 'You must have dealt with foreign companies. The world's getting smaller. Surely. you don't expect us to go alone?'

'I did have dealings with people in Europe

and, before I sold the company, I installed some of the new technology that's around now but it's the European measurements that I can't stand. I just can't seem to get my head around them. I used to enjoy watching athletics on the box but I don't now. I can never work out how far they are running or how high they are jumping.'

'You watched athletics meetings, did you? Some wonderful physical specimens around nowadays, don't you think? The female long jumpers do things for me. Such supple bodies.' Stuart's eyes were twinkling. 'I was quite a runner when I was young, can you believe.'

'Your legs are long enough so I'll believe you. Have you any trophies to substantiate your story?'

He shook his head. 'Alas, no. I went to sea early in life so I had to give the sport up.'

'I see.'

They grinned at each other and then Nina pushed back her chair. 'Just going to freshen up.'

'Oh, you women!'

'What do you mean?'

'Nothing.' He stood up. 'I need a pee, too. Meet you outside, by the car.'

When Nina came out of the cubicle, the ladies' room was empty. She went over to the basin to wash her hands. As she did so, she leaned forward and studied her reflection in the mirror. She pulled a face. The strip lighting made her look pale and the morning's well-applied make-up had all but disappeared. Her nose was shining and the fine lines around her eyes and mouth showed up clearly.

She frowned and searched in her handbag for her pressed powder compact but when her fingers touched it she left it lying there. She always presented herself as attractively as possible before leaving home but she was growing too old to prink and preen. She hoped Stuart found her good to look at but she wasn't going to act like a young girl, forever rearranging hairstyles and re-painting her lips. They were both mature people. At their age they ought to be concentrating on grown-up things; whichever way their relationship developed, she had a feeling it would be more than skin deep.

Helen was also travelling. She had threaded her way through heavy London traffic, concentrated on finding the right turn-offs and now she was on the road to Guildford. The miles behind her were growing and the time ahead was diminishing as she came closer to the entry to the village in which her mother lived. Even now, she might be staring out at scenes her mother was familiar with. The thought made her stomach jump. She hadn't experienced the feeling for years. Sometimes, when travelling on buses with Nina for long distances, her stomach had done the same little jump. It was a peculiar feeling, a nervy little twitch that had been almost enjoyable when it first started but which eventually made her feel sick.

The traffic had thinned out considerably during the last half-hour so Helen slowed down and allowed herself to breathe deeply. She couldn't relax entirely but she didn't have to concentrate so much. It suited her as it did the car in front of her.

It was an elderly but beautifully cared-for car. So was the driver – at least, the bits of her that Helen could see.

She was a tiny lady with hunched shoulders and she wore a large hat. She looked so small that Helen bet that she was sitting on a cushion to see where she was going. She drove very slowly. Instead of being irritated by this, Helen realised her own shoulders had begun to relax. The sun was shining and because her progress was now leisurely, she could glance around her. She could stop imagining what the end of her journey would bring and just enjoy the moment. Right at this very moment, she was appreciating the sheen on the two horses grazing in a paddock set back from the road. The paddock was next to an opulent split-level house and there was an expensive-looking car parked in the sweeping drive. Helen didn't note the make of car. Cars didn't interest her, people did.

She speculated about the kind of people who could afford such a house. Were they happy? Did wealth make for happiness? From the stuff you read in the newspapers, the wealthy had more troubles than most. Did the fault lie with the people or the wealth they possessed? Was her problem due to a genetic fault or her own unsettled childhood? Helen didn't believe in passing the buck. People, she reasoned, had been given choice and the power of reasoning. Every problem should, and could be, tackled and solved. Then, even if the solution was not what you wished, you could move on to the next stage of your life. She had been telling herself this ever since she got into the car.

With a start, she realised the elderly lady driver was leaving her. The right indicator was flashing merrily and the car was turning. Helen slowed down and was rewarded with a flutter from a wrinkled hand through the open window. The car turned off and bounced along a rutted, winding driveway before finally disappearing behind a clump of trees. Helen hoped there would be someone there to welcome the old lady; someone to sit her down and provide a fresh pot of tea.

Her journey, however, continued. She pushed up the speed and continued on her route. Twenty minutes later, the car developed a peculiar knocking noise.

Oh, no! Please don't do this to me!

She bit her lip and gazed apprehensively at the dashboard. No ominous red lights flickered. There was plenty of petrol in the tank. Helen tried to remember the various checks she was supposed to make but couldn't think of anything. She cut the speed back but the sound became even louder. She needed help. A little further down the road she was heartened to see a garage on the left. She nursed her car into the forecourt and explained what had happened to the mechanic in oil-smeared overalls who came over to speak to her.

'It was fine and then this awful noise started...'

The man rubbed his chin. 'Sounds like the exhaust.' He went to the back of the car to check.

'Sorry, miss.' He returned. 'It's the exhaust, all right.'

Helen got out of the car, glad to stretch her legs.

'Can you fix it?'

'Have to take a closer look.'

'Can you do it now?'

The mechanic scratched his head. 'Yes, I'll check it out. But it depends what I find whether I can...'

'Oh, thank you.' Helen flashed him a smile that made him blush. She looked around. 'Can I get a coffee anywhere?'

'There's a kiosk over there.' He waved his hand.

'Thank you.'

A proper cafe would have been nice but a kiosk was better than nothing. She put her money in the machine and collected a plastic beaker of black coffee and a vacuum-packed ham sandwich. If she'd been thinking properly, she would have brought a flask and her own sandwiches. But again, if she'd stopped to prepare a snack she might never have started at all.

She leaned against the vending machine, sipped her coffee and watched the mechanic who was now flat on his back on a trolley studying the undercarriage of her car. A tall, well-built young man came out of what looked to be an office and approached him. The mechanic rolled himself out of harm's way and stood up to talk to the man. Helen saw him shake his head and her stomach muscles clenched. She walked over towards them.

Please let it not be serious.

'This is Mr Urquart. He's the boss.' The mechanic gestured towards the young man.

'Hello.' The boss put out his hand and took Helen's, shaking it firmly. 'Not good news, I'm afraid.'

Her stomach spasmed again.

'Is it the exhaust?'

'Yes.'

'But that's not a problem, surely? I mean, I know it will be a bit expensive to replace but I have my credit cards with me. You must deal with this sort of thing all the–'

He cut her short. 'The trouble is, your car's a bit of a geriatric. I don't have spares to fit. We're rather more a specialised garage in that we tend to deal in up-to-date sports cars. We can order–'

Helen interrupted him. He may have softened his statement with a charming smile but she was furious.

'As far as I can see, you run a garage, not a car showroom. I can't believe you won't repair my car.'

'No, no. I didn't say we wouldn't, I said we couldn't. We'll have to order a spare exhaust and as it's already quite late, I don't suppose it will arrive until tomorrow lunchtime at the earliest. So you're looking at round two p.m. tomorrow.' He paused, studying her expression. 'It is an old car, you know.'

The colour drained out of her face. She nodded. 'Yes, it is. I'm sorry.'

'No, I am.' The young man's voice softened. He spoke in an aside to the mechanic and then turned back to Helen.

'Look, come into the office with me and

217

I'll ring round. See what I can do.'

'Oh, you mean you might be able...'

'No promises.' He took hold of her elbow. 'At least I can give you a proper cup of coffee or tea. That stuff out of the machine is diabolical.'

After a couple of swift phone calls, Mr Urquart admitted defeat.

'The earliest I can get the exhaust will be mid-afternoon tomorrow, then it has to be fixed.' He shook his head. 'I'm sorry, but whichever garage you stopped at, the result would be the same. However,' he studied Helen's pale face, 'I'm sure we could arrange an alternative. You could hire a car from me.'

She shook her head. 'No.'

'Why not? It wouldn't cost that much and if you're in a hurry?'

Helen rubbed her forehead. 'I was, but now...' Her voice trailed away.

She couldn't explain to this stranger. She hardly understood herself why the rush of adrenalin that had appeared and spurred her to undertake her journey had disappeared as quickly as it had arose. She just felt very tired. Fate seemed to be telling her it was a stupid idea. It wasn't meant that she should find her mother. Her car failing at this crucial time was an act of fate. Now, all she wanted to do was return home.

As if picking up an echo from her thoughts, the man behind the desk asked: 'Have you travelled far?'

'From London. I was heading for Thaxwalton.' She forced a smile. 'I'm sorry. I'm behaving like an idiot. Of course I must hire a car from you. I'll need one to get home.'

He looked at her curiously. 'You're very pale. Are you *sure* you're all right?'

'I'm fine.' She straightened her back. 'Now, can you let me have—'

He interrupted her. 'Is it essential you go to Thaxwalton today? I'm on the point of leaving for London. I have an appointment I must keep so I can't delay. If you like, I could give you a lift?'

She shook her head. 'Oh, no. Why should you? Anyway, I'll have to come back here to pick up my car.'

'Whereabouts do you live?'

She sighed, and told him.

He flipped open a map of London. 'That's OK. It won't take me far out of my way. And a guy who works for me will be transporting three new cars into the centre of London tomorrow evening. He can drop off your car then.'

'Oh, it's too much bother.'

'No, it isn't. I'll be sending a bill for the new exhaust, of course.'

She was still undecided.

Speaking rapidly, he explained. 'I've

recently started this business.' He shrugged. 'I explained why I couldn't fix your vehicle but it still doesn't look good. Now,' he grinned at her, 'if you tell your friends and colleagues how terribly helpful I've been, it could boost my business. Most of my customers work in or around London.'

She smiled, then nodded. 'OK.'

'Good. Just give me five minutes, then we'll be on our way.'

He dashed out of the room. Taking a sip from the cup of fresh coffee he had made for her, Helen revised her initial opinion of Mr Urquart. He was a little too full of himself but, deep down, he obviously had a kind heart.

Fifteen

Richard rarely ventured on the water but he saw the sea every day and he liked listening to the shipping forecast. He was listening to it now. So many of his favourite radio programmes had disappeared during the last few years and those that remained had been 'hyped up' or moved to other airwaves making them difficult to find, so he appreciated the ones that remained. There was something immensely satisfying in listening to the measured voice of the broadcaster as he intoned the familiar words: *'Rockall, Malin, Dogger and Finisterre.'* When he did so, Richard felt an echo of the feeling he experienced when he gazed up at the stars. But this day, even without the shipping forecast, Richard would have felt happy. The sun was shining and at three o'clock this afternoon, he was meeting June.

He put the jar of instant coffee back in a cupboard then switched the radio to another channel. An old pop tune was being played, one he knew. He crooned along with the music.

I beg your pardon. I never promised you a rose garden.

The telephone rang. He answered it.

'Hello. Is that you, Richard?'

The caller, a woman, sounded subdued. Richard had to strain to hear her.

'Afraid I can't–'

'It's me. Hope I haven't interrupted anything important.' Dear God! It was Helen. His daughter, Helen. *And he hadn't rung her back. He had forgotten.*

Richard was submerged in a wave of guilt. She was saying something but he couldn't concentrate on her words. All he could think was: first her mother deserted her and then me.

He cleared his voice. 'Helen, I...'

'If it's inconvenient, I can ring back.'

'No, no. It's a good time to ring.'

How hesitant she sounded.

'Give me a minute. Let me turn off the radio.'

He reached forward and somehow managed to drop the phone. There was a clatter as it hit the work surface. He snatched it up again, checked to see if they were still connected.

'Hello. Helen?'

'Yes.' Her voice was tiny.

'Just hold on.'

Something was wrong. He knew it. He replaced the phone on the breakfast bar. Two strides across the kitchen, a touch of a switch and the jaunty music was silenced.

Richard's hand was trembling as he picked up the phone again. He hadn't rung her back and now something was wrong.

His initial reason for not immediately contacting Helen had been sound. He had thought they both needed breathing space but then the days had rushed by and without noticing, his priorities had changed. Face it, he thought. When you met June you began to forget about Helen. I forgot about my own child. How long since they had spoken? He calculated the days. More than four weeks since Helen had called and left her new telephone number. Four weeks! An image formed in his mind. Helen's expression when the chap in the hotel in Liverpool ... what was his name? Warden. That was it! When Warden had said Nina had married McNulty, Helen's face had been ... desolate. Now, belatedly, Richard understood. Helen had never stopped loving her mother. That's why the news that Nina had entered into a bigamous marriage, only a few miles away from where Helen was living with Frank, had hit her so badly. So near, and yet Nina had not contacted her.

Now he, as her father, had to be there for her. But first, he had to find out what had been happening. He spoke down the phone. 'Helen.'

'Yes.'

'You've found out something about Nina's whereabouts, haven't you?'

'Yes.'

With his free hand he reached out for a kitchen stool, pulled it to him and sat down. 'Tell me.'

'You're sure you want to hear?'

'That's why you rang me, isn't it?'

'I guess so. But, as I've said before, it's my problem. I have to deal with it. I just need to talk to someone.'

'That's where I come in. So, tell me.'

She sighed and began. The words came slowly at first and then in a torrent. When she fell silent, Richard asked. 'You think your mother still lives there?'

'I know she does.'

He heard her painful intake of breath.

'When the garage owner drove me back to London and dropped me off outside my flat, I went inside and straight away phoned her.'

'You hadn't thought of doing that before?'

'Of course I had. I thought about ringing Nina every day since I found her address but something stopped me. Like ... what would I say? How would I start the conversation? "Hi, I'm Helen. Remember me?"'

Richard unaccountably felt a twinge in a back tooth, one he knew needed filling. He shifted the telephone to his other hand. 'So what *did* you say?'

'I asked her if she had enough life assurance.'

'What?'

'I pretended to be a phone researcher.' There was a silence which Helen filled. 'Pretty quick thinking, don't you agree?'

'I suppose so.' Richard shifted uneasily on his stool. Helen's voice was changing, becoming more strident. 'You're sure it was her?'

As soon as the words were spoken he wished them back. What a stupid, crass comment.

'I'm not an idiot, Richard. I know my own mother's voice.'

Her answer was sharp but Richard felt his shoulders relax. Better anger than despair.

'Anyway...' Helen was speaking again. 'Her reaction confirmed it was Nina. She gave me a frank opinion of her views on telephone sales. It was my mother, all right. The trouble is, what do I do now? What do *you* think I should do?' Her voice faded.

Richard gripped the phone tightly. 'Don't do anything in a rush, Helen. Wait until I come to see you.'

'No, Richard. I don't expect that of you. Please don't come.' Her voice was so vehement the phone crackled. 'I just want advice. You were a great help in Liverpool but this time it's different. I've found Nina and any talking has to be between her and me. I'd value your views, as an outsider, but you mustn't come to London.'

He winced. He had every right to be with her when she confronted her mother, but he couldn't tell her why. But she needed him. He *had* to find a way to persuade her... He took a deep breath.

'Helen, it's not easy to talk over the phone but I want you to know I *do* feel I have a stake in your search and I...' his voice trailed off. How could he convince her?

He started again. 'I told you my only child, my daughter, was stillborn. It was a great sorrow for me. I can't explain it, but when you and I met each other in the theatre and began talking, I had the strangest feeling of kinship for you. Yes, I know it sounds absolutely ridiculous – even a bit odd – but that's how I felt and I still feel. Then, when you showed me your mother's photograph and said you thought she might have stayed in the very house in which I now live, the link strengthened. I thought: maybe she did live here. I've thought about your words often, until I've almost imagined I've seen your mother in my house, when I was a boy.'

Richard's voice faltered and he shut his eyes. Against the blackness he reconstructed from memory the face of his love. Nancy, her lovely face when she was sixteen. Nancy, the mother of his child.

He spoke again, haltingly. 'All fantasy, I

suppose but that doesn't matter. What does matter is that I feel committed to you and your search for your mother. Let me come to London to talk to you. I'll drive over and you can use my car if necessary. You said your vehicle was unreliable. Let me help in a practical way, Helen. I could drive you over to see your mother and make myself scarce when you meet her. I just don't want to think of you all alone.'

He fell silent and held his breath.

A minute passed and then he heard her sigh.

'You *really* mean all that, don't you?'

'Yes.' He nodded his head vigorously, even though he knew she couldn't see. 'I'll sort out accommodation. I won't intrude on your space.'

'Oh, Richard. I don't know.'

He waited.

And then she whispered. 'It would be good to have someone on my side.'

His heart swelled. 'I am.' He hesitated. 'How well are you coping? Are you sleeping OK?'

She gave a short laugh. 'I do nothing else.'

His knuckles turned white as he gripped the phone. 'I'll drive to London tomorrow. Shall I give you a ring when I arrive and you can talk me through getting to where you live? I'm afraid my sense of direction is not too efficient.'

'Yes, ring me. Oh, I'll give you my work number, too. I might have to go in for an hour.' She did so. 'Is that OK?'

'Yes.' Richard studied the number on the pad and felt butterflies stirring in his stomach. The idea of driving in London terrified him.

Helen spoke again and her voice was soft. 'Thank you, Richard. I don't know why you're helping me so much but I do appreciate your kindness.'

His heart swelled. 'My pleasure. We'll speak tomorrow.'

He stared down at the telephone. Of course he'd manage to navigate the streets of London. He'd drive to Timbuctoo to make her happy. The question was, would finding Nancy, or Nina, as Helen called her, make his girl happy? Only time would tell.

He remembered June. He'd better get a move on. They were driving to Thornton le Dale for lunch and then June wanted to wander round a fruit and vegetable show. She'd seen the event advertised in the local press and thought it might be fun. He'd get changed and then check out the car. If he was going to London he needed to know he had enough petrol. Should he tell June he was going to London? It might be better to keep things vague. Tell her he was going to be away for a couple of days on business, pension stuff or something like that. Oh, hell! He smacked his forehead as he remembered he had purchased two tickets for a show at the theatre tomorrow evening and June knew about them. He'd have to say something unexpected had happened, something to do with ... what? He hadn't a clue, but he'd have to think of something. His relationship with June was progressing admirably but he couldn't see himself sitting her down and telling her about finding a daughter he didn't know existed and how the two of them were now on the trail of his past lover – his child's mother.

June came out of the hairdressers where she had been for a haircut and a rinse. Normally, she did a rinse herself, buying a packet from Boots every four or five weeks, but this month she had splashed out. The young stylist who attended to her had persuaded her to have her eyebrows darkened and her new rinse had an exciting name: craze-cool blonde. Viewing the finished result, the stylist had enthused over June's new image.

'You look wonderful, Mrs Greening, and much younger. Your fella won't recognise you.'

'I sincerely hope he will,' June had retorted and she had swept out of the salon wishing she hadn't confided in the girl about her 'man friend'. Waiting for attention, June had been amazed at the conversations she overheard as women leaned back to have their hair washed and gave up their hands to have their nails painted blood red. When summoned, and as she followed the pert girl in the skimpy overall to have her own appearance enhanced, she told herself she would remain mute but after five minutes she found she was speaking about her new gentleman friend and how she might try a bit of a new 'image'. Maybe it was something to do with the clouds of hairspray, she thought.

'Fella' sounded like something out of a musical from the era of *Guys and Dolls*, she thought as she let herself into her house, patted Reg and looked at herself through the kitchen mirror. She turned her head one way and then the other. The shape of her new haircut looked good but the bits of hair falling over her ears looked a slightly different, colour from the rest. June tugged fretfully at the offending pieces of hair. They were a much lighter colour and, she realised, it didn't take a genius to realise why. She had more white hairs in that area of her head. Oh, dear. Would Richard note the difference? Worse still, would he know the reason?

Richard. There he was, back in her mind. She tried to push him out but her effort was half-hearted. She enjoyed thinking about him. It was great to have a man in her life again. Anticipating their next meeting gave her a lovely warm feeling and she rather felt he experienced the same sensations; he always had a huge grin on his face when they came face to face. Why then, did she also feel apprehensive?

The year after becoming a widow, June's feelings had been strangely muted. She missed her husband's presence but didn't feel the gut-wrenching pain she had expected. She felt, instead, a sort of numbness at his absence. She had to rouse herself to do all the tasks John had previously seen to. She missed him most when she had to sort out awkward financial details, reset the video or alter the clock on the central-heating system. John had never taught her how to do those tasks.

'It's man's work,' he had said.

She didn't even miss the sex most of the time, just his absence from the bed at night. Without him beside her she had difficulty in sleeping. She thought more of burglars and checked all the locks before going to bed. But she had her son to look after and so she strove to become self-reliant, competent. It had been difficult, but she had done it. She learnt to re-wire a plug, deal with minor water leaks and, eventually, enjoy the space of her double bed.

Then Chris had grown up and decided to

live his life in another country and she had bitten back her tears and waved him off with a smile. Now she had only Reg, her child's dog, to look after.

Pets were easy. Oh, your heart could crack if your dog had to be put to sleep, but you got over that. There was no true heartbreak with a dog or cat because they lived in the moment, they put no pressure on you. Feed them, walk them, and they adored you. People were different. People made demands on you. People, if you allowed them to get too close, could break your heart. June wasn't sure she cared for the risk. Richard was such a lovely man. She was lucky he was interested in her, but things were moving quickly. She already loved his voice, his good manners, his hazel eyes and the way he walked. That was enough to keep her awake nights. Add to these attributes his consideration and the way his face lit up when he smiled, and she was already swimming in deep water. Was it wise? There was so much she didn't know about him. She should go more slowly. Yes, that's what she would do. She told herself this, knowing she was already committed to more foolhardy behaviour.

He jumped out of the car and walked towards her. His smile was as wide as ever and she responded by smiling back. She felt her pulse quicken.

'You look different.'

'I've had my hair cut and styled.' She said nothing about the rinse but she touched the offending portion of her hair with her fingertips. 'Do you approve?'

'Yes. I do.'

But his gaze slid over her and he glanced up at the sky. 'We should be all right, I think. There's a few clouds around but the forecast was good.'

She was silent. There was a tenseness about him. He was abstracted. Something was bothering him. She told herself not to be silly. Who did she think she was? Gipsy Rose Lee from her booth at the bottom of the town? She shook her head. There was so much she didn't know about Richard. But why should she? They had only known each other for a short time. It was probably nothing.

'Where's Reg?'

'What?'

'Reg. What have you done with him?'

'He's in the house. I didn't think you'd want him with us. You know he barks when he gets excited and...'

'Oh, let the old chap come. We can keep him on the lead and he can stay in the car when we have lunch.'

He was smiling his good-natured smile. June allowed her shoulders to relax. 'You're sure?'

'Yes.'

She went to get her pet.

They walked round the lovely old village and enjoyed the fruit and vegetable show. The tent in which it was held was full of glorious colour and heavy with scents from the many varieties of fruits and autumn blooms. The lunch was good, too. It was as they were leaving the restaurant, Richard told her he wouldn't be able to escort her to the theatre. He handed her the tickets.

'Unforeseen circumstances mean I have to be away for a couple of days. Sorry, but I didn't get much notice.' This time, his smile was more pinched. 'Look, I'll give you the tickets. Maybe you can take a friend?'

'Yes. I probably can.'

She accepted the tickets. Instinct told her something was worrying him. She wanted to ask him what it was but their relationship was too new. As she stepped out of the car outside her home she gave him a dazzling smile.

'Thanks for a lovely day, Richard.'

She opened the rear door and yanked Reg from his seat.

'See you when you get back.'

'What? Oh, yes. Of course. See you soon.'

He drove away.

She watched the car turn the corner at the bottom of the street.

Richard didn't wave to her.

She jerked at Reg's lead. 'Come on, old boy.'

He gave her a jaundiced look and marked his slab of paving stone with a few drops of urine before waddling into their home.

'You don't help,' she told him.

Sixteen

Helen cleaned the flat. She had only been in the place for a few weeks, but somehow she had accumulated a pile of black bin bags full of rubbish. One by one she manhandled them down the stairs and dumped them by the dustbin in the back garden, thinking: five bin bags. It was ridiculous. Why on earth had she transported the debris of her past life to her new home? She rubbed her forehead, leaving a grimy streak.

That ghastly vase Phil's auntie had given them for a wedding present; no wonder her ex-husband had generously said she could keep it, but why had she? And the piles of clothes? Flowing skirts and platform shoes ... stuff she had worn as a teenager. God, what a fright she must have looked. An autograph book signed by a couple of teachers she got on with and some of her classmates, and a school photograph with the image of herself, solemn faced and plain, sitting in the middle of the second row; she remembered why she had kept that. It proved she had stayed long enough at one school to be included in a group photograph. These things were so *pathetic*.

She was pathetic for hanging on to them.

But not any more. Tomorrow morning the relics would be carted away in the council's dustcart and the old Helen could go with them. From tomorrow, she was going to be a different person. And Richard was coming.

Richard would be a comfort if not a tremendous help. She knew he wasn't a macho hero, in fact she worried over him driving to London, but his prompt offer to come and see her had cheered her up immensely. With Richard to talk to she wasn't completely alone and, she remembered, he had proved his worth in Liverpool.

By the time Richard left the M1 motorway and was passing the Brent Cross Shopping Centre, he was completely shattered. Dear God! What had happened to this country he loved? He was in hell! All he could see was acres of roads, thousands of cars and lorries and enormous roundabouts. Was he doomed to spend the rest of his life trying to get off this gigantic conveyer belt? He took his eyes off the road ahead for a split second to glance at his wristwatch – the clock in the dashboard was no good – he had forgotten to adjust the time at the last change-over. No, he was all right for time. He should be able to get to where he was meeting Helen without too much delay.

'Bottom of Hampstead Heath,' she had

said. 'Outside the swimming baths.'

Thank God he had spoken to her before setting off, and admitted his nervousness. 'Take me out of North Yorkshire and I'm out of my depth.' He had hated saying the words but they had to be said.

She had been tactful, pointing out that many experienced drivers hated travelling to the capital. She had told him to get paper and pencil and she had talked him through the route.

'Will that help?'

He had thanked her but warned that he might be a little late arriving.

She had laughed. 'Tell me about it! I've never known anyone to arrive early.'

Now, Richard realised he had sold himself short. He had actually made good time. He glanced at the written instructions which he had taped to a convenient vantage point in the car. He'd have to turn off in a couple of minutes. He wiped the sudden sweat off his upper lip. Yes, yes. This was the place. He signalled, checked his mirrors and swung his car into the appropriate lane.

OK. He blew a gusty sigh of relief. Maybe he wasn't such an old relic, after all. He'd coped with the traffic. Would he be able to help Helen cope with meeting her mother? Would *he* be able to cope?

He had last seen Nancy, or Nina, as she called herself now, when he was fifteen.

There was no way she would recognise him but how would *he* cope with the meeting? Suppose she was a raddled old hag? Would he be able to suppress his shock and horror? Suppose she was still beautiful, a mature version of the lovely girl who had lived in his heart for so long? That might be even worse. He concentrated fiercely on the road. More likely, Nina would be a perfectly ordinary housewife. Of course, she wouldn't recognise him. She'd have forgotten him years ago.

If Helen asked him to accompany her to Nina's home, he would go with her, up to Nina's front door. After that, the two women would be far too busy struggling with their own emotions to consider him. He could make himself scarce, drive around for a while and then come back to take Helen home. Of course, it all depended on how the initial meeting went. He wondered how Nancy would feel and, for the first time, a feeling of anxiety for the mother swept over him.

When he had listened to Helen talk during their trip to Liverpool he had never managed to match Helen's Nina to *his* Nancy. His memories were of a slim girl, light on her feet, dashing around the hotel, working hard and flashing him cheeky smiles when no one was looking. On the few occasions they managed a short conversation he had been struck by her confidence and what she knew about the world. He had felt a babe by comparison. She had called him a baby once.

'You want to clear out of here as soon as you can, Richard. You'll be a baby when you're fifty if you don't. You're dad's not too bad, a bit miserable. But your mother...'

He remembered he had felt he had to object. 'Mum's OK. She saved my life when I had rheumatic fever. Never left my side for weeks.'

'But you've not got rheumatic fever now, have you?'

She'd winked at him and whisked away to answer a guest's ring for attention.

And then, as always, his special memory.

The rustle of the sheet as she slid into the bed to lie beside him, and the way they had clasped hands and watched the stars. The sound of her breathing and then the softness of her body as she had turned to him. She had, he remembered, touched his face with the tips of her fingers.

Richard jerked as a car horn blared behind him. The past was dead. Long live the future. Helen was his priority now. He was getting close to the designated meeting place. He wondered what plans she had made. What would she say when they met.

'What will you say to her?'

Helen shrugged. 'I've rehearsed dozens of

openings but, honestly, I don't know. I'll wait to see if she opens the door and I'll take it from there.'

'Probably best.'

Richard looked down into his glass, swirling round the remainder of his red wine. Helen had met him as arranged. After grasping his hands for a long moment and smiling at him, she stepped back and asked him about the journey. He told her, making light of the more horrendous moments and they had decided to go for a coffee. Skirting round the reason for their meeting, they discussed Helen's new flat and how busy she was at work. He thought how tired she looked but she answered his questions with composure.

She seemed disinclined to move so Richard ordered more coffee. When it arrived, Helen explained to him how she had found the file containing Nina's address. When she finished he was about to comment when she completely turned tack.

'I've hogged the conversation. Tell me how your life is going?'

'Oh, pretty good.'

Startled, Richard wondered whether to tell her about June, but as his daughter had made no reference to a particular friend, he decided not to. Instead, striving to introduce a lighter feeling to their conversation, he told her about the latest exploits of his cleaner.

'Amy's hell-bent on getting concessions on the local bus service for old age pensioners. She's bending my ear trying to get me involved. Yesterday, she brought a letter to me to check for mistakes before she sent it to the local press.'

Helen smiled. 'Good for her. I hope you encouraged her?'

'I keep very low key. Amy doesn't need encouragement. She's a complete power-house.'

Helen leaned back in her chair.

'And what about you, Richard? Are you still a stargazer?' Her smile was a little strained. 'I should have asked you to take a look through your telescope before coming to see me. Maybe you could have picked up some pointers as to how I should behave when I confront my mother.'

Richard frowned. 'I hope you're joking. You know my interest is astronomy, not hocus-pocus. You *are* joking, aren't you? Surely after our trip to the planetarium you know the difference between astronomy and astrology?'

'Of course I do. I was joking, Richard.' Helen pushed away her empty coffee cup. 'Although, just lately, I've been reading my stars in the newspaper every day. Curious, isn't it? When things go well, we don't bother but when things aren't so hot...' She paused for a moment. 'Perhaps we're all pagans under the skin. We turn money over in our pockets when we see a new moon and avoid walking under ladders...' She pressed her lips together and glanced at her watch. 'Let's go.'

Richard watched her. 'Where?'

'Back to my flat. I'd like you to see it. Then I'll cook you a good meal. That's the least I can do. We'll talk about where you'll sleep later. There's a couple of local B&B places that fit the bill.'

Richard admired the flat and ate heartily of the meal Helen had prepared. Now, comfortably ensconced in easy chairs facing each other, they were drinking wine. Both knew it was too late for him to be leaving in search of bed and breakfast and both were comfortable with the thought. Richard thought Helen's face, in repose, was worn and tired and he, himself, felt shattered but, if she wanted company, if she wanted to talk, that was fine by him. He'd be whatever his daughter demanded of him.

On the table between them lay the McNulty file.

'Every working day I tell myself I'll take it back but I don't.'

What could he say to make her feel better?

'I think it's perfectly logical of you to want to hang on to it. The file's the first concrete evidence that your mother's still alive, as well as giving her present whereabouts.'

Delicately, with her middle finger, Helen removed a tear from her cheek. 'You don't think I'm behaving in a crazy manner?'

'Far from it. You're a strong lady, Helen.' He frowned, trying to pick the right words. 'You've had to be. An unsettled childhood, deserted by your mother when you were in your teens.' He paused. 'You must have set up a lot of lurid scenarios in your time?'

'Tell me about it.' She managed a weak smile. 'Every time a newspaper reported a woman's body uncovered I went into shock. I'd shut myself in my bedroom for a day and then grab the paper and pour over every line. Of course, my stepfather found me hard work. In the end, he refused to discuss anything to do with Nina.'

'Did he? You never told me that.'

She shrugged. 'I couldn't blame him. He'd married Nina and welcomed us into his home and then she left. He never said much but he was bitter, of course he was. Nina's presence hovered like a ghost in our house, never acknowledged but always there.'

He was silent, imagining how stressful her teenage years had been. Abruptly, he asked.

'What about your husband? Did he know your history? Could you tell him how you felt?'

She hesitated. 'I told Phil. Not straight away but when we decided to get married. Obviously, the question of the bride's mother cropped up. Phil's family were as normal as apple pie. He was quite intrigued to hear my mother had gone missing. Before that, he had assumed there'd been what is called "a normal break-up". He knew Frank was my stepfather.'

'But wasn't he concerned for you?'

'I suppose so. But it had happened so long ago. To be honest, he wasn't too interested.' She saw Richard's expression and hurried on.

'It was all right, honestly. You see–' she swallowed I wasn't thinking about Nina then. I was *happy*, really happy for the first time in years. I'd decided to forget about my mother. I was grown up. I was marrying the man I loved. I had a good job I enjoyed. It was only later...' Her voice petered out.

Richard lowered his eyes and resisted the impulse to rush across to where she was sitting and put his arms around her. Instead, he cleared his throat.

'It was the break-up, wasn't it? Your divorce was the trigger to your desire to find out what had happened to Nina?'

'I guess so.' She linked her hands on her lap and stared down at them. 'Pretty pathetic, eh?'

'Christ, no.'

The emotion in his voice made her look up.

'Richard?'

Oh, God. He wanted so much to tell her. She did have one parent she could rely on. He'd never let her down. He loved her so much. He had thought he loved Nina. He had thought he loved his wife and, God forgive him, he was beginning to think he loved June, but the emotion raging within him was stronger than anything he had ever experienced and it was devastating because he knew he *couldn't* tell her. Her reaction to such a revelation would be shock, even horror. He had been living a lie. Was there no end to the wickedness and deceit of her parents?

He could imagine the questions. Why was he masquerading as her friend? How long had he known? Why hadn't he told her before? How could he possibly explain? Oh, God. Why hadn't he been honest with her the day she had shown him her mother's photograph? He could have done it then. It would have been difficult but not impossible. A sob threatened to break out of him. He felt sweat bead his forehead.

'Richard? Are you ill?'

Her voice penetrated his pain. He brushed his face with a shaking hand and forced his voice into normality.

'Sorry. I guess I'm just tired. It hit me all of a sudden.'

Helen jumped up at once, concern shining on her face.

'Oh, I've been so selfish. I knew you'd find the car journey awkward and yet I've kept you talking for hours. Look, I'll just...'

'Please, Helen. Don't fuss. I'll be fine.'

One day, he promised himself, one day Helen *will* know of our true relationship and somehow I'll make her understand how I care for her. But not now, not yet. He took a deep breath and, miraculously, his voice came out firm and steady.

'I'm all right, Helen. Stop fussing. I'll go to bed in a minute but there's something I want to say to you first.' He drew a deep breath. 'You're not weak, Helen. You're strong. You've endured uncertainty and abandonment as a child and heartbreak as an adult, and yet you're still in there, fighting to find out the truth. It's people like me that are weak.'

A frown creased her brow. 'I don't know what you mean, Richard.'

'Hearing about your life has made me think about mine. You've made me realise that all my life, I've stood on the sidelines. I've blamed everyone else for my boring, unsatisfactory existence. I've blamed my parents for being too protective, my wife...' He paused. 'God forgive me. I knew our marriage was failing but I never lifted a finger to try and save it. When our little girl was stillborn I wallowed in my own emotions. I never even considered what she was going through.'

'But, Richard, you...'

'No, hear me out.' He smiled at her. 'Meeting you, watching you struggling to make sense of things has caused me to come to a conclusion. I want to help you as much as I can, but without intruding too much on your life. You see, you're helping me to grow up.'

In the short silence that followed, Helen twisted her hands together.

'I'm not sure what to say.'

'When unsure, follow the golden rule.' Richard's voice was a little unsteady but his smile was sure. 'Say nothing. How about I wash up and you go and find me a pillow and a blanket and then get off to bed. I shall be perfectly happy on the sofa.'

'Oh, no. I've a fold-up bed in the box-room. I can–'

'The sofa will be fine. After all that red wine I'll sleep like a log.'

'You're sure?'

He nodded. 'How about you? Will you be able to sleep?'

On her way out of the room, she paused. 'Do you know, Richard ... I think I will.'

She managed a tentative smile and disappeared.

Richard cleared his throat, went over to the dining table and began stacking the crockery to take through to the kitchen.

Seventeen

Nina believed she had a certain amount of precognition. She had been intuitive about behaviour of certain rival agents during her business life; she had pulled off a couple of spectacular *coups d'état* and she had realised, long before Alex did, that his illness was serious. Why then, she thought later, on a bright but chilly autumn morning, when she had opened her front door in response to the bell, did she have no inkling as to the upheaval the man and the woman standing on her doorstep would cause to her life?

'Good morning.' She smiled pleasantly, hoping they were not Jehovah's Witnesses. Nina believed everyone had the right to their own religion and she quite enjoyed a ten minutes amiable argument but she didn't fancy a lecture before she'd had her coffee break.

'Good morning.'

The man replied. He had a pleasant voice with a touch of northern accent. The woman with him just stared at her. She was attractive-looking and smartly dressed but there was a strained look about her eyes which made Nina feel a little uncomfortable.

251

There was a pause.

To get things moving she said. 'Can I help you?'

She'd keep the door open for another two minutes, she thought, then she would close it. Really, there was too much disturbance of people in their own homes nowadays. If it wasn't envelopes for your loose change it was coloured plastic sacks to fill for 'the less fortunate among us'.

And when you'd complied with the message, spent ages raking through your wardrobes, what happened? More often than not no one returned to collect the donated goods. And what about unsolicited phone calls? Dear God, they never stopped. There'd been the girl on the telephone last week. She'd been an odd one. Remembering the call, a chilly feeling clutched at Nina's stomach. There'd been something about the voice of the telephone researcher that had disturbed her, disturbed her so much she had been very rude before slamming down the phone. And now there was this stranger; standing silently on her doorstep and staring at her with hazel eyes.

Nina clutched at the opened door with her hand as her stomach heaved. It couldn't be! She numbered the years. A tall, dark-haired woman with hazel eyes. Feverishly, she calculated her female visitor's age. Approaching forty. That was about right!

Her throat went dry and she swallowed with difficulty. She managed one word.

'Helen?'

A pause, and the woman nodded.

Oh, dear God.

She repeated the word. 'Helen!'

A sudden rush of tears blinded her. She put out her hand and touched the fabric of her daughter's jacket. She paused, terrified Helen might pull away from her; terrified that she might turn away and leave her without a word. She wouldn't blame her. She had every right and yet...

She whispered: 'Will you come in?'

She saw Helen's shoulders slump and sensed, rather than heard her slow exhalation of breath. Nina opened her eyes wide to stop tears falling. 'Please?'

The man and woman looked at each other. There was a brief, quiet exchange of words. Nina made no sense of what they said. Her gaze was riveted on Helen's face. Somehow Helen had found out where she lived. Had she come to castigate her mother for her desertion? Did she come just to verify that it *was* her mother? Did she want to spit in her face or hold out her arms? Anything was possible. Please, God, she thought: don't let her turn away, walk down the path and out of my life. To her huge relief it didn't happen, only the man turned away and walked back to the car parked in the road outside her house. Tears blurred Nina's eyes. She brushed them away impatiently. Tears were superfluous in a situation like this. Tears were for stubbed toes and trapped fingers. Heartache was tearless. Besides, tears blurred her view of her daughter's face. Timidly, she dared to ask a question.

'Is he your husband?'

'Of course not.'

Helen's voice was sharp.

Nina lowered her eyes. What right had she to ask personal questions? She stammered. 'Sorry'.

'He's a friend.' Helen laughed but it wasn't really a laugh. 'I take after you, mother. I'm no great shakes at keeping a husband.'

Nina accepted the rebuff. It would be the first of many and she deserved every one of them.

'Please come in,' she said in a small voice. She led the way into the sitting-room. 'Shall I take your jacket?'

'Yes. Thank you.'

They were so formal, it was ridiculous.

Nina carried the jacket into her cloak-room. She held it to her for a moment before placing it on a hanger. She returned to the room where Helen waited for her. There was an uncomfortable silence as the two women stared at each other. Then Nina asked: 'What do we do now?'

Her daughter shrugged. 'I'm not sure. We could fall on each other's necks, but I don't feel like doing that. You'll understand why?'

Nina bowed her head. 'Yes, I do. But I think you should decide. After all...' she paused and stared into Helen's eyes, 'you came looking for me.'

'That's true.' Helen sighed. 'I could do with a cup of coffee.'

'Of course.' Glad for something to do, Nina hurried towards the door. 'How do you like it?'

'Strong. No sugar. Just a dash of milk.'

'Like me.' Nina nodded. 'I won't be long.'

She brought back a tray which held cups and saucers, milk and a large coffee pot. She placed the tray on a coffee table near the sofa and they sat together and, haltingly, began to talk.

During their conversation, they drank three cups of coffee each. Helen said she knew coffee wasn't good for you and Nina said: 'What the hell.' The conversation during their first cup was inconsequential. They asked careful questions and talked about things they partially knew, or had guessed. In response to Nina's questions, Helen told her that Frank had been a limited but well-meaning stepfather. He had encouraged her to continue with her studies after which she'd found a decent job in

London and moved there. His sister, she added, with remarkable restraint, had been 'a bit of a pain'.

'She always was.' Nina commented. 'Tell me, did Frank ever mention me?'

'Hardly ever. A few times just after you left us.' Helen watched Nina's flinch without emotion. 'And then, not at all.'

'That must have been hard for you.'

Helen glanced at her mother. 'It was hell, but you can hardly blame him, can you?'

Nina was quiet for a moment and then, changing the subject, she asked: 'You said you were married?'

'Yes.'

'And it didn't work out?'

'No.'

'And you blame the break-up on me?'

Helen gasped. 'No! At least, I didn't. But when you come to think of it, I hadn't much of a start. You weren't a great role model.'

Nina replaced her cup and saucer carefully on the tray. 'No. I wasn't. But you never knew what *my* childhood was like and, although I never pretended to be the marrying kind, I was always a good mother to you.' She gave Helen a pleading look. 'We had good times, didn't we?'

'Yes, we had wonderful times and that's why it was so horrible when you left.' Colour rushed into Helen's face and she leaned forwards. 'God, Nina, I missed you *so* much. You've no idea. You can't have had any idea how hurt I was, otherwise you wouldn't have left me.'

Nina, grim-faced, poured out more coffee.

'I owe you an explanation, Helen and I'll give you one. Now that you're a woman it might be easier to explain. I hope so. But you'll have to be patient and listen to me. Will you do that?'

'I suppose I'll have to. I've waited all these years, I can hang on a little longer.' Helen accepted her coffee cup from Nina and sat back.

'Thank you.' Nina hunched her shoulders and sat, clasping her knees with her hands.

'You think I'm a hard bitch, I suppose?'

She stared at Helen and their eyes locked. It was Helen who looked away.

Nina continued. 'At least you have some happy memories. That's what I kept thinking about when I left Frank. And you were growing up. I knew that, before too long, you'd be out in the world, living your own life.'

She sighed. 'I guessed you'd hate me for a little while but I thought "She'll get over it".'

'You thought it would be that easy?'

'No. I knew it would be hard, but children get over anything.' Nina paused then said softly: 'Children have suffered much more hurt than you suffered and they've survived.

I know. I wished my mother in hell.' Nina wrapped her arms around her body. She did not look at Helen.

'I always hated my mother. She was a small-minded, prim-mannered sadist. She enjoyed inflicting pain, particularly on her children. I don't remember my father. He must have been around for a while but I can't visualise him. When I was about seven, my mother told me he had left when I was a toddler and I remember thinking "Good luck to him". There was just mother, me and my little brother. I didn't know anything about his father, either. God knows how my mother got pregnant. I couldn't, and still can't imagine any man kissing or cuddling her. In fact, I don't remember any man setting foot in our house.'

She sighed. 'We lived in a small village on the Yorkshire Wolds. It was an isolated place and people kept themselves to themselves. Mother saw I was clean and well turned-out to go to school. I always wore blouses buttoned up to the neck and long sleeves. Mother was considered quite a pillar of the community. She went to church regularly. She probably told everyone who asked that she was a widow. Then one day...'

Nina's voice trembled. She gripped her hands tightly together.

'One day I came home from school and David, my little brother, was laid on the settee. Mother was in the kitchen, banging about and stoking up the old boiler to do some washing. She was a great one for washing, my mother. I didn't worry about David at first. He was always quiet. He'd already learned that, but then later, when I spoke to him and he didn't answer or open his eyes I was worried. I touched his hands and they were...' Nina cleared her throat. 'They were flaccid. His face was cold. I got hold of him and shook him and his head fell back and I saw a huge bruise.'

Helen was sitting upright. 'Was he...?'

Nina looked at her.

'I ran into the kitchen. I screamed at my mother, the first time I had ever dared, but she didn't even turn her head. She just kept putting clothes into the copper. I ran out of the house and went to our nearest neighbour. I told her about David and she sent her husband round to find out what had happened. After that, everything was a bit of a blur. I remember the neighbour putting me to bed next to her own daughter. Betty, she was called. She wanted to talk to me but I couldn't. Next day the neighbour ran me a bath and I remember her intake of breath when she helped me undress. Then a woman in a navy blue uniform came and took me off to a children's home. I remember being taken to David's funeral. The coffin was so small.'

Helen made a small noise of distress. Nina pressed her fingers to her temples and then smiled at her daughter.

'I'm all right now. It was so long ago. Things like that happened then. People go on about the "good old days". They have no idea.'

Helen nodded. 'No wonder you never talked about your childhood.'

'But I did.' A smile touched Nina's lips. 'Don't you remember. I told you about living in a country cottage with roses round the door and a beautiful garden. You see–' she lifted her shoulders '–I was fibbing from an early age.'

Helen's forehead wrinkled. 'So you stayed at the children's home?'

'Homes.' Nina corrected her. 'You got moved around quite a bit when you were in care. It wasn't too bad. I had fights with the other kids from time to time. There was always a strong pecking order. The worst thing was schooling. Without conceit, I knew I was bright. I would have made a good scholar but what with the moves and the fact I was in council care, no one thought beyond getting me into a domestic job when I was fourteen. It killed two birds with one stone, you see. Accommodation came with domestic work which looked after my moral welfare and provided another vacancy at the children's home.

There was always a clutch of little bastards needing to be cared for.

'Trouble was, in my case the moral bit didn't quite work out.'

'You mean, when you got pregnant with me?'

Nina looked at Helen and nodded.

'Yes, but we needn't dwell on that. I've told you before. I looked at you and realised I loved someone more than I loved myself. I wasn't sticking you in a council home. That's the truth.'

Helen nodded. 'Yes, I believe you, and you were a terrific mum but why then...' Helen dashed the back of her hand across her face. 'Why did you go away and leave me with Frank?'

'I was coming back. I had every intention–'

'You didn't. You didn't come back, and I was still a kid. My whole world fell apart, Nina. I couldn't believe you'd gone for good.'

Nina opened her mouth but Helen seemed unable to cut off the flow of words. She leaned forward and spoke passionately.

'I had a Girls' Own pocket diary then and every night I ticked off another day without you. Every day I expected you back. I didn't sleep properly. Two o'clock, every morning, I woke. I sat up in bed and listened. I kidded myself I heard your voice and I'd creep on to the landing but it was always Frank's sister speaking. You never came. Then I decided you were dead. I thought that would be the only thing that would stop you coming back for me. I was *sure* you'd been murdered. Every news item about a woman's body being found terrified me but I had to get hold of a newspaper, read all the gory details.'

With eyes burning with emotion, she looked at Nina. 'Then I got wise. For years you had walked away from boyfriends, why shouldn't you walk away from me? Perhaps I'd got to be a drag. I wasn't a cute toddler any more. Maybe I was getting old enough to be a rival? A good-looking woman like you didn't want a teenage daughter hanging around.'

'Stop that.' Nina's cheeks were flaming. 'You've got it all wrong.'

'Have I?' Helen pressed her hands to her cheeks. 'Then tell me. That's why I'm here.'

Nina clasped her hands together and leaned forward in her chair.

'I never meant to stay away permanently. Things had been difficult between Frank and myself. He was so damn boring! So. I took myself off to Scarborough for a weekend break. I needed some space.'

'You got that all right.' Helen's voice was sullen. 'You got over twenty-five years of space. Anyway, what made you visit Scarborough?

Nina hesitated before speaking. 'I worked there for a while when I was young. In fact, if you want the truth, you were conceived in Scarborough.'

'At last. I get to know something.'

'Don't be flippant, Helen.' Nina's brow wrinkled. 'When you are, you sound like I was, before I met...'

'Don't tell me! You met your one true love.'

Nina's mouth tightened. 'Yes. That's it, exactly. But that can wait until later. What I want you to know is that I did come back to talk things through with Frank. I was going to take you away with me. Didn't Frank tell you?'

Helen's eyes widened. She sat upright. 'You came back? To the house?'

'Yes.'

'Where was I?'

'At school. I deliberately picked a time when I knew you were out. I thought that would be best.' Nina sighed. 'Now I realise I made a mistake.'

'But if you came for me, why did you go away again?'

'Frank pointed out other possibilities. We had to decide what was right for you.'

'Dear God. You make me sound like a puppy needing a home!'

'No, no. It wasn't like that.' Nina grabbed at the coffee pot and drained the remainder of the coffee into their cups. She whispered, as if to herself. 'How can I make her understand.' She stared into Helen's face, willing her to listen.

'I went to Scarborough,' she said. 'But it was no good. Too much time had gone by. I decided I had to return to Frank. I had to settle down and be a good wife and mother. I knew you were enjoying your school and wouldn't want to move again and I was sick of drifting from one bedsit to another and looking for my one, perfect, guy. He didn't exist. Or so I thought.

'Then, I saw a poster advertising a pop concert in Liverpool.'

She paused. 'You'll remember how I loved the Beatles' music. Well, I knew it was silly. I was too old to go to POP concerts but I thought, I'll do this one last silly thing. I'll go to the concert and then accept middle-age. I was coming home. I could stop off in Liverpool for the day, go to the concert and then travel back to Chester and you and Frank.'

'But you didn't come home?'

'No.'

'Why didn't you?'

Nina stared into space for a moment before answering Helen's question. And then she said: 'For the first time in my entire life. I fell in love.'

Eighteen

Silence enveloped the room. As Helen seemed disinclined to break it, Nina did.

'Don't you want to ask me something?'

'What?'

'Well, I've just told you about...'

'Falling in love?'

'Yes.'

Helen shrugged. 'But what was so unusual about that, Mother? As far as I can remember, you were always falling in love.'

Nina looked at her daughter and felt chilled. How could a child of hers be so cold? She thought of the boy who had fathered Helen. So far as she could remember he had been shy, almost timid. If it hadn't been for his looks she would never have noticed him. She remembered his polite way of speaking to her. She had liked that, and the way his eyes followed her whenever their paths crossed. When she had gone to his room that night, she had acted out of devilment. His mother had driven her mad – picking her up on everything she did and forever finding fault. She had told her one day it was time she bought a decent bra. Nosey old cow. Maybe Helen had inherited some of her grandmother's genes. That would explain her cold expression.

Nina studied Helen's face, particularly her eyes. She had her father's eyes all right. When she had tiptoed along to Richard's room, slipped into bed with him, she had imagined a few clumsy kisses and a cuddle but he had surprised her. And the sky had been full of stars. They had seemed to be all around them. Their youthful coupling couldn't be called love... It was nothing like the times she shared with Alex, but it was a good enough start for a child to be conceived. Now Helen was middle-aged. She had been married. Surely she had experienced passion? Surely, she had been in love? If she hadn't, how could she understand the emotions that had driven her mother to do the things she had done? And how could she make Helen understand why she couldn't leave Alex and go back to Frank?

Thinking of Alex had distracted her. She asked Helen: 'How *did* you find me? How did you know I became Mrs McNulty?'

'You're not, are you. Not legally.'

Nina gasped. She had honestly forgotten her marriage to Alex had been bigamous.

'Helen, you must realise that when I was with Alex–'

'It was sheer chance I found you.' Helen interrupted her. 'After my divorce...' Helen paused for a moment and when she resumed speaking, her voice sounded harder. 'I went to Scarborough to try and pick up your trail. I'd found a photograph of you in Frank's belongings after his death. That's what started me on the search. You'd sent it from Scarborough. I didn't have much luck with my enquiries but I made a friend. You saw him today. He had the photo enlarged so we could see the poster in the background. Then we went to Liverpool.'

'But we left Liverpool years ago. How did you...?'

'We found a man called Warden.'

Nina started. 'Terry Warden?'

'Yes.'

'My God. I thought he'd have died years ago.'

'No. He's alive and well. He manages a hotel now. He told us about you and...'

'Alex.' Nina provided the name Helen couldn't, or wouldn't say. She clasped her hands together. 'Did he tell you about the night Alex and I met?'

'I think so. It was the facts I was interested in. He told us you got married and went to live in London.' Helen paused. 'Sorry, Nina, but I can't get fired up about someone who stirred your pulses years ago. Later, I found out Alex died.' Her voice softened. 'I'm sorry.'

Nina lowered her head. 'How did you find out?'

'That's the strangest thing. After Liverpool the trail ran out and we gave up. Richard went back to Scarborough and I returned to London. I work for an insurance brokers and, lo and behold, while reorganising the office filing system, an old file turned up on my desk – labelled McNulty's Musical Agency. Your present address was in it. It's absolutely ridiculous, isn't it? I was flying all over trying to find you and the information I wanted was in my place of work. Of course, I wouldn't had connected the word McNulty with you without the contact we made in Liverpool.'

'The man who befriended you, the one from Scarborough...' Nina twisted her fingers together. 'What did you say was his name?'

'Richard. Richard Argyle.'

Nina closed her eyes.

Helen frowned. 'Are you all right, Nina?'

She didn't answer.

A moment later she felt her cold hand being taken and held in a much warmer clasp. 'What is it? You've gone quite white.'

She opened her eyes. Helen had moved closer to her. Her face held concern.

'What's wrong?'

'Nothing. No, really. I'm fine.'

Nina pulled her wits together ... but she kept hold of Helen's hand.

'What sort of man is this Richard?'

'Richard?' Helen sounded puzzled. 'He's all right. He's the man who brought me—'

'Yes, yes. I realise that. He's not ... he's not important to you, is he?'

'I don't understand. Oh.' Helen shook her head. 'Did you think he was my boyfriend? No, I'm sorry to disappoint you, but I have no man in tow. Richard and I met by accident in a theatre in Scarborough and somehow, almost without us knowing how, he's got involved in my search. It sounds a bit peculiar, I know, but he's kind and helpful, has a lovely home and quite a bit of money so he doesn't have to work. I think he finds life a bit boring; helping me gives him something to do.'

She looked at her watch. 'God! The time's flying. Maybe we ought to pack in all this soul-searching for now. We've made a start, haven't we? If you will allow me to come back...?' She looked enquiringly at Nina.

'I think you're right, Helen. We need space to consider what's happened. I've hundreds of questions to ask you and there's a great deal I need to tell you but you look tired and I feel as though I've been run over by a train.' Nina put a hand up to her face. 'There's just one thing I'd like a bit more information about. You're sure your meeting with Richard was an accident?'

'Yes, I'm sure. Why do you ask?'

'Oh, no reason.' Nina prepared to get up

from the sofa but Helen put out her hand and stopped her.

'May *I* ask one more question?'

'Of course.'

'Please tell me, briefly, what happened when you came to see Frank. That time when I was at school.'

There was a pause. Nina ran her fingers through her hair. 'Before I do, I want you to realise, Helen, that there's a great difference between me and you. You were strong as a child and now that you're a woman, I can see you have learned to be even stronger. I'm not like that. I always needed approval from someone. I always needed a man in my life. It's only since Alex died that I...' She caught a slight hardening of Helen's expression and she stopped. She began again.

'I met Alex and fell wildly in love with him. For over a week I thought of nothing but him. We were besotted by each other. In bed, out of bed, it was as if we were two halves. It was wonderful. When I finally thought about you, I knew you would be missing me but, it was as if you were on a different planet. And, if I can call it an excuse, I knew Frank and his sister would look after you. Remember, I didn't know what was going to happen next. I was half geared up for Alex to get tired of me. Tell me to go home. It had happened to me before. But he didn't. You see, he felt the same as me. I really couldn't believe it. I reasoned you were safe with Frank for a couple of weeks. I was irresponsible, I admit it, but it was as if I was having the honeymoon I'd missed out on when I was young. I still loved you and I missed you but,' she paused, 'I didn't want you around, not then.'

Staring down at her hands, she continued. 'But then, after two weeks I realised I couldn't imagine life without you. I was missing you badly. I missed your serious little face and your grown-up comments. I wasn't sure what I'd say to Alex, but I knew I had to get you back, so I got on the train and came back to Chester.'

'Frank never told me you came back for me. Even when he was dying, he never said a word.'

Nina shook her head. 'I was a fool. I was so enclosed in my own happiness I didn't realise how badly he'd react to my news. He'd been gruff and miserable for quite a while, I thought he didn't care about me any more. And there was always his sister, dripping poisonous remarks in his ear. I wouldn't be surprised if she was the one who got the idea of taking his revenge out on you. When I met him at the house, I felt sorry for him. We were chalk and cheese together but he was desperate for me to stay. I said I couldn't. Our first half-hour together was terrible. He called me foul words which, I suppose, I deserved. But then, he went quiet. He seemed to accept the situation, but he said you should stay with him.

'I told him no. I said there was no way I'd leave you behind. He lowered his head for a moment and then he said he'd changed his mind. I was right. A child should be with her mother. He said he'd explain everything to you, that I was coming the following weekend to get you and he'd inform the school and get your belongings together. I believed him. I reckoned that a man like Frank wouldn't want the responsibility of bringing up a child. We parted on reasonably good terms.

'But three days later, he sent me a letter. He told me you were hurt and disgusted by my behaviour. He wrote that you never wanted to see me again. He said you wanted to stay with him. You were settled at school and had good friends for the first time in your life. You were sick of moving around. He said you didn't want to hear from me or see me ever again.'

Helen gasped. 'How could he be so cruel?'

Nina shrugged. 'Frank was very deep. I never did understand what went on in his mind.'

'But you believed him? How could you believe him? You knew me better than you knew Frank!'

'I thought I did, but reading his letter brought it home to me what a rotten mother I'd been. I'd done exactly what I wanted. For years. Dragging you around the country. New schools; no time to make friends; living in bedsits. It wasn't the right kind of life for a small girl. And you were starting to grow up. Everyone knows mothers and daughters fall out around that time. I'd dragged you from pillar to post and if you'd come to live with me and Alex, there would have been even more travelling. The pop-music world was hardly stable. I remembered how *I'd* missed out on proper schooling. I didn't want that to happen to you. I wanted you to have choices when you grew up. So, I decided, if you really wanted to stay with Frank, I would agree. I wrote you a letter. I don't suppose...?'

She looked at Helen who shook her head.

They lapsed into silence.

Then Nina picked up the coffee pot and shook it.

'Sorry. It's empty.'

Helen nodded and then she smiled. 'No damn wonder.'

Nina yawned. 'I'm exhausted. I'm sad and angry but I'm happy, too. So many misunderstandings sorted out.' She held her head on one side. 'I'm also hungry. Shall I make us a sandwich?'

'Well...'

'When are you expecting your friend back?'

'I suggested two o'clock might be an appropriate time.'

'Good.' Nina stood up. 'We've got time. Chicken all right?'

'Perfect.'

'What about a glass of white wine to go with it? I think we deserve one.'

'OK.' Helen nodded. 'On one condition.'

'What's that?'

'You allow me to help you.'

'Agreed. Come through to the kitchen.'

Helen followed her mother into the kitchen.

Nina took the chicken from the refrigerator. 'There's some salad in the bottom compartment but I don't want any. I've been trying to get some weight off but I'm sick of the damned rabbit food.'

A faint smile touched Helen's lips. 'You don't need to slim.'

'You're joking?'

'No, you look fine.'

'Well, thank you.' Nina glanced across and studied Helen's appearance.

'Obviously you don't have problems with weight. You must have inherited your build from your father.'

She watched Helen's face for a change of expression but saw none. Helen took lettuce and tomatoes from the refrigerator without comment. Nina poured out the wine and handed Helen a glass.

'Here you are.' She sipped at her own drink. 'You know,' she gave a faint smile, 'when you and your friend appeared on my doorstep, I thought you were Jehovah's Witnesses.'

'Did you?'

'Yes, and I must say, after this morning, when it comes to revelations, we beat them hands down!'

Richard returned to Nina's house on the dot of two p.m. He was full of worry for Helen. His daughter, he sensed, had already been stretched to the limit through anxiety and lack of sleep even before meeting her mother. How would she cope? She was like brittle glass, he thought, easily shattered. And Nina, what about her?

Away from the house, he tried to remember Nina's face but it was a blur. His Nina had vanished years ago. He had hung on to her memory through foolishness. Another face surfaced in his mind. June, on the beach, her hair blowing, the corners of her eyes crinkling as she put up her hand against the sun. She was a real woman. One he could love. But first, he had to help Helen. Please God, let things be going right for her.

Abstracted and tense, he drove round the

village twice before spotting a pub, although he knew there would be several of them within the vicinity. He went in, ordered half a pint of beer and a ploughman's meal. He ate and drank although he couldn't remember tasting anything. Then he walked round the streets bordering the Market Square, noticing nothing.

He continually checked his watch until it was time for him to collect Helen. He was sweating when he drew up outside the house. He wondered whether just to sound the horn but that seemed rude. He got out of the car and went up the path.

Nina opened the door. This time, he really looked at her. She was a good-looking woman but older and not as slim as he remembered. Richard felt a fleeting sense of disappointment until he realised the absurdity of his thoughts. *He* had been fifteen years old. It was forty years ago! My God, he thought. If she realised who he was, she'd probably die of shock. Forty years ago he had been a schoolboy.

And then she looked into his eyes and smiled and he realised, she *did* know. The colour flooded into his face.

'Nina, I...'

She put her forefinger to her lips and then glanced over her shoulder.

'She'll be with you in a minute. She's upstairs, in the bathroom.'

'Right.' He fumbled for the right words, any words.

It was Nina who spoke, quietly and rapidly.

'We've made a start. We're sorting things out. She mentioned your help and gradually, I realised...' She glanced behind her again. 'I haven't said anything. You will have to tell her sometime, but not now. There's been too much... We're both exhausted.' Her voice faded again. 'I feel so much guilt. I've hurt her.'

Richard saw Nina's eyes go shiny. He wanted to touch her, say something to comfort her, but he dared not.

He muttered, rapidly. 'You gave her love, too. She's told me. The two of you, together against the world.'

Nina nodded. 'Yes, that, too.'

Richard heard the sound of Helen's steps on the staircase. He stepped back, then whispered. 'How did you know?'

'About you?' She reached forward and touched his cheek for a single moment. 'Your eyes, Richard. You gave our daughter your beautiful hazel eyes.'

Nineteen

Richard was in his car heading homewards. He was listening to the radio but for once he'd abandoned Radio Four and was now tuned into some unknown channel. A man who talked very fast – indeed, he occasionally sounded demented – was playing various tracks from artists Richard did not know. After a bemused ten minutes, he decided he had suffered enough and he was reaching for the turn-off switch when another voice came over the airwaves. The disc jockey had mentioned the name Smokey Robinson. Richard relaxed and listened. He liked him. So he left the radio on, closed his eyes for a moment and slumped in his seat. It was quite safe to do that because he was going nowhere. He was stuck in the middle of a traffic jam.

There was a line of stationary cars in front of him and a huge lorry behind him. Nothing had happened for at least ten minutes. Richard yawned. He had been a long time going to sleep last night, and it wasn't because of the sofa. His thoughts had kept him awake until the early hours. Images of Helen swirled in his head. How weird, but how absorbing, it was, stepping into other people's lives. He was glad, so glad he had come to Helen's assistance because he now knew more about his daughter. He had seen where she lived. He now knew that Helen was neat in her habits. There were no tights draped about in *her* bathroom. No shoes kicked under chairs. The cap was on the toothpaste. Richard liked that. His ex-wife had been messy.

And he'd seen Nina. And seeing her in the flesh had banished his ghost. Now he could think of her without anguish. He would remember the young Nancy with affection and gratitude for his daughter. As for the middle-aged woman she was now, it was a woman he didn't know. He found himself wondering... Did she have a man in her life now? He smiled. Of course she did. He'd bet money on it. There was an overt sexuality about Nina that would last until she was an old, old lady, but it was not for him. He would treasure his memories of her but that was it. He'd rather think about June, and that's what he did.

A horn blared behind him. He looked in the mirror at the man behind the wheel of the lorry and then checked ahead. The traffic was beginning to move. Richard released the car's handbrake. He glanced again at the lorry driver and the young man grinned and stuck his thumb up signalling victory. Richard felt a glow of pleasure. He felt part of something. A 'fellowship of the road'. Stupid, he supposed, but why not. There was another pop tune on the radio. It was from years ago. He remembered he had liked the song the first time round but he hadn't been happy then. He was now. As he drove off, he sang aloud the first line of the song, the only words he remembered.

'In the summertime, when the weather is fine...'

He picked up speed.

In the evening Helen rang Richard to see if he had arrived safely. He had. She talked to him for a little while and then she put down the phone and wondered who to ring next. She was restless. She felt she'd been wrapped up in a cocoon for ever and now it was time for her to break out. She had arranged to meet Nina in a week's time. She was going over to spend the day with her but, a week was a long time. She had her work to go to but nothing else planned. She wanted company. She had lived with ghosts for too long.

She looked through her telephone book and rang a girlfriend who had been close to her during her divorce but was now almost a memory. Val was in. She was a little abrupt at first but Helen told her she had been rushed off her feet at work and lots of things had been happening in her private life and she perked up, asking: 'Like what?'

Helen said she didn't want to discuss it over the phone. That was true. She would tell Val a doctored version of what had happened to her but not yet. She decided she was sick of the past. There'd been too many post-mortems.

They arranged a day to meet for lunch.

She wandered into the kitchen and took a yoghurt from the fridge. She stared down at the cutlery drawer remembering the advances made to her by the new man at the office. She picked up a spoon half-wishing she had responded to them. Martin Horton. He was undeniably attractive but now he was taken. Pity.

She frowned and ripped the top off the yoghurt pot. She was ashamed at her own thoughts. All Martin Horton was interested in was sex. When she turned him down he'd immediately propositioned another female member of staff. Was that the sort of man she wanted? No, of course she didn't. She wanted a decent relationship. Something that would lead on to better things. Or did she? She put down the tub of yoghurt and pressed cold hands to her burning face. Dear God! She was forty years old and she was thinking like a sex-obsessed teenager. Still, forty wasn't old. A thought jumped into her mind.

I bet Nina has a lover.

Her doorbell rang. She jumped. She wasn't expecting anyone. She glanced into a mirror before going to answer it. A man stood on her doormat. A good-looking man. For a moment, she didn't recognise him. Then he smiled.

She felt her pulse leap. It was the owner of the garage she had stopped at. What was his name? Urquart. Ian Urquart. 'Hi. Hope you'll forgive me for calling on spec. I looked up your telephone number and I rang you ... twice, but the line was engaged.'

She drew a deep breath. 'What do you want?'

'I wondered ... will you come and have a meal with me?'

They dined in an Indian restaurant. Helen, presuming he had dashed up to London on business, had offered to knock together a snack meal for them at the flat but Ian had demurred.

'I had no right to call on you without notice, but circumstances...' He shrugged. 'Let me take you out for a meal, please.'

The Bay of Bengal restaurant was quietly luxurious. Soft lights, graceful women in saris, tinkling music and gorgeous smells. Helen, wishing she had put on a more glamorous outfit, glanced around her. She had passed by the restaurant on several occasions but had never been in. It was a place, she thought, for couples.

Their table was set back in a corner which gave a good vantage for observing the other diners. They all seemed relaxed, sleek and confident. She looked down at the menu.

'Have you decided?'

Ian Urquart was watching her. She blushed. 'Not really.' She closed the menu and placed it on the table. 'Will you choose for me? To tell the truth, I don't know much about Indian food. Chinese, I enjoy and I've also sampled Greek food but–' she pulled a little face '–I tried Indian once and I didn't like curry.'

Ian laughed. 'There's a whole lot more than curry on offer. I love Indian food. I'll choose carefully and I'm sure you'll enjoy what I order.'

He was certainly masterful. Helen pressed her lips together, suppressing a smile. Normally, she couldn't abide bossy men but, tonight, she felt differently. It was a good feeling, being looked after.

When their order had been taken, she asked Ian: 'Why did you turn up on my doorstep?'

'Two reasons.' Ian drew lines on the tablecloth with his fork. 'First, I wanted to see you again.'

'Why?'

'Why the questions? Does there have to be a reason?' He put the fork down.

'Yes.'

He sighed. 'Well, let's see.' He raised one eyebrow. 'I kept wondering about your car. Was the exhaust behaving itself?'

Helen laughed. 'Yes, it's fine.' She paused. 'Do you give this kind of follow-up service to all your occasional customers?'

'No. Only the attractive ones.'

'You must be kept busy then.' She smiled and looked down. She thought: I'm flirting!

The wine arrived, it was tasted by Ian and deemed acceptable. He poured out two glasses and raised his in the air.

'Here's to an enjoyable evening.'

She touched her glass to his but made no comment.

A waitress brought the food.

When she left them Ian sat up straight in his seat: 'Actually, Helen, my trip to the city was two-fold. One, I wanted to see you again but I also wanted to contact a customer of mine. Have you ever heard of Terry Watersmith?'

She considered for a moment and then shook her head.

'I didn't suppose you had.' Ian swallowed a mouthful of wine. 'Mr Watersmith's big in the City. He's a millionaire. The word in the motor industry is that he's looking for a very special car and I–' he grinned '–I know where I can lay my hands on one.'

Helen felt a twinge of disappointment but

she managed a smile.

'Good for you. Did you see him?'

'No. I phoned when I got to London and his wife informed me he was out of the country, but he's due back early tomorrow. He has his own helicopter, lands on a pad on top of his business block and he'll be in his office by eight thirty tomorrow. At least, that's what she said.'

'I see.' Helen put down her fork. 'So you really called round to see me because you needed a bed for the night. Actually,' she paused, 'you didn't have to buy me a meal. I would have said yes because you helped me out when my car broke down.'

Ian stared at her.

'You've got it all wrong. I wanted to see you again.' He stirred his food so vigorously some split over on the table-cloth.

'Damn.' He mopped up the sauce with his serviette. 'I've a good business, you know. This car I've got for Watersmith is rare and top of the range. That's what I do, Helen. I find the right car for the right customer at the right price and I do very well from it. I don't need to beg for a bed from a girl-friend. I could book into any one of the best hotels.'

'Oh.' Helen's cheeks reddened. 'I didn't realise...'

'No, you didn't. Although I can understand your confusion. The garage doesn't look anything special, I admit. But it suits me to keep it like that. It confuses rivals and it does well as a garage. I use it mostly as my base. Anyway, let's forget business.' He gestured towards Helen's plate. 'You haven't eaten much. Don't tell me you don't like it.'

'Some of it's OK.' She paused, seeing his expression change. 'No, it's very good, really.' The corner of her mouth twitched. 'There, do you feel better?'

'Sorry?'

'Oh, nothing.' She picked up her glass and drank. 'I get the feeling your parents spoiled you, Mr Urquart. Am I right?'

'Not entirely. My mother died when I was quite young and my father was at sea.'

'Oh.' Helen's face now wore an expression of contrition. 'I am sorry.'

'It's all right. It was a long time ago. Dad's still alive. Very much so.'

Ian had now demolished the rest of the food on his plate. He looked towards Helen's plate. 'What is it that you don't like?'

'Sorry?'

'The food.'

Her face went pink. 'Oh, for God's sakes. I don't really know. Perhaps the flavouring's too rich.'

He snorted. 'Ridiculous.'

A waitress, gliding passed their table, looked at him reproachfully.

Helen tried hard not to grin but Ian saw her. He threw down his napkin and stood up.

Alarmed, she asked, 'Where are you going?'

'To pay the bill.'

'But don't you want something else?'

'Not if you don't.'

He signalled to the man behind the counter at the bar.

Anxious not to cause a scene, Helen whispered. 'But where shall we go?'

'We'll find a Chinese restaurant.'

'What!'

'I'll take you to a Chinese restaurant. You like Chinese food.'

She started to laugh. 'Don't be an idiot.'

His eyes narrowed. 'I mean it, Helen. If you thought I was just free-loading on you, I'll have to prove I wasn't.'

She looked around. One or two people were watching them.

'Sit *down*,' she hissed.

He stared at her for a moment and then he did.

She breathed a sigh of relief, and ate some rice. He was a little alarming but he certainly wasn't boring. 'So why did you come to see me?' She asked.

'I was attracted to you. I told you. I *am* attracted to you, Helen. Why is it so difficult for you to understand?'

He stared at her and she felt herself blush. 'There's so many girls–'

He interrupted her. 'I prefer women, particularly a woman with a mind of her own. Girls can be hard work. They're forever touching up their make-up, eyeing other men and giggling. When they're out with you they have no conversation but they spill their guts out talking about you to their girlfriends over the phone. I bet you don't do that!'

She smiled. 'That would be telling. Still, I'm surprised you pick your female friends because of their conversation.'

'Not entirely, I don't.' He stared into her eyes.

She looked away. 'Anyway, you don't know anything about me. How do you know I have a mind of my own?'

'You've just proved it.' He grinned. 'I find you most attractive and I think you're very brave.' His smile widened as he saw her questioning look. 'Driving that car of yours.'

He laughed out loud at her expression. 'Come on, Helen. Show me that you're brave. Let me order a sweet course. If you don't enjoy it,' he paused, 'I'll never darken your doorstep again.'

She did enjoy the food and she enjoyed their subsequent conversation. An hour and a half later, as they left the restaurant, she felt happy. They walked towards a nearby taxi rank. Ian said he never drove after having a drink. It was drizzling with rain when they arrived and Ian had slipped his arm around Helen's shoulders.

'Thank you for coming out with me.'

She moved closer to him. 'No, thank you. I was wishing for company and then, lo and behold, you appeared on my doorstep.'

He smiled. 'That's me. Merlin the wizard.'

'No, no. You're much too young.'

His gaze lingered on her lips. 'I guess we're about the same age. Both adults.'

A taxi was there. The cabbie wound down the window. 'Where to?'

Helen gave him her address and opened a rear door. She looked enquiringly at Ian. 'What about you?'

He hesitated.

'Bit late to start looking for a hotel,' she said.

They both got into the taxi.

The next morning, she woke up feeling wonderful.

Monday morning Stuart Urquart walked up Nina's path carrying a cardboard box containing a rather tatty-looking shrub. He went round to the back door and rang the bell.

Nina opened the door.

'I thought you might like this.' Stuart thrust the cardboard box into her hands.

She studied the plant. 'What is it?'

'Don't know the name but it's very attractive. I thought you could plant it in front of your sitting-room window.'

She turned the box round to see if the other side of the plant was any more appealing. It wasn't.

'My gardener will be coming in a couple of days time,' she prevaricated. 'He'll know how high it grows and whether it will suit the soil. I'll ask him about it.'

Stuart assumed a hurt look. 'Your soil's the same as mine and it grows about three foot tall. I'll put it in for you if you don't want to do it. And if you don't want it at all, just tell me. I'll take it back and plant it next to my hydrangea.'

Nina looked at him over her glasses. He was being a little tetchy. What had brought that on? She suddenly remembered she was wearing her glasses. She had been reading the daily newspaper when Stuart interrupted her. She could feel herself blushing and she balanced the box with the plant in it in one hand so she could remove the offending specs from her face, and then she realised he hadn't even noticed them so she left them on. It was disconcerting but rather reassuring that Stuart took no notice of the spectacles. She thought: if Stuart had to wear a hearing aid, would that bother me? She decided it wouldn't. She put her free

291

hand on his arm. 'Fancy a drink? I know it's a bit early but–'

He cut her short. 'Now you're talking.'

On her second gin and tonic, Nina found she was confiding in Stuart. She was telling him about Helen's visit. The words were tripping out of her mouth. She heard them and she was horrified but she couldn't stop them. What was the matter with her? It wasn't as if she was drunk. Two gin and tonics were nothing. She could drink a navvy under the table. What was she doing? She snapped her mouth together and the silence in the room grew heavy.

Stuart stirred, but did not speak.

Nina was curled up against his shoulder. He was a very comfortable man to curl up to. Not too fat, not like an old sofa that collapsed when you laid down on it, with squashy cushions sliding away from beneath your bottom, and not too hard and boney, so you were bounced off a too rigid support. Stuart was a wonderfully supportive sofa. She sighed and turned her face into his neck.

He tightened his arm around her. 'Feel better now?'

'I think so.'

'Liberating, isn't it? Telling secrets.'

'I've never told any before but, yes, you're right.'

He rested his chin on her hair. 'What do

you want to do now?'

'I don't know. I'm happy here. I feel all light and floaty.'

'I'm glad, my love.'

A pause.

'What did you say?'

'I said...'

'I know what you said.'

'Then why ask?'

'Well...' Nina strove for sensible words but they came out in a disorderly rush. 'I've been a terrible mother. I caused mayhem. I had a bigamous marriage. I deserted my child.'

'She came looking for you.'

'Yes, but...' She started to sit up. 'You can't care for me. I don't deserve it.'

He pushed her back down.

'Logic's nothing to do with feelings and I do care for you, Nina. As for misdemeanours, what about me? I sowed wild oats when I was young. Quite likely there's a couple of kids somewhere I'm responsible for and, now that I'm older and more sensible, I'm sorry. But you have to live in the "now" and right now...' He paused.

She twisted her head and gazed up at him. 'Yes?'

'Right now, I'd like to take you to bed.'

She put her finger to her lips, thought a moment and then smiled.

'I'd like that, too.'

Twenty

There was another special offer on chickens, but these were not in the free-range category. The young lad with the trolley stopped opposite to where June stood and began grabbing the pathetically small corpses, trussed in plastic, and slinging them on to the waiting empty shelves. June averted her eyes. On days like this she wished passionately she could have returned to working at the local building society after John's death, but it didn't work like that. She had been too old and times had changed. When she had first stood behind the counter of the building society, staff had used brain power to calculate interest rates. In her neat saxe-blue overall, she had filled in passbooks, handed out money and had time to ask after the newest baby or commiserate on the passing of an aged relative.

It wasn't like that any more. The last time she had been in the building society she noticed the staff had quadrupled, machines buzzed as passbooks and plastic cards were inserted and the queues of people waiting did not talk, they watched the TVs above their heads, advertising mortgage rates and telling them new ways to borrow money. Still, even with the changes, it would have been preferable to working at the super-market, staring at hundreds of factory-reared slaughtered chickens.

She finished her checklist and went to collect the money from the girls on the tills. Only another hour and she could go home, have a bath and prepare to meet Richard. Her head throbbed. Would he be pleased to see her? Would he tell her anything about his sudden trip?

Richard didn't even mention being away but he did seemed delighted to be with her again. They went to a fish restaurant at the bottom of town and he chatted throughout the meal. Afterwards they drove around the Marine Drive which connected the south and north bays. On the south side, the amusement arcades had closed and only a few couples strolled along the beach. Travel-ling round the Drive the sea was calm and, through the partly opened window of the car, there was only the soft swishing sound of the sea. The moon was full.

When June suddenly shivered, Richard looked at her with surprise.

'Are you cold? If you are, we'll close the windows.'

'No. It was just a feeling, like a ghost walking over my grave.'

'Good grief.' He reached for her hand,

and held it. 'I hope you haven't caught a chill. The weather has turned much colder this last week.' He glanced at her face. 'I'll get you home.'

After parking outside her house, he kissed her. It was a pleasant kiss but not enough.

June moved away from his embrace and asked. 'Would you like to come in?'

He smiled. 'Yes. Just for a little while.'

He waited as she unlocked the front door. They stepped into the hallway. Reg, alerted by the noise of the key in the lock appeared in the kitchen doorway. He gazed at Richard and wagged his tail.

June smiled. 'He always preferred men to women.'

Richard bent down and tugged his ears. 'Silly dog.'

June led the way into the sitting-room. 'Will you have a whisky?'

He hesitated.

'Oh, go on. You've only had one glass of wine.'

'Yes. All right. I will.'

He sat down on the sofa. June poured out two whiskies and carried them over. She sat next to him, handing him his glass.

'You haven't mentioned your trip. How did it go? Was it successful?'

'Yes.' He raised the glass to his lips.

She glanced at his profile. 'Business, you said?'

'In a way it was.' He smiled. 'You wouldn't be interested, June.'

She felt rebuffed.

He drank a little more whisky and then put the glass down. He turned to face her. 'It's lovely being here with you,' he said. He slipped his arm around her and gently, but firmly, drew her closer to him. He kissed her. His lips were warm and smooth.

She shut her eyes and kissed him back. Her body leaned into his.

His arms tightened.

It's happening, she thought. After reading all the books, watching all the films, it's happening to me. I love this man.

The warmth within her spread and glowed. She gasped as Richard continued to kiss her. She slumped against him and opened her mouth, flickering the tip of her tongue against the soft inner part of Richard's mouth.

He stiffened. She felt him withdraw from contact with her.

She opened her eyes. 'Richard?'

He didn't look at her.

She sat up straight, feeling foolish. All her passionate feelings fled. Richard sat beside her looking embarrassed. Had she misread his feelings? She pushed her fingers through her dishevelled hair, trying to tidy herself. She felt bewildered, wondering what she had done wrong. She stared at him, willing him to meet her eyes but he did not. Instead, he stood up.

'I'm sorry, June. I'd better go.'

'But, why?'

'Oh. Reasons.' He shuffled his feet. 'It's getting late. You must be tired. I'll ring tomorrow and we'll fix something up. It's OK.' He flipped his hand. 'I'll let myself out.'

And then he had gone.

Half an hour later, June made a move to her bedroom. She had drunk another full glass of whisky. Once in bed, she lay rigid, wondering what was wrong with her. Did she give out some signal saying she was frigid, or was it the opposite? *Something* must be wrong with her. Her husband had been less than passionate and now Richard had let her down. What could she do?

She was just a normal woman with normal feelings. Surely she wasn't, without realising, giving out messages that she was desperate for sex? She began to shiver and tears oozed from the corner of her eyes. She was lonely. Night after night she sat alone and watched endless scenes of seduction on the television. Oh, she knew real life wasn't like that. She knew the actors were faking and many of the love scenes were ludicrous but she was sick of being alone. And Richard was so nice. He was courteous and kind. He was good looking, too. She was proud to be seen out with him. He was certainly masculine. She could have sworn he was attracted to her. So, what was wrong?

She was so tense, she was shaking. She shut her eyes and imagined Richard was lying next to her. She cupped her breasts with her hands and imagined it was he who was caressing them. She felt her nipples begin to harden. Damm it! She was pathetic. Her eyes flew open and she stared into the darkness. No, she wasn't pathetic. She was normal. She brushed the palms of her hands over her nipples again and they responded immediately to her stimuli. She began to breathe more deeply and her hands moved downwards. If no one loved her then she would have to love herself. She touched and stroked until her breath came in huge gasps. Oh, dear God. She moaned as her body spasmed and then relaxed. She lay, staring into the darkness then the tears came. Her face was soaked in them.

Why? She thought. Why am I so un-lovable?

Richard drove straight home. He put the car away, went up to his flat and went to bed. Lying still and straight beneath the bedcovers he felt like a counter on a board game. The game was Monopoly and his counter always landed on one particular square: 'Go straight to jail'.

He put his arms behind his head and stared into the darkness. He felt let down and confused. He had thought he'd be all right with June. He thought she was gentle and shy. But tonight, she'd shown him there was another side to her nature.

When she had slipped the tip of her tongue into his mouth, he had been startled. He hadn't expected it and it had taken away his confidence. Oh, he knew from what he read in the newspapers that women nowadays had become more demanding with regard to sexual behaviour, but he had thought the articles referred to young people, not people like him and June.

Still, he'd upset her and that, he regretted. He shouldn't have left so abruptly. What if she wouldn't agree to meet him again? That thought made his stomach lurch. He had to see her again. He had to make her realise that he did love her and he wanted to make love to her. He did want that – but how could he tell her he was scared? What if he wasn't good enough? He was no expert at making love. His ex-wife had told him that, several times. And June had been happily married. What if she compared him unfavourably with her ex-husband? What if she took a lot of satisfying?

Richard flung his hand over his sweating forehead. June had been a widow for a long time. She seemed gentle and quiet, but he'd heard other men talking about 'the quiet ones'.

'My Missus wouldn't say boo to a goose but when the light's out...'

A postman had said that one day, ages ago, in Bill Bretton's pub. Richard remembered it had been the man's birthday and he'd had a lot to drink. He had been stood at the bar and he suddenly pulled up his shirt to show off his back.

'How about that for a night of passion?'

His mates had cheered when they saw the long, deep, scratch marks.

Richard had been sitting at his usual table but he had glimpsed the weals and thought: My God. What sort of love is that?

But life was changing so quickly. From the stories you read in the newspapers and the things they showed on TV it seemed that sort of behaviour was what people wanted. But not June, surely not June!

He buried his face in his pillow.

They met three days later. June hadn't gone to the theatre when Richard had left for London. She had managed to change the tickets for another night – this night.

She rang Richard in the morning.

'I did mention it when we were at the fish restaurant but...' she coughed. 'I thought you might have forgotten.'

A great wave of relief washed over Richard.

'No, I hadn't forgotten. I was going to ring you to arrange a time to meet. I can pick you up–'

She cut in. 'No, don't bother. I'll meet you there, in the foyer.'

'But why can't I come for you?'

'I'll meet you there,' she repeated. 'Around seven fifteen.'

He was ten minutes early, waiting for her.

'Hello. You look nice.'

'Thank you.' She produced the tickets. 'Shall we go in?'

The play was fast-moving and witty. The audience laughed a lot. Richard and June were mainly silent. When they emerged from the theatre, Richard suggested a walk. She nodded. They headed towards a neutral area of town, away from their respective dwelling places. After a while, as it was a cold night, they went into a small pub with few customers. They sat by a window.

Richard brought over the drinks. He sat opposite her.

'Are you all right, June?'

She stared at him.

He saw slow tears form on the lower lashes of her eyes. She blinked them away.

'Oh, hell.' He said. He leaned over and grasped her hands in his. 'I'm so sorry, June.'

She sighed. 'What happened? It was me, wasn't it. It was when I–'

He cut in. 'Nothing. You did nothing wrong. It was me. I just can't...'

Her forehead creased. 'You were married, Richard. You're not telling me you're...'

'Gay? Good God – no!' He clutched her hands more tightly.

'What then? Is there someone else?'

'Of course not. I can't imagine being with anyone but you. It's...'

He struggled for the right words.

'I've not been very successful with women, June. When I was very young, too young, really,' he paused. 'I had a particularly intense–' he groped for the proper words '–I was with this girl and, without really understanding we...' He looked at her helplessly.

She studied his face, then helped him out. 'You slept with her?'

'Yes.'

'Well, it's happened before and it will...'

'No. It was more than a couple going too far after a dance. You see, we were at home and my parents caught us.' Richard choked, remembering the look in his mother's eyes and the words she had used. His father had stood at her shoulder, a dark, speechless bird of prey.

'What happened?'

'Sorry?'

'What happened.' June tried to wriggle her fingers free. 'Sorry, but you're hurting...'

He released her and stared down at the table. 'I can't honestly remember. They threw...' He choked. Somehow, he couldn't say Nancy's name. 'They got rid of the girl. They blamed everything on her. I was fifteen and she was a bit older than me. She had been working for them as a skivvy. She had "led me astray".'

'Fifteen? That *was* young. At least, it was in those days. What did they do to you?'

'Oh, they told me I was an innocent child. None of what happened was my fault. She had been a "harpy". She had corrupted me.' Richard took a deep breath. 'But they changed towards me. Nothing was ever the same again. In fact,' he exhaled a long breath, 'now that I think about it, they treated me as though I was a pervert.'

'Poor Richard.' June leaned across the table and impulsively kissed Richard's cheek. 'No wonder you have hang-ups about sex.'

He stiffened. 'I have no hang-ups.'

June looked at him.

'I haven't. I've had a few girlfriends. For God's sake, I've been married.'

She said, quietly: 'And it didn't last.'

'How many marriages *do* last, nowadays.' He hunched his shoulders. 'I'm a perfectly normal man.'

'I'm sorry. I was only trying to help.'

They sat in silence for a few minutes.

She sighed. 'Maybe we should go.'

'Yes.'

They walked side by side but not touching.

Then Richard asked: 'Will you see me again?'

She tried to read his expression in the half-light. 'Do you want me to?'

'Oh, yes.'

'Then I will.'

She reached out and caught hold of his hand.

'We'll go slowly, Richard. I do value your friendship but...' she stopped walking and turned to face him. 'My feelings for you are more than seeing you as a friend. You must have realised that.'

He nodded. 'I feel...'

She stopped his words with her hand. 'Don't promise anything, you can't deliver. Let's take a little more time. Agreed?'

He kissed her cheek. 'Agreed.'

Twenty-One

After a full Sunday dinner consisting of Yorkshire pudding, roast beef, and all the trimmings, Stuart and Ian Urquart were slumped in easy chairs, sipping whisky and chatting. Ian had arrived late morning, with no prior notice and in a flurry of hailstones. His sudden appearance was unexpected but the hailstones were not. It was the middle of November and the beautiful weather experienced in September and October was now nothing but a memory.

As his father moved around the kitchen preparing the meal, his son followed him, chattering away about a variety of things and more specifically, describing a particularly spectacular coup he had just pulled off, to do with a couple of top-of-the-range Mercedes Benz.

'Fowler suggested I contact him again in the New Year. The business is taking on new men so...'

Beating up the batter for the puddings and chopping carrots, Stuart had listened and observed. Now relaxing, the meal eaten and the dishes washed up – Stuart always demanded a tidy galley – he asked his son a question.

'So, if the business is going from strength to strength, what's making you so itchy?'

'I'm not itchy.'

Ian shifted uneasily in his chair.

Stuart stretched out his long legs and gazed down into his whisky glass, then he glanced across at his son.

'Come off it, Ian. Ever since you were a little kid I could tell when you were uneasy about something. If you've just pulled off a good business deal, you can't be short of cash so,' he paused, 'I guess it's a woman?'

'That's ridiculous. I just thought it was time to pay a visit to my dad.'

Stuart shrugged. 'Have it your way. Are you staying for the night?'

'I hadn't really decided. A mate of mine phoned just before I set off. There's a party; he suggested we go. It seemed a good idea at the time but that was before this weather started.' He stared out of the window. 'Maybe I will stay.'

Stuart smiled. 'That's fine with me.'

Ian lay in bed and listened to the hailstones chattering on the windows. Stuart's spare bedroom was immaculate, swept and dusted. A bowl of pot-pourri stood on the window-sill and scented the air. Ian put his hands behind his head and stared up at the ceiling. No cobwebs anywhere. How did the old man do it?

He had a cleaner in twice a week. He was hardly ever in the flat and yet, the place always looked a tip. That's why he took his occasional girlfriends to hotels for seduction. It made life easier.

He sighed and turned over on his side. It was time he changed his ways. He wasn't young any more. He was verging on middle-aged. Pubs, clubs, one-night stands, they were all losing their power over him. He wanted to move on, but move on to what? He still couldn't imagine settling down with one woman. He'd be bored silly in a couple of years. And yet he wanted kids. He would like at least three. He'd been an only child and he hadn't liked it. He decided he would sell his flat and buy a house. Then, in a couple of years, he'd find the right woman and marry her. He'd marry a strong woman, someone who would keep him on the straight and narrow.

An image of Helen Stephens came into his mind. She was older than his usual girlfriends but she wasn't that old. She'd still be able to have babies. Look at the newspapers, women in their fifties were producing kids. And he could afford for them to hire a nanny. He didn't fancy broken nights. Christ! He stirred. Where were his thoughts taking him.

Still, in ten years' time, he didn't want to be living as he was now. In ten years, he'd have *real* money. He could become a pillar of society. His eyes began to close. But maybe not. Maybe he'd live luxuriously but tastefully, in France, perhaps. He wanted ... he drifted into sleep.

He wanted to be like his father.

Next morning, as Ian was putting his overnight bag in the boot of his car, in preparation for leaving, he heard the crunch of boots. The driveway was carpeted with last night's hailstones. The frail, winter sun had, as yet, done nothing to dispel the evidence of yesterday's bad weather.

He turned round.

'Oh, hello. It's Ian, isn't it? I didn't know you were coming this weekend.'

It was his dad's girlfriend. He hadn't seen her for some time. She was wrapped up in trousers, thick jacket and a pull-on hat in bright red with a matching scarf. She looked slightly eccentric and totally delightful. Ian thought: How does dad do it?

'Is your father about?'

'Yes. He's in the kitchen.'

Ian closed the car boot, moved to the back door, opened and yelled: 'Dad. Someone to see you.'

'Who?' Stuart appeared in the doorway. A checked tea-cloth was slung over one shoulder.

'Who indeed!' The woman laughed out

loud. 'How many women beat a track to your house this early on a Monday morning, particularly in this weather? Are you holding out on me?'

'Never, my love.' Stuart pulled the tea towel off his shoulder and wiped his hands on it. He put his arm around her and gave her a hug. 'I wouldn't dare.'

'Cheeky bugger.' She shook her head at him. 'I came to see if you want to come for a walk with me but as you have company...'

'No. Stay for a little while. Ian's setting off soon. I'm making coffee. Why not stay for one?'

'I shouldn't. I drink much too much of the stuff.' But she shuffled her feet and looked undecided.

'Please stay, Nina.' Ian flashed his most becoming smile. She and his dad looked good together. He was happy for them. Also, it was a plus, Nina had money. The Saab she had admired was long gone but there was always another car. Anyway, he liked her. She had a bit of go about her.

'Please?' He coaxed.

'All right.' She nodded.

Seated in the kitchen, they chattered like old friends. Nina asked Ian if his dad had looked after him.

'Sure. He always does.' Ian gave his father a cheeky but affectionate grin. 'Best Sunday dinner I've had in ages.'

Stuart grunted. 'You mean the *only* Sunday dinner you've had in ages.'

'He's a fly-by-night, my son.' He looked at Nina and shrugged his shoulders. 'He only comes to see me when he feels the need for a bit of parenting or when he's on the horns of a dilemma.'

Ian rolled his eyes. 'Horns of a dilemma. Honestly, Dad, you're turning into an Old Testament character. People don't use phrases like that any more. You ought to get out more.'

'I get out quite a lot, thank you.' Stuart stared at his son. 'Look me in the eye and tell me you've not got something on your mind. I know you, my boy. What is it? Woman trouble?'

Nina, looking from father to son thought how much they resembled each other. Maybe too much. She tried her act as peacemaker.

'At least he comes to see you, Stuart.'

He frowned. 'Yes, but he hasn't told me why he came.'

Ian thumped down his coffee cup with unnecessary force. 'I'm perfectly happy, Dad. I've plenty of friends. My business is booming, and as for women, I'm in a neutral zone at the moment. I don't even have a girlfriend.'

'Ah, that proves my point.'

Nina, her eyes lighting up with curiosity

and interest, switched her attention from Ian to Stuart.

'What do you mean?'

Stuart shrugged. 'My son habitually has two girlfriends on the go. If he hasn't, something's happened to change that. Has someone failed to fall for your charm, Ian. Is that it?'

'No, it damn well isn't!' Ian glared at his father. 'I've told you. I'm concentrating on the business. Truth is–' he glanced at Nina, then shrugged '–I'm getting a bit sick of playing the field, Dad. It's time I grew up. I've only been out with one woman these last few weeks and that was someone whose car broke down near my garage. I fitted a new exhaust for her, or Andrew did.'

'Is that right.'

'Yes. And I'll tell you something else. Helen's not a bimbo. She's intelligent as well as attractive. I enjoy her company.'

'Are you seeing her again?'

'I hope so. It depends on her.'

'Does it, by God!' Stuart smacked the table. 'I'm vindicated.' He looked at Ian's unresponsive face. 'Don't you see? This woman's got you dancing to her tune, instead of vice versa.'

Nina glanced at Ian and saw he was not amused. She attempted to defuse the atmosphere building up between the two men.

'You're being aggressive, Stuart. Not all couples fight for supremacy in a relationship. My own marriage was a successful partnership and–' she blushed a little, glancing at Ian '–*we* get along as equals, don't we?'

Stuart reached across to her and pressed her hand. 'You're quite right, Nina.' He looked at his son. 'I apologise.'

Ian shrugged and stood up. 'You're entitled to your own opinions about me. Anyway, it's time I was on my way.'

Nina also stood up. She gave Stuart a reproving look before turning to Ian.

'Don't let your dad rile you, Ian. He thinks the world of you, really. Anyway, I think it's good you're attracted to a real woman instead of...' Her words trailed away. 'Maybe, we'll get to meet your new ladyfriend?'

Ian shrugged on his coat, only partly mollified. 'I doubt it. Although' he paused, 'now I come to think about it, she was travelling here when her car broke down. She was very upset about it. I gather she was coming to see someone special.'

There was a sudden pool of silence. Ian, glanced from Nina to Stuart.

'What is it?'

'Is your Helen tall, with dark hair?' It was Nina that spoke.

Ian nodded. 'Yes. How do you know?'

Nina brushed her hand over her mouth.

She took a deep breath.

'Oh, nothing. I just thought... I mean, I saw a tall, dark attractive woman in the newsagents a couple of days ago. I hadn't seen her before. When you were talking, I remembered her. Still, it can't have been her, can it? She never made it.'

Ian thought. 'She might have come another day. She never mentioned it when I saw her in London, but there again, why should she?'

'Yes, of course. Anyway, it doesn't matter.' Nina stood up. 'I really must go and have my walk.'

'If you wait a minute, I'll come with you.' Stuart also rose to his feet. 'We'll see you off, first.' He put his hand on Ian's shoulder. 'Don't pay too much attention to me. Actually, I'm glad you're taking a more responsible tack with regard to your life. I wish you well with all of your ambitions.'

They walked out of the house and stood by the car. Ian got in.

They waved. 'Drive carefully.'

'I will.'

They watched him go and then they stared at each other.

'What rotten luck. Who would have guessed a coincidence like that?'

Stuart took Nina's hand. 'Don't worry.'

'How can I not?'

'It might be another Helen.'

Ignoring him, Nina chewed on her fingernail. 'She must have come on her own and then the car broke down.' She sighed. 'It must have been her.'

'Just leave it, Nina.'

'If Ian finds out about me from Helen...'

'He won't.'

She stared at him. 'You don't know that.'

'I've listened to you talk about her. She wouldn't tell Ian about her childhood. Not yet. Of course, if they got serious, then she might.'

Stuart gave Nina a hug that lifted her off her feet.

'That would be something, wouldn't it? You and me and Ian and Helen. It mightn't be that bad. A real "keeping it in the family".'

'Oh, you.' She punched his arm, feeling more cheerful.

They walked through a landscape rimmed in white. All was silence. Nina jumped when a blackbird flew out of a hedge with a flurry of wings and powdery frost. Stuart caught her and held her to him.

'It doesn't matter. You and Helen have come together. That's all that matters.'

'Yes.' Nina stood on tiptoe and kissed his cheek. 'You're right.'

'Of course, I am.' Stuart took her gloved hand, pushed it into his jacket pocket and held it tightly.

'Our children are grown-ups, love. They will have to sort out their lives. They'll be happy. They'll be sad. We must concentrate on us. We haven't as much time left as they have. We must make the most of it. That's not selfish, it's sensible.'

She smiled up at him.

'You're right. That's what we'll do.'

Twenty-Two

Helen woke up with a sense of anticipation although, just for a moment, she couldn't remember what she was anticipating. Then she remembered. She had booked a day's leave because she was going Christmas shopping with Val. She jumped out of bed and went into the bathroom. She used her most expensive moisturising cream when she showered and, although she dressed in sensible clothes – shopping demanded that, particularly Christmas shopping – she topped her outfit with her most colourful jacket. Val, she had rediscovered, was lively; she was fun and Helen wanted to be like her.

They had met years ago while working for a large publishing company. They worked in the same office. They sent out monthly sales statements to the company's authors.

'Bloody boring job,' Val had grumbled. 'I chose publishing because I had this picture of me finding a book in a slush pile and discovering a genius author.' She had thrown out her hands in an extravagant gesture. 'The book gets published, a bestseller, of course, and I'm feted as the person responsible. Immediately, I'm promoted to editor-in-chief.'

Helen had smiled, then said: '*You* have no desire to write?'

'God, no. Too much sweat and tears.'

Helen had been cautious about making friends with Val because Val had been to university. A large proportion of staff were university graduates but most of them worked as editors or in the publicity department.

Val was different. She was a wild card. She had done many things. Worked abroad, married and divorced before she was twenty-two. When she and Helen became closer, she talked about her checkered past.

'I'm just restless, I don't know why. Maybe I'll settle down when I'm older. As for my marriage, you don't have to look at me as if it was a tragedy, it wasn't. It was fun while it lasted. I'm still in touch with my ex but as a friend. He's married again. I guess we were just too young.'

Val was the closest thing to a friend that Helen had ever experienced. She had told Val something about her childhood. Not all, but a little. Val had commiserated.

'Poor love. No wonder you're a bit cautious. Still, you've got to look to the future. Make up for the past.'

Val had left the publishers first. She had got fed up of waiting for the literary scoop of the century. She went to work at a wholesale wine importer. Helen left soon after. They kept in touch, if only spasmodically. Val had turned up when the news of Helen's divorce came out.

But today, they were meeting in happier circumstances.

Helen rummaged in the bottom of her wardrobe for a pair of low-heeled shoes; essential for shopping. But she'd take a pair of high-heeled shoes with her because she'd decided, after the present-buying and if time permitted, she was going to treat herself to a new outfit. Something a bit different, something smart, even a little glamorous.

Nina had intimated she would like her to spend part of the Christmas holiday with her. She'd have a few friends round and introduce Helen to them. Then there was Ian. He had been quite insistent that they keep in touch. Helen found the shoes she wanted and stood up. She stared into space for a moment. Ian was lovely but a bit overpowering. He liked his own way. Well, she'd make sure she wouldn't be pushed. She thought of her ex-husband. She wondered what he would be doing over the festive season.

Anyway, she'd better get a move on. There were presents to buy. That, in itself, was a new experience for her.

She met Val off the tube and they hit the shops. Oxford Street to start with but not for long. Christmas fever was building up. The shop windows were being dressed with stars and Father Christmases. Already there were crowds on the pavements and queues. They agreed Knightsbridge would be better. They worked their way through the department stores and the boutiques. Helen bought a cashmere scarf for Nina and a pair of gold earrings. She also bought cuff links for Nina's gentleman friend.

She had met Stuart on two occasions but only briefly. She didn't even know his surname but she liked him. She wondered if she was going over the top, buying him a Christmas present, but she wanted to. And it was obvious Nina and he were close. She understood why. There was a warmth about him that disarmed her, as well as her mother. He had broken through her natural reserve. She had noticed he wore cuff links and the pair she bought for him were unobtrusive in design, a pair of small, plainly carved pewter dolphins. She knew he had been at sea for many years; dolphins seemed somehow appropriate. She hoped he would like them.

She hadn't got a present for Ian yet. He seemed to have everything he needed. She hadn't found anything for Richard yet either. She knew she wanted to buy a present for him too, but what? Theirs was such a strange relationship; it was like an almost completed jigsaw with one crucial piece missing. She still couldn't understand what had triggered his regard for her but she knew it was genuine.

When she and Val collapsed in a cafeteria for a coffee break, she spoke of her difficulty. Val listened to her and did not immediately speak when Helen stopped talking.

Then she said: 'You say he's never put a foot wrong?'

'Not once. And he could have done. When we went to Liverpool there were plenty of opportunities.'

Val shrugged. 'You said he lived alone?'

'Yes.'

'He sounds odd but not threatening. Maybe, as you say, he's just lonely. He told you his daughter died at birth. I suppose you're filling the gap. You'd better watch out, though. If he gets a bit pushy, wants to see you more, then I'd terminate the relationship.'

Helen nodded. 'And you think I can buy him a Christmas present?'

'If you want. Not anything personal, though.'

'Yes, but what?'

'What's he interested in?'

'I can't think. Oh, yes. He likes astronomy.

He has a telescope in his attic.'

'There you are then.' Val drained her coffee cup. 'Get him a book on that.'

They used their credit cards in the small boutiques. Val bought some black, slim, slinky trousers and a delicate silver-grey top.

Helen told her she looked a knockout. 'Just right for an intimate party.'

Val sighed. 'Maybe. But I'm not sure what I'm doing this Christmas.'

'Oh?'

'I've got a choice. I've been invited to a friend's bash in a very exclusive nightclub in the West End for Christmas Eve but,' she paused, 'I've also heard from my ex.'

'Have you.'

'No, Helen.' Val shook her head. 'It's not what you think. I've kept in contact with Miles. You know that. But I'm sure I told you that he'd married again; just over a year ago.'

'I don't remember.' Helen looked at her friend. 'Did it upset you?'

'Not at all. Perhaps I didn't tell you about his marriage. We were out of touch for a while, weren't we? Anyway,' Val shrugged, 'they were happy, until fate intervened. Lorna, his wife became pregnant very quickly, which was what they wanted. Things were fine until she went into labour. She had eclampsia, undetected until it was too late. The baby was born but Lorna

324

didn't make it.'

'Oh, God. That's terrible.'

'Yes. It is.' Val nodded her head. 'But life's like that. It rears up and kicks you in the teeth.' She sighed and rubbed her forehead.

'Miles has been remarkable. I would never had guessed...' Her voice went husky and she turned away for a moment then she turned back to Helen and smiled. 'His mum's still alive and well. She stays with him a lot, helping with the baby, but I gather he'll be on his own for part of the Christmas holiday. He didn't ask me if I could give him some time, but I think I should.' She shrugged. 'Not that I know much about babies.'

'But you'll be company and you are a woman.'

'That doesn't mean I'm a dab hand at nappy-changing.'

'He doesn't want you there just for that.'

Val sighed. 'I know.'

They sat in silence for a moment. Then Helen said, 'You never know, do you? You think you've got everything covered and then something awful happens.'

'It's not always bad things.' Val roused herself. 'Sometimes marvellous things happen. That's life. And we've got to try and handle everything that fate chucks at us.'

'I suppose so.' Helen glanced shyly at Val. 'Forgive me, but you and Miles?'

Val shook her head. 'Don't go working out the plot, Helen. We're dealing with real life here. I don't want to get together with Miles and I'm sure as hell he's not thinking about taking up with me again. We're different people now. We've moved on. It's just ... we've got a history and we're there for each other, when necessary.' She sniffed, then glanced at her watch.

'Christ! Look at the time. We've still got things to do. We have to find something glamorous for you to wear this Christmas. You'll want to impress all these new characters you've found. Come on, girl. Onwards and upwards!'

They staggered into Helen's flat around five p.m. Val collapsed on her sofa.

'I'll get my breath and then I'll be off.'

'No, I won't have that. I think you should stay overnight.'

'Well,' Val rolled her eyes. 'It sounds attractive. I can't face another shop and I'm too tired to eat out.'

'That's how I feel.' Helen kicked off her shoes. 'We'll flop for a while, then I'll send out for a take-away. We'll open a bottle of wine or two. You can sleep in my spare bedroom. I have one, you know, although it's more of a cupboard.'

'My heroine!' Val flung her arms out wide. 'I can think of nothing better. And it will give us time to talk some more.'

Helen smiled. 'There's *more* to talk about?'

'Of course. I've saved the best bit to the last.'

'Oh! It sounds like good news.'

'Yes, it is. In fact, if things work out, it could be fantastic news.' Val's smile split her face. 'Like I was saying, you never know what's round the corner.'

'So, when are you going to tell me?'

'Oh, not this minute. I want to set the scene first.' She paused. 'Can I ask a favour?'

'Yes, of course.'

'Can I have a bath?'

'Sure. Have it now. There's plenty of hot water. The immersion's on.'

'No wonder you're my favourite friend.' Val stood up and trailed in the direction of the bathroom. 'I'll see you in two hours.'

'Make it half an hour. I could do with a bath myself.'

'Will do.'

Helen laughed.

She heard the water being turned on as she stood up and went to check her answerphone. There was one message, from Ian. He asked if he could take her out to dinner tomorrow. She thought for a moment and realised she wanted to see him. More important, she wanted to go to bed with him again. She visualised his face, his ready smile. He certainly was an attractive man. She dialled his number. There was no reply. She could have contacted him on his mobile but she always forgot to ask him for his number. She told his answerphone she would be delighted to dine with him.

As she replaced the phone, she smiled, a little grimly. *What a long way we've come from love-letters.*

Twenty-Three

In the second week of December, North Yorkshire was hit with an unexpectedly heavy snowfall. The coast area suffered most; the road linking Whitby to Scarborough was closed for three days. Trains to and from York to Scarborough still ran, but were late arriving. On the streets, the snow turned to ice and pavements were treacherous. Elderly people were not to be seen.

In Scarborough, Amy Langton railed at the council.

'It's all right for the mayor. He's got his blooming limousine. What about the pensioners? And why can't the council put some salt or sand down on the streets? It's not as if it's in short supply. We've got two blooming beaches full of sand. They clear the roads, don't they, but they don't think about the pedestrians.'

Richard stared out the window, watching the waves racing each over the hard-packed, empty beach. He could see the sun in the sky but it was a pale sun, devoid of power, veiled by the fast moving wispy clouds. He sighed and turned away from the view. He looked at Amy. *He'd* thought about her. He had telephoned her and told her not to come today and then, when she insisted, he had taken the car out of the garage and gone and fetched her. He wished it was time to take her back again. He began to seriously wonder when he could persuade her to retire.

The telephone rang. He went to answer it. It was Helen. She wanted a chat.

'Hello!' His spirits began to lift and his voice regained vigour. 'How are you?'

'I'm fine. How about you?'

'Me? Oh, all right.' He twisted the telephone cord with his free hand.

'Richard, is it true you have snow?'

'Masses of it. We were on the TV news last night. Didn't you see it?'

'No. A colleague at work mentioned it, though. I've been too busy to watch the telly.'

'Have you.' Richard paused. 'Christmas stuff, I suppose?'

'Partly. I've more or less finished the gift buying. Oh, and Nina's invited me to her place for Christmas Day. She's entertaining a few friends.'

'That's great, Helen.'

He thought: Why the pang of disappointment? Helen was never going to come here. Why should she? I guess I'll just get a Christmas card and her best wishes. And Nina's hardly likely to consider me for a house guest. Anyway, I couldn't go. There's June.

'Richard?'

'Yes.'

'Are you terribly busy this coming week-end?'

'No.'

'You're sure?'

He had nothing planned. He was seeing June on the Saturday but no specific arrangements had been made.

'Why do you ask?'

'I thought I might come up and see you.'

His spirits soared. *'Really?'*

'Yes. I won't come if you've something planned...'

'No, I haven't. I'd love to see you, Helen.'

'Good.' She paused. 'I'm not sure how I'll travel. It depends on the weather.'

'Even if the snow lasts, you could still come by train. The line between York and Scarborough has stayed open. There's been a few problems but nothing too serious and the forecast says the weather will clear by the weekend.'

'I might do that. I'm still stuck with my unreliable car and if I come by train, I'll be retracing my steps, won't I? You know, Richard,' she hesitated, 'I've been thinking lately, going over all that has happened, and I know I owe you so much. I would never have managed on my own.'

'Nonsense.'

'It isn't nonsense. That's why I want to come and see you. I've made a decision about my future and I'd like to discuss it with you before I actually go ahead. Is that all right?'

Richard cleared his throat. 'I'd be honoured.'

'Oh.' She laughed. 'You're a lovely man. I don't need a father when I have you to talk to.'

She paused.

He could not speak.

'Richard?'

'Yes.'

'Oh, sorry. I thought the line had gone dead.'

'No.' He cleared his throat. 'You'll stay over with me, won't you? You won't have to sleep on the sofa. I've a very nice spare bedroom.'

'Thank you. Of course I'll stay at your place.'

June was in her kitchen; on her knees and scrubbing away at the bottom of her cooker. Cleaning the oven was her most hated household job. She hated wearing rubber gloves. She hated the way baked-on grease refused to be separated from the inner casing of the oven, and she hated the God-awful mess that the task entailed. No matter how television voice-overs cooed and praised various brands of oven cleaner, she knew better. Her kitchen floor, the kitchen sink and she herself, always ended up filthy. There'd even be grease spots splattered on the window blinds – she knew she ought to remove the blinds before starting the job, but she never did; and when she'd finished, she knew that even her kitchen cupboards would look as though they'd contracted the plague. Because she knew all this, she *always* cleaned her cooker when she was in a bad mood. Why waste pent-up emotion in dusting?

Today, she felt totally fed-up. She was fed-up with her life, her job and, if she was honest, she was fed-up with Richard. Time was passing but where were the two of them going? They saw each other. They went to see films. They took Reg for long walks and they talked about television programmes they had watched. Now and again they went for a meal.

June sat back on her heels and closed her eyes. But Richard didn't cook for her any more. He didn't ask her round to his home. He was scared. He was scared she might be too much for him. She sighed and wiped her gloved hand across her forehead, leaving a black mark. But how could they resolve anything until he loosened up? He rarely touched her now and he seemed nervous if she leaned against him or showed him any affection. She wondered why he bothered seeing her any more. They were going nowhere, and yet, when they were parting, he panicked if they hadn't arranged their next meeting. She'd tried to force the issue, hoping that would make him open up a little. She'd said she couldn't plan ahead because she was busy. She'd ring him, she'd said. But no. He had to confirm the day and the hour they would meet. She had to face it. The man was a complete menace.

The more crucial question was, why did she put up with him? Was there something equally peculiar about her? No. There was not! Deep down, she knew the answer. Neither of them were peculiar but they both had hangups. Despite the 'oh-so-careful' conversations and his averted glances, she knew, she was *positive*, that Richard loved her. She also knew he was a kind and considerate man.

It showed all the time she was with him: when he slowed the car to allow a pensioner to cross the road, when they were walking on the beach and he paused to watch and smile at the comical antics of a couple of toddlers. He was a *good* man but this business with the girl, when he was young, had scarred him.

From what he told her, his parents' reaction had been horrific and after that...

June shook her head, imagining the meaningful silences and the watchful eyes of his parents. He'd been a lonely boy, you could tell that. And if he had no one to talk to, the emotional scarring must have grown and festered until he felt isolated. She sighed. No wonder his marriage broke down.

She got to her feet, picked up the bucket of dirty water, carried it into her back yard and poured the water down the drain. At least the oven was halfway decent again. Good enough to put a small turkey inside. Would she be eating on her own again? Surely not. As she walked back into the kitchen she found her eyes filling with tears. She wanted Christopher at home. It was all wrong. Families should be together for Christmas. Her son should be celebrating the festive season with *her*, not eating turkey sandwiches on a sunny beach in Australia. Life was so bloody unfair. She blinked away her tears and looked up at the kitchen clock. Oh God. She was going to be late for work.

As arranged, Richard waited outside the supermarket. At three thirty, June came out of the staff entrance. He went across to meet her.

'How was it today?'

'Hectic.'

He took her arm. 'The car's over there.'

With his free hand, he gestured. 'Mind this bit. It's very slippy.'

'Yes, I will.' June looked up at the sky. 'Do you think it will snow again?'

'Maybe, but the forecast said it will clear tomorrow.' They approached the car. 'You haven't got any shopping with you today?'

'No. I'm the only woman in Scarborough without a shopping bag.' Her laugh was hollow. 'You know, I'll never understand shoppers.' She shook her head. 'The Christmas break is, what? Two, three days at the most. Yet half the population seem hell-bent on stocking up enough groceries for the next two months. I saw one woman with a large trolley full of loaves of sliced white bread. I wonder who she's expecting for the holiday? Gabriel and all his angels?'

Richard smiled and opened the car door for her to get in. She smiled back at him. One thing Richard had in abundance was good manners.

She asked: 'Where are we going?'

'Nowhere special. Just out for tea.'

He took the road to York. After ten minutes, June, looking out of her window, frowned.

'Are you sure this is a good idea? The road's pretty snowed up and it will be worse when it begins to freeze. Once it gets dark...'

'We're not going far. We'll be back before it's dark.'

Twenty minutes later, he turned into the drive of a well-known stately home, one which the National Trust maintained.

June was puzzled. 'We can't get tea here.'

'Yes, we can. It's a one-off.' He drove into the public car park and brought the car to a stop. He consulted his wristwatch. 'Come on. We'll have to get a move on.'

The Grand Hall was not as large as some stately homes but it was wonderfully decorated and full of atmosphere. Holly-wreathed lights burned in candle-sconces all round the walls. A Christmas tree stood in one corner of the oak-panelled room and, facing the tree, a trio of musicians wearing festive red jackets tuned their instruments. In the main body of the hall, tables were set up for afternoon tea. The table covers were holly red and there was a posy on each table made up of winter anemones and ivy. The beautifully carved staircase was also decorated with ivy. All the tables were taken. A gentleman in livery came to escort June and Richard to theirs.

June sat down and looked about her. She felt an urge to giggle but she managed not to. Instead, she said: 'Good God, Richard. Look at all these people. They look so smart. You should have warned me to dress up. I feel an absolute frump.'

'I wanted it to be a surprise. I saw an advertisement in a York newspaper and I thought it would make a nice change for you. You've been working so hard and I wanted you to enjoy yourself. Get a bit of Christmas spirit. Anyway, I think you look very nice and quite in keeping with the surroundings.'

'Ancient, you mean.' June was touched by his words but she couldn't resist a pun. However, when she saw his face cloud, she was sorry. She covered his hand with her own.

'It's a lovely idea. I'm very flattered you arranged it. Thanks, love.'

Richard squeezed her hand and kept hold of it as the waiters arrived and began serving the food.

Tea was poured out into fine china cups from silver teapots. There was a choice of fancy-cut sandwiches. Mince pies with brandy butter and slices of Christmas cake. The musicians struck up with an old-fashioned carol and June, partly easing off her left shoe under the cover of a long red table-cloth, began, for the first time, to feel a touch of the festive season.

They drove back to Scarborough late that frosty evening and under a canopy of stars.

The road was virtually deserted so Richard slowed the car and glanced through the windows.

'Aah!' He checked his mirrors and stopped the car. 'Look, over there. That's the Andromeda constellation.' He glanced at June. 'You can usually see Andromeda without the aid of a telescope but tonight it's particularly fine.'

'Where?' June twisted her head, looked at the myriad of twinkling points of light and gave up. She opened the car door and got out.

'Be careful.'

'Don't fuss. Which one, did you say?'

He got out of the car and joined her. He put one hand on her shoulder and pointed with the other. 'There.'

They looked in silence.

'It's lovely. Particularly looking at it somewhere quiet and peaceful.'

'Yes.' Richard turned June towards him and kissed her.

'You did enjoy the Christmas tea party?'

'Very much.' She nodded. 'I'm enjoying this, too. Just you and me, together.'

She felt something, a tiniest recoil.

She moved away from him and said, a little too heartily. 'You promised me you'd teach me about astronomy.'

'Yes, I will. After Christmas.'

He opened the car door. 'We'd better get in. We don't want a mad lorry driver to bear down on us, do we?'

She shivered. 'No.'

They resumed their journey.

Richard asked if she had finished her

Christmas shopping.

'More or less.' She sighed. 'I've sent Chris a money order. It's not satisfactory, but I haven't seen him for so long. I don't know his interests any more.'

'Oh, surely you do? He writes, doesn't he?'

'Occasionally. You know what young people are like. More often, he phones me, but forgets the time over here and he wakes me up in the early hours of the morning. Reg barks and the call gets a bit scrambled.'

'I see.' Richard hesitated. 'Do you ever think about visiting him?'

'Of course I do. But it's a matter of expense.'

'You know I would–'

'Stop there, Richard. Don't say another word.'

He sighed and changed the subject. 'The ice is going.'

'Yes.'

He drove in silence for a few minutes. Then, he asked. 'Are you working extra hours at the weekend?'

'Of course. We all are.'

'So, you won't have much free time?'

'I doubt it. Why?'

'Oh, nothing.'

She strained to see his face in the dim light of the car.

His profile gave nothing away.

She said. 'I did enjoy myself, Richard.'

'Good.' He smiled at her. 'You've had a busy day, why don't you close your eyes for a bit, have a rest. I'll have you home in twenty minutes.'

She was tired so she did as he suggested. As she drifted off to sleep, she thought: Maybe, as we get older, we'll be happy to be just good friends. At some point in your life you must see love-making is a ridiculous activity. You must stop wanting sex at some time. Then we'll meet up and chat, play cards or something. She yawned and put her head on Richard's shoulder. As she drifted off to sleep she thought: Not yet though. Not if I can help it.

Twenty-Four

Helen arrived in Scarborough on Friday evening. Richard was on the station platform, waiting for her.

The train arrived. Doors were opened. Richard spotted his daughter and waved to her.

She looked round, saw him and waved back. He hurried over to her.

'It's good to see you.'

His voice was husky with emotion. He realised, so he coughed and said, 'I've a bit of a cold.'

She smiled. 'No wonder, with the weather you've had up here. I see the snow's gone. I'm disappointed. I was hoping for a Christmassy landscape.'

He reached for her suitcase, disregarding her protest that she could carry it herself. 'Afraid not. Scarborough's reverted back to being cold and draughty,' He hunched his shoulders. 'Particularly in this station. Let's go to the car.'

They spoke about general things as he drove home. Helen spotted the coloured lights festooned in the trees near the top of the main street and admired them. She pointed out a particularly beautiful Christmas tree in the window of a major shop. She sounded happy and lively. As she looked around her, Richard looked at her. He thought she had turned into a completely different person. She was at ease with herself, and happy. At least, she sounded happy. His own heart lifted.

When he turned into the Esplanade and parked the car outside the flats she had the door open and was out in a flash, running across the road to look at the sea. A strong north-easter was blowing, agitating the waves which flung themselves about, twisting and turning restlessly. Above the tossing mass of water, the gulls screamed as they swooped and dived and opened their wings to ride on the wind.

'Oh,' she cried. She glanced back at Richard. The wind caught her hair and blew it across her face. She pushed it back, impatiently. 'I've missed the sea.'

Richard, watching her, thought, *And I've missed you.*

Back home, they shed their coats and relished the warmth of the central heating. Richard made a pot of tea and toasted muffins. They sat either side of the fire, smiled at each other, ate and talked. They kept the conversation light.

Helen laughed when Richard described

his tenants, Mr and Mrs Shapley. Captivated by a dimple that appeared in Helen's chin – did she have that before? Richard began to elaborate.

'They're so weird, Helen. They're like something out of a film.' He paused. *'Night of the Living Dead.'*

She put her hand over her mouth and then shook her head. 'Oh, Richard. It's not like you to be unkind.'

He reflected. 'You're right. I suppose I was being unkind. Actually, they're perfect tenants. I ought to be counting my blessings.'

She sobered. 'We all should.'

There was a pause which Richard took advantage of. He said: 'Are you able to tell me a little about how you are getting on with your mother? I can't help wondering...'

Helen put down her cup and saucer. She sat back and clasped her hands together.

'It's going well, Richard. Better than I would have dreamed. We're very different of course. We always were but now that I'm a grown woman, I can understand certain things. I can cope better. Also,' she paused, 'I've found out a lot more information. Nina didn't actually leave me, you know. At least, she did for a little while, but then she came back for me. Frank kept that secret. I could hate him for that. I did, when I first found out, but...' She shrugged. 'Life's so complicated.'

She stared at Richard. 'You know, when you left me with Nina and went off ...' She paused. 'Where did you go, by the way?'

'Oh, just round and about.'

She smiled at him. 'We talked for a while and then Nina opened up to me. She told me about her own childhood and, honestly, Richard – it was horrendous.' She sighed. 'The papers are full of violence to children by strangers, but I think some of the worst crimes are perpetuated by family members.'

Richard bent his head and remained silent.

'Anyway, we talked and talked and it helped. I'm not saying we're completely besotted with each other. I think Nina's finding it difficult to realise she has a daughter of forty. And I, well...' She shrugged. 'I'm very glad we found her. In many ways, she hasn't altered much. She has a boyfriend, you know. I've met him, briefly. He's very nice and good for her, I think. I suppose he'll be there, at her house, for Christmas.'

'You've definitely decided to spend Christmas with Nina?'

'Oh, yes.'

She looked across at him.

'What about you?'

'Christmas, you mean?'

'Of course.'

'Oh,' he thought about June. 'It depends.'

A frown creased her forehead. 'What does *that* mean? You won't be here on your own, will you?'

He forced a smile. 'Now you're sounding like *my* mother, Helen!'

She flushed. 'I'm sorry.'

Richard stood up. 'Come on, I'll show you your room. Maybe you'd like a bath after your travelling?'

'That would be nice.' She got to her feet. 'And I'll unpack.' She smiled and Richard thought how much younger she looked when she did.

'I've bought myself a rather slinky dress, Richard. A zany friend I was with talked me into it. I shall wear it on Christmas Day but, I'm a bit nervous about it so I thought I'd have a rehearsal. I'd feel much happier wearing it when I have a male escort, so I wondered...' She held her head on one side. 'Will you take me out this evening?'

She laughed at his expression.

'Nothing drastic. Not a nightclub, or anything like that; but I thought surely there's a decent hotel where we can dine and have a drink beforehand? And it's going to be my treat. No, I absolutely insist on it.' She held up her hand, anticipating his rejection. 'I owe you so much, my dear friend. Indulge me over this, please.'

What could he say?

It took a little arranging. The pre-

Christmas parties had started, but Richard pulled some strings and managed to book a table for two at the Royal Hotel. When he and Helen walked into the cocktail bar he spotted two men he knew. They were not really friends, but they had worked at the Town Hall when he was based there. He stiffened a little, then nodded to them as he guided Helen towards a table. He realized the men's conversation had come to a sudden halt. He glanced across and registered their expressions and, all at once, he found, difficulty in keeping a smirk off his face. In that miraculous split second he realised he had changed from excessive nervousness to complete confidence.

With a flourish, he pulled out a chair for Helen, saw her seated and sat down himself. *My daughter,* he thought. *My daughter is a complete stunner.*

Helen's dress was made out of shiny material. It was quite long, it draped, rather than clung to her slim figure. It was a sort of mixed-up colour. Greeny-blue, he supposed would be a correct description. Whatever it was, the colour matched her eyes. She wore a little jacket too, which matched the dress, and high heels. He wasn't so sure about those. It made her about half an inch taller than he was.

A barman came over to them and he ordered drinks. He glanced across at the former work colleagues and saw they were still watching him. He smiled, leaned towards Helen and told her she looked absolutely fabulous. She laughed. Then she looked serious.

'I don't suppose you get out to places like this very often, do you, Richard?'

He stiffened. 'I've never been a social animal.'

'No. I didn't mean...' She sighed. 'It's this Christmas thing. The party season and all that. I've had some lonely Christmases, Richard. Some of them were totally dire. This year, everything's different. I'm looking forward so much to the holiday. I've found my mother. That's the top prize, and you helped.' She leaned over and pressed his hand. 'And other things are happening. Somehow, I don't quite know how, a very good-looking man's interested in me and also...'

She stopped talking. Reddened slightly at Richard's change of expression.

'Don't worry. I'll let you meet him. You can check him out for me, if you like, before I'm tempted to do anything silly.'

She glanced away. She traced her finger against the slight misting on her wine glass. 'I suppose, I'm *being* a little silly. It's because I'm happy. There's nothing wrong with that, is there?'

She looked at him but he was staring

down into his glass of wine.

'Richard?'

He looked up.

'I'm happy for you, Helen. I'm just a bit worried that you...' His words trailed off.

'Make a mistake?' She shook her head. 'Maybe I will but I'm forty years old, my dear. I'm entitled.'

'Yes, you're right.' Richard sighed and drained his glass. 'Tell me to mind my own business.'

'I don't want to.' She leaned forward and touched his hand. 'I want you to be happy, too.'

He looked over her head. 'I'm happy at this moment.'

'Yes, but maybe that's the trouble. Richard.'

His gaze focused on her face.

He said. 'It's all right. You don't have to worry. Yes, I'll admit you've become very dear to me but not in the way you seem to think...' He paused. Started again. 'I do *have* a life of my own, Helen. In fact, I'm seeing a very nice woman.'

Her face went scarlet. 'Oh, God. I'm so clumsy. I didn't mean to upset you. That's the last thing I want to do.'

'You haven't upset me.'

Richard looked away from her. He saw a man walking towards them and thanked God for sending a waiter at absolutely the right moment.

'I think we're being called for our meal. Shall we go through to the dining-room?'

Later that night, when they were back home and Helen had gone to bed, Richard sat in his favourite armchair and thought about the changes the last few months had brought. A snippet of conversation surfaced in his memory. Something Amy had burbled on about when the comet had been in the news.

'Change,' she had said. 'Change for the better.'

Had it been for the better? For Helen, yes. She was a different person from the woman he had talked to at the theatre. She was so confident and happy. And, from the sound of things, Nina was delighted to have found her daughter again. And that left June and himself. He sighed and rested his head on the back of the chair. June wasn't too happy. And who could blame her? He loved her. He really did. But... His mind veered away, to something he could handle.

In a few more days, it would be Christmas. Then, after Christmas, New Year. Dear God! What would that bring? More problems? Who was this new man in Helen's life? Was she falling in love with him? Was he good enough for her? Did Nina know about him? He could ring Nina. Find out what she did know. No. Better leave it.

June re-imposed herself in his conscious-ness. He rubbed his hand over his forehead. Let it go for now. He was tired. It was time for bed. Helen said she had to go back to London tomorrow afternoon. She said there was some kind of interview she had to attend. Was she thinking of changing her job? Surely, she wasn't going to dash off and marry this new man in her life? No, she had too much sense.

He wouldn't think of the future. He'd go to bed and re-live this evening. That, at any rate, had turned out all right.

Twenty-Five

Saturday morning was bad. The shop was heaving with customers, two counter staff hadn't turned up, and now Stan Wilkins was messing about rearranging a display – when there were a hundred and one more important things to do. June Greening stormed down the aisle and appeared before him. She was like an angel, not a Christmas angel but an avenging angel, very much Old Testament.

'Bloody hell, Stan. What are you playing at?'

'Mrs Wharton told me to do it. It was in the centre of the middle aisle but some kids pushed it over and she thought it would be better to–'

'Leave it, Stan.'

'But Mrs Wharton–'

'*Leave it.*' June breathed deeply. Next year, she swore, I'll celebrate Christmas in Australia, even if I have to remortgage the house.

'Look, I've been informed someone's dumped a whole load of tangerines at the back. They're blocking the fire exit. Go and shift them. Bring a couple of boxes into the shop and move the rest to the store. You'd better fetch some more bananas through. We're almost sold out. Then help with stocking up the shelves. After that, go for some more till rolls from the office. Two of the cash operatives are down to their last roll.'

'If you're sure, Mrs Greening.'

'I'm sure, Stanley.'

She turned on her heel and made her way to the bacon counter where, two women were arguing loudly over a large bacon joint.

'We've plenty more in the back, ladies. Just give me a minute and I'll fetch them.'

She hurried to the meat store, grabbed a trolley, filled it with bacon joints and dashed back to the waiting customers. On the way, her foot slipped on something gooey. A harassed young mother with a baby in the seat of her loaded trolley and holding a little girl by her right hand, spoke to her. The woman blinked her eyes nervously and looked on the point of tears.

'I'm so sorry. We were just passing the eggs and Tracey showed me her latest ballet steps and,' she sniffed. 'Her arm caught some of the boxes. I'll pay for the damage, of course.'

June looked at the mess then patted the woman's arm. 'Don't worry about it. We'll write them off.' She forced a smile as she addressed the little girl.

'Just keep hold of Mummy's hand, won't you, Tracey?'

The girl stuck her thumb in her mouth and remained silent.

Lunch was a cup of coffee and a Kit-Kat, after which, June retreated to the ladies' room for a moment's peace. She went into a toilet, closed the door, sat down and closed her eyes. But then she realised she was on the point of going to sleep so she came out again, splashed her face with cold water and returned to the arena.

Around three o'clock, there came an unexpected but blessed lull. As if by magic, the store became almost deserted.

'Uncanny, innit.'

June looked down. It was Ginny Bean speaking to her.

Ginny was approaching eighty and spent a part of every day in the shop. She didn't spend much but, as she said to those who would listen, she liked being where there was a bit of life. She had a room in a council home for the elderly but she wouldn't stay there in the daytime.

'Everyone's bloody asleep or falling to sleep,' she told the store assistants. 'That's what they do, snore all day. I can't be doing with it. I'll get enough rest when I'm dead.'

Ginny was tolerated in the shop because she didn't get in anyone's way. She wandered about a bit but, usually, she sat on one of the low tiled alcoved window-sills and watched the customers come and go. There were times she was an asset. She marked the many teenage kids who wandered in looking innocent. If she was suspicious, she would trail them. She was very good at that. If things disappeared off shelves and into pockets she would leap out at the culprits; curse them in ripe language and say she would put a spell on them. She terrified them. More often than not, they dropped the pilfered cans of lager and fled the store. This suited the company. Taking them to court was a waste of time.

Today, Ginny was in a mellow mood. She told June about the group of schoolchildren who had visited the Home and sung carols for the residents. Ginny said it had been lovely.

'"Away in a Manger". That's a lovely carol. My favourite. You can just imagine it, can't you? The baby with his mother, the shepherds and that lovely hush when the angels came.' She glanced round the store. 'That's what it's like now ... a hush before the angels come.'

'Yes, love.'

June wondered if Ginny had started celebrating Christmas early. She had been known to like a spot of gin. It was strange about the lull in proceedings. Maybe it was the calm before the storm? She knew she ought to check the poultry department, Stanley might have skived off again, but she had a better idea. She'd nip into the rest room and get herself a cup of tea. Ten minutes off her feet would prepare her for the next influx of happy shoppers.

But luck was not with her. The store manager spotted her as she passed his office. He shouted through his open door. 'June. Can you spare me a minute?'

She sighed and turned back.

He had stood up and was rummaging in a cupboard. He turned round holding a parcel in his hands. A substantial parcel, wrapped in brown paper.

'I've glad I spotted you. I've been trying to track down a storeman for the last half-hour.'

June nodded.

'The thing is, it's imperative this parcel is put on to the London train today. Head Office are waiting for the contents to finalise some important documentation. I would be quite happy to take it to the station myself but I'm awaiting an important call, so I can't leave the office. I want you to take it to the station for me.'

'Well, I...'

'Have you a car?'

'No.'

'Ah.' He thought a moment. 'No problem. I'll ring for a taxi.' He put the parcel on his desk, felt in his pocket and placed two twenty-pound notes on top. 'That should pay for the taxi and the parcel.'

June hesitated. 'We've been dreadfully busy, Mr Blackmore. It's quietened down now but it won't last.'

'Let's hope so.' He beamed at her as he dialled the number for the taxi firm. He covered the mouthpiece of the telephone. 'I'll tell them to send the taxi to the staff entrance as soon as possible. It will be cutting it fine, but I'm sure you'll be able to get there and register the parcel before the London train comes in.'

'And I'd better go and tell the chief supervisor.'

'No, no.' He waved his hand. 'I'll see to that. Go and get your coat.' He turned his head, spoke into the phone and replaced the receiver. 'There. That's done.'

He gestured to the parcel and June picked it up.

'You might as well go home after that, June. Put your feet up for a bit.'

'Oh, thank you, Mr Blackmore. Thank you very much.'

There was quite a crowd waiting for the London train. Leaving the parcel office, June glanced across at them. She supposed most of them were the lucky people able to start their holidays early. She noticed some of the cases had brightly coloured airline tags attached to them. Their owners would be flying off to the sun. She wondered, just for a moment, what her son was doing right now. Sleeping, probably. She saw a couple she knew. They were regular customers at the shop. The woman noticed her and raised her hand. June waved back.

She was almost at the exit when she spotted Richard. He emerged from the kiosk that dispensed tea and coffee and sold newspapers and sweets. A tall, dark-haired woman walked beside him and they were chattering in such an animated way Richard never noticed June, even though they were only a few yards apart.

Who the hell was she?

June came to a sudden stop. There was an explanation! Of course there was. A perfectly rational explanation. She would ask Richard and he would tell her. Richard had lived in Scarborough all his life. So had she, but Richard had been more involved with people. He had worked at the Town Hall. Maybe the dark-haired woman was a friend who had previously worked with him? He was entitled to have friends.

One thing June noticed, the woman who might be a friend was not staying, her suitcase, which Richard had carried, was now deposited near her feet. She must be waiting for the London train.

June felt herself beginning to panic. She didn't want Richard to see her. He might think she was spying on him. She looked round and moved to stand behind the board showing the times of departures and arrivals. He couldn't see her now. She realised her hands were trembling so she pushed them deep inside her coat pockets. She was behaving in a ridiculous manner, but she couldn't help it. Was this woman just a friend?

She thought of the recent difficulties that were spoiling their relationship. Richard had spoken about things in his past but what if a more recent development had caused his reluctance to commit? And he had never really explained his sudden trip to London. June's eyes narrowed as she watched the unknown woman smile at Richard. Now she was touching his hand.

She thought she ought to stop spying on them but she couldn't drag her eyes away. Richard's companion was now taking something out of her hand luggage. It was a parcel, seasonally wrapped. She gave it to Richard. He said something, obviously protesting about the present and then he leaned forward and kissed his companion on her cheek.

June caught her breath. There was the

sound of a whistle along the track. The train was coming. There was activity on the platform. Earlier arrivals, who had managed to get a seat on the few benches on the platform, stood up, picked up their suitcases or adjusted their backpacks. June saw Richard and his companion move a little closer together. They even held hands. They made a handsome couple. June's eyes stung but the train came into the station then with a clashing of brakes and she told herself she had picked up a piece of grit from somewhere. Anyway, she didn't want to see any more. She didn't want to see Richard kiss this woman goodbye.

She rushed away from the scene and blundered her way on to the station forecourt where she narrowly missed being knocked over by a taxi coming in to pick up a fare. She muttered an apology to the irate driver and took to her heels. She wanted to go home.

After three days trying unsuccessfully to contact June, Richard called in at the supermarket determined to see her. He pushed his way through the crowds of shoppers and finally saw her talking to a customer. He waited until she had finished and then he went up to her and tapped her on her shoulder.

'Hi, June. Why haven't you been in touch?'

She turned round and looked at him. He was shocked by her appearance.

The first thing he registered was that she was wearing make-up, quite a lot of make-up. June was a great one for moisturising her skin but she rarely bothered with make-up. Today, for some reason, she had really gone to town. In particular, she had rouged her cheeks. Rouge wasn't a word that was used now, but Richard always thought of cheek colour as rouge. His mother had used it and he had always thought it made her look worse, not better – awful bright spots of colour standing out on her gaunt, pale face.

June didn't look awful but she looked sad, weary and dejected. The pink colour brushed on to her cheeks and the eye make-up she had used merely emphasised her pale skin and the shadows beneath her eyes.

'June, what have you done to yourself? You look so tired. You're working too hard.'

She gave him a peculiar look. 'I'm busy, Richard. Too busy to talk.'

As if to emphasise her words, a bell rang on one of the check-out stations near to where they were standing and the operator raised her hand.

'I have to go.' June turned on her heel and went towards the woman.

Richard fell in step with her. 'When can I see you?'

'Do you want to?'

'Of course I do.'

She stopped walking and looked through him. 'We can't talk now.'

'I know that. But I want...' He shook his head. 'May I call round to see you this evening? Even if you're too tired to go out, we can have a chat.'

She shrugged. 'If you like.'

'I do like.' He studied her face. 'Something's the matter? I wish you'd tell...'

A shopper approached June, asked her where the brandy butter was kept.

She answered the woman's query then looked directly into Richard's eyes.

'Richard.'

'Yes.'

'Do you think I'm stupid?'

He started. 'What?'

She turned her back on him and walked away.

He didn't telephone before he went round to her house because he thought she might tell him not to come. When he rang the bell he heard Reg break into a torrent of barking. He almost smiled.

She opened the door. She was in a housecoat, her face was free of make-up and her hair was damp and slicked close to her head. He guessed she had just got out of the bath. At least she had a little colour in her face.

She said: 'You were going to ring first.'

'I know, but I thought you'd refuse to see me.'

She stepped back to allow him to enter.

Once inside, he stopped in the hallway and asked: 'What's upset you, June?'

'You realised I was upset?'

'Of course I did.'

'How perceptive of you.' She pulled a wry face.

Nonplussed, he just stood there. He felt stupid and inadequate. Dear God, he would never understand women. Yet, at the same time, at this very inappropriate time, he felt a powerful surge of desire. He thought about her naked body beneath the house-coat; it would be warm, even sweating a little, soft and perfumed with bath oils.

He swallowed. 'May I come in?'

She stood back to allow him to enter. There was no Reg to come bouncing along, defusing the difficult atmosphere. June must have shut him in the kitchen. Richard followed her through to the living-room.

June pointed to an uncomfortable chair that was rarely used, at least to Richard's recollection. He sat down. June sat on the sofa.

She stared at him for a moment and then she said: 'I had to go to the railway station.'

Richard looked at her but did not speak.

'I took a parcel to go on the London train.

I saw you there. You were saying goodbye to a woman.' June's voice shook a little but she steadied it. 'You seemed very close. She gave you a present before she left and you kissed her.'

'Yes, I did.' Richard leaned forward. His hands were clasped tight. 'Her name is Helen.'

'I don't think I want to know.' June turned her face away. 'You told me I was the only woman in your life but there was a definite warm relationship between you and that woman.'

'Yes, there is and I'm glad of it.'

Richard wanted so much to go to June and take her in his arms but looking at her unresponsive face, he knew he could not. Not yet. He had to tell her the truth and pray she believed him.

'You see, there's two women I love. One is you. I truly love you, June. The other woman,' he paused. 'Her name is Helen and she's my newly found daughter.'

He told June everything. Halfway through his confession, she held out her hand to him and he knew she believed him. He went to sit next to her on the sofa. He sketched in the trip to Liverpool and their failure to find Nina. He spoke of how Helen had found out where her mother's present home was and how he had been there when mother and daughter met.

'That's when you went to London?'

He nodded. 'I should have told you but it was so complicated and difficult.' He sighed. 'So many old emotions surfacing. I didn't want to involve you. I didn't want you to worry.'

June was now curled up beside him, her head on his shoulder. She moved to look into his face.

'And when you saw Nina?'

Richard touched her face with his hand. 'Nothing, although she is still an attractive woman. Our meeting was good for me, in fact. I finally shed the idealistic picture of the angel that came to my room so long ago.'

June smiled. 'But you haven't told Helen you're her father?'

He shook his head.

'But you must, Richard.'

He sighed. 'I don't know how. And what if I lose her?'

'You won't.' She snuggled in to him again. 'You could write and tell her, if you think that would be better.' She sneaked a look at him. 'I'm good at letters. Maybe I could help you.'

'I'll think about it.'

The warmth of June's body was getting to Richard, distracting his thoughts. Also, the skirt of her housecoat had parted and he could see her slim, white legs up to her thighs. He trailed his fingers over her silky skin.

'Richard!' June began to sit up.

Very gently, he pushed her down. 'Can we forget about family relatives for a bit, June?'

She widened her eyes. 'With pleasure. Shall we go to bed?'

'No, it's nice here.' Richard continued to stroke her legs. He felt relaxed and happy. He had given his secret to his love and she, with her usual good sense, had blown away his fears and fancies. She is good for me, he thought, and she loves me. His hand moved higher. He put his free arm around her shoulders and pulled her close to him.

'Tell me what you like.'

She gasped. 'I think ... that ... and that.'

She began to participate in their love-making. She unbuttoned his shirt and stroked his bare chest. She guided his head down to her breasts so he could kiss them. They were almost falling off the sofa. There was a pause where they giggled like children and pulled the sofa cushions down on to the floor so they could stretch out before the fire. They stripped each other. June clasped her hands behind Richard's neck when he finally entered her, back arched. When they climaxed together, she cried out.

'Dear God.' She moaned. 'Why did we wait so long?'

He smoothed her hair back from her fore-head and kissed her lips. Then he gathered her up in his arms and they stared into each other's eyes.

'It was never like that with my husband.' June whispered.

Richard looked gratified. 'Nor me, with my wife.'

He touched her cheek. 'We're so lucky. We're going to have a wonderful Christmas.'

Twenty-Six

Helen drove over to Nina's on Christmas Eve. She arrived just before darkness fell. After taking her suitcase from the car, she walked up the garden path towards the house. She noticed the evergreen bushes and shrubs crowding against the pathway looked somehow different from her last visit. They seemed more dense, as if they had drawn together and squatted closer to the earth. The fanciful thought made her shiver and she was pleased when she reached Nina's front door. She took care mounting the two steps. The weather was cold. There had been icy patches on the roads but fortunately, no snow. In *her* car, Helen hated driving in snow.

She rang the doorbell, looking forward to the welcoming warmth of Nina and the comforts of her home. The flat was all right but she would have hated to spend her Christmas holiday there alone. Also, she had been extremely busy in the period coming up to Christmas and she relished the idea of a rest.

While waiting for Nina – she could have walked in but she didn't like to, she wasn't confident enough – she took another look at the garden. There had been no snow here, either. Plenty of frost though. Beautiful white, lacy patterns of frost were everywhere. In the half light, the shrubbery had suddenly turned into a row of dumpy Spanish widows, their black clothing shockingly relieved by their wonderfully intricate frost mantillas. Helen smiled. She was getting fanciful in her middle age.

She wondered when would be the right time to announce her recent decision. She wondered how the people she was sharing Christmas with would react. She frowned. She had her mother to think about now and quite a few good friends. Richard, of course, and Ian and Ian's father Stuart. It was wonderful to know people cared for you, but closeness brought responsibility.

Helen jumped as the front door was flung open and the strains of 'Oh come All Ye Faithful' sounded in the night air. Nina stood on the step. She was wearing slim dark trousers and a sparkling top.

Helen smiled. Nina had started Christmas with style. Of course she had. Her mother had always managed to conjure up Christmas magic, even in dismal bedsits or crummy rented rooms. She bet Nina had gone wild getting this house ready for Christmas, particularly with the guests she was welcoming.

'Come in. Come in.' Nina pulled her through the door.

She'd want an instant reaction.

Helen dropped her case to the carpet and looked round.

She caught a glimpse of a magnificently dressed Christmas tree through the opened door of the sitting-room. She saw Christmas cards everywhere: on window-sills, inter-twined with sprigs of holly, on the top of radiator shelves and pinned to lengths of holly red satin ribbons dangling from the staircase. She looked at her mother.

'It's truly magnificent, Nina.'

Her mother kissed her cheek. They were getting better about things like that.

'Sorry I kept you waiting. I was looking for the Christmas tapes I wanted to get a proper atmosphere.'

Helen gave her a hug, while continuing to look round.

'So many cards. You must have made a lot of friends here?'

'A fair amount. A few of them are coming round at eight thirty. I invited them for a Christmas drink. That's all right, isn't it?' Nina glanced at her daughter. 'They're easy people to get on with. Most of them are from my writing group.'

Writing group? Helen didn't know her mother had literary aspirations. She shook her bemused head. Nina should have enough material to draw on.

She opened her mouth to speak but Nina was rattling on. 'Stuart's coming, of course.' She smiled. A cheshire cat sort of smile. 'And my next-door neighbours, and Ian's invited, if he arrives before bedtime. Did he say anything to you?'

'Yes. He hopes to be here around nine p.m.'

Helen expected to meet up with Ian over the holiday. They had spoken about Christmas just over a week ago when they had last spent time together.

For some reason, Nina had been extremely worried as to how much Ian knew about Helen's early life. She had phoned up in a panic.

'You can imagine how I felt, Helen. *You* were Ian's mysterious new girlfriend. Stuart recovered before I did. He was quite pleased. He said if Ian was finally getting serious about a woman, he was pleased he'd picked you. He likes you. He said it was time Ian set his sights a bit higher than...' Nina coughed 'But it's more complicated, isn't it? We don't want Ian knowing our business.'

When Helen finally discovered what Nina was talking about she had remained unruffled.

'Stop worrying, Nina. Ian will assume the fact that I'm your daughter is pure coincidence. It is. It *was* a coincidence, me stopping at his garage. And yes, I did tell him I was searching for someone, but I never said who. I never mentioned a name. It could have been anyone. An old school-friend, for instance. Just try not to worry.'

'But I do. And keeping your past from him is a bit like lying, isn't it? You know,' Nina's voice had lowered, 'I've told Stuart about my past.'

'That's different. Forgive me for saying so, but your past is much more chequered than mine. Anyway, you and Stuart are important to each other.'

'But, I thought Ian was important to you?'

'He's a very good companion.'

Helen found it difficult to talk about Ian with her mother. Indeed, there was several topics of conversation she found awkward. Nina was such an emotional person. She acted impulsively and cried easily. Helen loved her but she knew they were miles apart characteristically. Why, she had found it easier communicating with Richard, particularly when she paid that flying visit to Scarborough.

She knew she couldn't tell the truth to Nina.

I like Ian's company and sex with him is terrific, but I'm not sure that I like him.

'He's a good business man, has good prospects,' Nina said.

373

Helen had laughed out loud. 'Oh, Mother. How can you say that? Since when did good prospects influence your choice of man?'

'Oh, well. I was a fool' Nina paused. 'You're not.'

They had talked a little more and then Nina had rung off. Helen had put down the telephone wondering which of them was right.

After a cup of tea, Helen took her suitcase upstairs to her allotted bedroom. She had a shower, then came downstairs in her housecoat to help Nina with her preparations. When all was ready, she went back to her bedroom, applied her make-up and put on her new outfit. She stared at her reflection in the mirror and worried about Richard. She hoped he was not on his own. When they had met, he had let drop that he was seeing someone. Helen hoped strongly that she was good enough for him.

The drinks party started without the appearance of Ian. Helen came downstairs and circulated. Nina introduced her as her daughter and a few eyes popped but everyone was very welcoming. Nina caught, Helen's eye and they both smiled. Helen thought: we do have a few things in common.

A little later, she sat down next to Stuart. 'It's going well.'

'Yes. Nina's in her element.' Stuart pressed Helen's hand. 'The fact that you're here has made Nina so happy.'

Helen nodded. 'It does a lot for me, too. I have to pinch myself to believe it.'

For a few moments they sat quietly. Helen thought how pleasant it was to sit beside someone who was restful. He'll be good for Nina, she thought. She saw he was observing her so she grinned and said, 'Nina tells me she's involved in a writing group.'

'She is. So am I.'

He laughed at Helen's expression. 'It's all right. We're not very good. It's just a hobby. I'm trying to write about my experiences at sea but when I read my stuff I find I sound like a poor man's Hemingway. No originality at all. Most of the group are like that – but for your mother,' he paused. 'She's an original. When she finishes the book, I won't be the least bit surprised if it gets published.'

'Really?'

'Yes. Why do you sound surprised?'

'I am surprised. I can't remember Nina showing any literary talent.'

Stuart's eyes narrowed. 'Writers usually start writing when they're middle-aged. You were a child when you were parted from Nina, but she was young, too. She wasn't even thirty years old.'

With a shock, Helen realised he was right.

'Then consider your mother's life.' Stuart leaned forward. 'First a scarred childhood and lots of disastrous experiences before she met Alex. On the plus side, her involvement with the music scene during the exciting sixties. That in itself would add interest to her writing. After that, another phase. Alex's death and her move here to another, different life. Your mother's a survivor, Helen, and survivors make for a good story.'

Stuart sat back in his chair. 'When she finishes the book – and she will – I think it will be a damn good one.'

'And where do you fit into the story, Stuart?' Helen spoke softly. She smiled at him. 'How do you feel about my mother?'

'That's easy. I love her. I think she loves me but she isn't over Alex yet. Not completely.' Stuart put out his hand and touched Helen's fingers. 'So don't say anything and don't go asking about wedding plans.'

'I won't.'

They smiled at each other, totally in tune.

Around midnight, guests began to depart. Stuart stayed behind to help Nina and Helen put the house to rights.

'Bung the crockery and the glasses into the dishwasher.' Nina instructed Helen. She put a pile of plates on the draining board and then paused. 'Why the huge grin?'

'I was just thinking, Mum, and remembering all those grotty places we lived in.' A dimple appeared in Helen's cheek. 'Did you ever, for one minute, think you would own a dishwasher?'

A huge grin spread over Nina's face. 'No. I'd never even *heard* of a dishwasher so how could I want one.' She paused. 'But you know what, at this very moment, makes me even happier?'

'No?'

'You've just called me "Mum". That's the first time since...' She choked.

The two women stared at each other. Stuart, who was bustling about putting food into the fridge turned and looked at them. Then he removed the tea-cloth from his arm, dropped it on to a chair and said: 'I'm off, now.'

Nina started and mopped her eyes. 'There's no need, Stuart.'

'Oh yes there is. I can see a weepy session coming on.' He collected his jacket from the back of a chair. 'Remember you're coming to me for Christmas dinner. One o'clock sharp.'

'Are we?' Helen looked at Nina.

'Yes, he's much the better cook.' Nina looked from her daughter to Stuart with shining eyes. She blew him a kiss. 'Happy Christmas, Stuart.'

'The same to you, sweetheart.'

The door closed behind him. There was a

moment of silence.

Nina brushed a tear from her face. 'I've all I want now,' she tried to smile, 'including a dishwasher; but the best present you've just given me.'

She held out her arms.

A slight hesitation and then Helen went into them. She felt clumsy holding her mother until she realised she was so much taller, so she kicked off her shoes and they clung together.

A moment and then Nina said: 'Do you forgive me, Helen, really forgive me?'

'Yes.' Helen cleared her throat. 'Yes, I do.'

A moment's silence. Then Nina spoke again. 'Happy Christmas, Helen.'

'Happy Christmas, Mum.'

Twenty-Seven

Christmas Day dawned and Helen was up early. It was a momentous day for her, for many reasons. She got up, drew back her bedroom curtains and looked out. The view was unchanged. There had been no snowfall. She felt a pang of disappointment. Today the sky should be full of swirling snowflakes. There should be children shouting, building snowmen and groups of carol-singers going from house to house. She gave a rueful smile. She was getting romantic, she must be picking up vibes from her mother. She bet Nina would have Bing Crosby crooning 'White Christmas' within a few minutes of going downstairs. Maybe she could beat her to it?

She grabbed her dressing gown, put it on and hurried downstairs. She checked through Nina's music collection. Yes, there it was. She knew it. Nina had always loved that record, only Bing was on cassette now. She slotted it into the music centre and switched on, then sneaked upstairs and took possession of the bathroom before Nina appeared. She stripped off, stepped into the shower cabinet and held up her face to the flowing water. Her hair was soaked, it didn't matter. She was with family today. She didn't have to dress up or put on a show.

Stuart had announced he was cooking the Christmas dinner. Helen and Nina didn't have to do a thing. Helen's face sobered as she remembered how finicky her ex-husband had been over the cooking of the Christmas dinner. Thank God she didn't have to go through that. She wondered how his new blonde girlfriend would cope and then she forgot about them.

Instead, she thought with keen anticipation of the pile of presents, beautifully wrapped and waiting to be given and received. She hoped Ian would like her present to him, although it wasn't the kind of present you could wrap. Choosing his gift had caused her more headaches than the rest of her presents put together. As far as she could tell, Ian already had everything he wanted. Finally, she had paid for a weekend for two at a health spa. They – she assumed she would go with him – could go any time during the month of January. The place was within easy reach of London and boasted a golf course as well as indoor tennis courts, the obligatory indoor swimming pool and saunas and well-equipped gyms. Ian had mentioned he wanted to tone up in the new year so she thought she would encourage him. He had been looking strained during the last couple of weeks but he had assured her his business was going well. She supposed he had arrived safely at Stuart's house last night. No doubt he would be sound asleep now in the spare bedroom. As she knew, he was not normally an early riser.

She stayed under the shower and scrubbed herself until her skin was red then she got out and pampered her body from a selection of Nina's formidable array of creams and lotions. Back in her room, she blow-dried her hair, put on a minimum of make-up and dressed in well-cut trousers and top. She went downstairs.

Nina, still in her dressing gown, was eating toast and marmalade. Helen helped herself to coffee and sat down opposite her mother.

Nina smiled at her. 'Sleep well?'

'Like a log.'

'Good. Come and have some breakfast.'

'If you don't mind, I won't. I'm not great on breakfasts.'

'I remember.' Nina reached across and patted her hand. 'But you should, you know. Breakfast should be the most important meal of all.'

She waited until Helen shook her head and then asked: 'Well, if you're not eating, will you go and put on the Bing Crosby cassette again, please.'

After a leisurely hour and when Nina was ready for the day's festivities, they put their presents into a large dust sack and walked over to Stuart's home. Ian greeted both women with a kiss and brought them drinks. Stuart came out of the kitchen to say 'Happy Christmas' and disappeared again. Carols sounded from the radio.

Christmas dinner was a culinary delight. Helen particularly admired the cooking of the large turkey, which was pleasantly moist, and the gravy. She knew how awkward gravy could be, particularly when you were also wrestling with bread sauce, herb stuffing and three kinds of vegetables at the same time. She ate so much she had to pass on the pudding and mince pies.

'Oh, surely...?'

'Sorry, Stuart. I couldn't eat another thing. Maybe later.'

'Good idea. Perhaps we could all do with a breather. You lot go into the sitting-room and I'll–'

'You'll do nothing.' Helen grabbed Stuart's arm and propelled him in the direction of the sitting room. 'You've done your bit. Sit down and relax. I'll clear away the pots and Ian will help, won't you Ian?'

He groaned. 'Not straight away, Helen. Let's sit down and let the food settle.'

'Let the dregs of food and the gravy dry on the dinner plates, you mean.' Helen gave him a vigorous dig in his ribs. 'Come on lazybones.'

Groaning he lumbered to his feet but as soon as the kitchen door closed on them, his manner changed. He flung his arms around her and kissed her.

'Happy Christmas, darling.' He kissed her again. 'I've been waiting to do that since I woke up.'

She relaxed against him. 'Where were you last night? At a party?'

'A very boring party, Helen. I would much rather have been with you.'

He kissed her again, a slower more sensuous kiss.

They stood close together for a moment and then Helen moved away.

'Wash or dry?'

'What?' He whispered in her ear.

'Do you want to wash or dry?'

'Oh, Helen.' Ian moved away from her and clutched at his hair. 'Why do you do that?'

'What?'

'Change so quickly. One minute you're soft and loving, so much so I want to whisk you off to bed and then you're...' He paused.

'What?'

'Like a bloody school matron.'

The colour rose in her cheeks. 'That's not fair. I'd like to go to bed too. In fact, I can't think of a better way of spending Christmas afternoon, but there's your father and my mother in the other room.'

Ian grinned. 'They could be thinking the same thing.'

She blushed and then laughed. 'Touché, but that's not the point. There's Christmas presents to exchange and–'

He interrupted her. The good-humoured smile returning to his face. 'You're right, of course. We'll make time for us later, but talking of presents, can I give you mine now?'

'What? Here in the kitchen surrounded by washing-up?' Helen shook her head. 'No thanks. Let's shift this stuff first and then we can go for a walk. That's if we can walk, after Christmas pudding. You can tell me though–' she put her head on one side '–is it a large present, or a small one?'

'It's small.' He went to the sink and turned the tap on. 'And what about mine?'

'Very mysterious.' Helen tapped the side of her nose. 'It involves pleasurable exertion.'

'Oh, we're back to that, are we?' Ian smiled and plunged dirty crockery into the sink. 'Let's press on. I'll wash, you dry.'

An hour passed and then the pudding was consumed. There was a ceremonial giving and receiving of presents and lots of Christmas paper, smiles and hugs. By four o'clock, everything was tidy and Stuart, sitting in his favourite chair, was trying hard to keep awake. Nina whispered to Helen:

'If you and Ian want to slip away now,

that's all right. I shall get myself a brandy and gloat over my gifts, especially your scarf, which I love. Stuart can have a nap.' She pulled a little face. 'He's not into the habit of sleeping in the afternoon, but he's had a couple of brandies and he did work hard preparing the meal. You go and enjoy yourselves. We'll see you later.'

They took the path behind Stuart's back garden which led away from the buildings and wound through a small wood. The light was already waning and the tops of the oak trees on either side of the path seemed to lean towards each other, whispering secrets. Helen shivered but not from the cold. The weather had turned milder and all the frost had gone. Ian had taken hold of her hand and as they approached the end of the path, he stopped walking, turned to face her and asked: '*Now* may I give you your Christmas present?'

'Yes. Of course you can.'

She looked up at him feeling a little uneasy. Ian was always laughing and joking but now he looked serious. She wasn't used to seeing him so solemn.

He took a small packet from his pocket and handed it to her. 'Happy Christmas, Helen.'

'What is...?' Helen opened the wrapping and saw a small, leather jewellers' box.

She looked up. 'Oh, Ian. It's not...'

'Open it.'

She did and stared in silence at the seven stone diamond ring. 'I don't know what to say. I...'

'"Yes", would be nice.' His eyes were fixed on her face. 'I thought you might have guessed. Didn't you?'

She shook her head.

He wouldn't look away. 'Don't you like it? I wasn't sure whether...' He took a deep breath. 'We can always change it. We can go back to the shop and you can make your choice...'

'No, Ian. It's not the ring. It's...' She shook her head. 'I didn't realise you felt so seriously about us. This has come as an absolute bombshell.'

'How can you say that.' Ian snatched the box back from her. 'You know how we are together. I've never looked at another woman since I started going out with you. I thought you felt the same.'

'I'm sorry.' Helen's feet felt as though they were rooted to the path. She couldn't think of any other words. She felt she had stood there for hours, saying how sorry she was.

There was silence. For a long, drawn-out minute they stared at each other and then Ian swore. He turned away from her and flung himself down the path without a second look.

Helen waited a moment before turning round and walking back to Stuart's house. Oh Lord, did Stuart know about this, and Nina? It was going to ruin Christmas. Nina would probably think she was deranged turning Ian down. She'd see an engagement between her daughter and Stuart's son as a fairytale ending to a lovely Christmas. But it wasn't like that. Friendship between her and Ian might possibly last for years but marriage would be disastrous for both of them. They were so different. She'd had one rotten marriage. She didn't want another. Heavy-hearted she retraced her steps.

When she re-entered the house she found Stuart and Nina seated on the sofa, hand-in-hand and talking together. Stuart jumped up at once. 'Enjoy your walk?'

She gazed at him.

'Would you like a drink?'

'No. I...' She suddenly wanted to burst into tears. She struggled against giving in to her weakness. 'Yes, I'd like a brandy, please.'

He looked at her, gave a little frown but went to pour out the drink without saying anything. He handed it to her.

She accepted gratefully.

Nina asked: 'Where's Ian?'

'Oh, he wanted to walk further than I did. He'll be back soon.'

I hope, she thought. Surely, he won't get in the car and go back to London? He thinks too much of his father to do that.

She drank the brandy and bolstered up by the spirit, decided to tell Nina and Stuart the news she had been saving.

But first, she wanted to thank them.

'I've had a lovely Christmas,' she started. 'You've been...'

'It hasn't finished yet,' Stuart reminded her.

'No, that's true, but there's something I must tell you and now seems a good time. I don't know how you'll feel about it,' she looked at Nina, 'but I hope you'll be happy for my sake.'

Nina sat upright. 'Oh dear, this sounds like a change?'

'Yes, it is rather.' Helen decided short and brutal was best. 'I've accepted a rather wonderful job that's been offered to me. I've resigned from the insurance company and, in February, I'm moving to France to work.'

'France?' Nina's eyes opened wide. 'What will you do there?'

'A friend of mine put me on to it. Val's worked abroad before and she heard through the network that people fluent in French were being recruited to work on a two-year contract in Paris. It's to do with the European Parliament. Val applied and was accepted. When she was visiting me, she mentioned there were still a couple of vacancies to be filled. I thought about it and decided to give it a go.'

'But ... do you speak French?' Nina's forehead was marred with a frown.

'Yes, I do.' Helen's smile was a little forced. 'I'm a bit rusty but I passed the tests and when they found out I could also converse in German, although not as fluently as French, they offered me a job. The money's good and a flat's provided.'

'A job and a flat, eh?' Stuart had been watching Helen's face intently. He walked up to her and put his arm around her shoulders, giving her a hug. 'You must be so excited. Well done, Helen.'

'Yes, yes.' Nina still looked worried. 'But have you thought it through? You might be lonely. You might...'

'I've been lonely in London, Mum.' Helen used the word unselfconsciously this time, without realising. 'And I've been wanting a change for ages. I've played safe too long. It's time I struck out. If I don't do it now, I never will. Anyway,' she managed a smile, 'I'm only following in your footsteps. You were always on the move.'

Nina hunched her shoulders. 'I didn't go abroad. I stayed in my own country.'

Stuart left Helen and went to sit beside Nina. 'Paris is just a hop across the Channel. We live close to London. We can easily go by plane or simply drive there via the Channel Tunnel. Once Helen is settled we'll visit and she can show us the sights.'

'I suppose.' Nina sighed. 'It's such a shock.' She thought for a moment: 'What did Ian say? You have told him?'

As if on cue, the back door banged. Helen stiffened. 'That will be him. If you'll excuse me for a minute.'

She rushed into the kitchen.

Ian was standing by the sink. He stared at her.

She said: 'I'm so sorry, Ian.'

He shrugged. 'I should have known. I took too much for granted. It was my fault, I'm used to getting my own way, you see.' His voice thickened. 'I wanted you, Helen. I wanted you for my wife. We're good together. In bed and out. I thought you and I would...' He sighed. 'It's the first time I have ever contemplated marrying anyone. You're the only woman who made me feel that way.'

She shook her head. 'It would have been disastrous, Ian.'

Flags of colour flared in his cheeks. 'How can you say that. We're great together. We're....'

'We're great when we dine out. We're great friends for short periods of time.' Helen's voice dropped. 'We're completely compatible in bed, but that's not the same as being married. We'd drive each other insane. Believe me, I've been married. You'd be flying about. I would never know where you were. You'd want to date other women.' She ignored the shake of his head. 'You like ruling the roost and so do I. I can be a bossy cow, you know. Anyway, I don't want to marry anyone. In fact, I've made plans of my own. I'm going to live in Paris.'

His head came up. 'What?'

She told him.

He sighed, stared out of the window for a moment and then came across and embraced her.

'At least I'm not losing you to another man.'

'No.' She touched his face.

'You'll come and visit, Ian?'

'I might.'

She nodded. 'French girls are very lovely, or so I've been told. And, of course, if you read the newspapers, there are apparently hundreds of women in London looking for a husband. If you're serious about settling down, I'm sure you'll find someone suitable. Only, take your time won't you? Stay clear of the airheads.'

He shrugged. 'I'll think about it.' He looked thoughtful. 'Still, there's no rush. Maybe you'll change your mind. Anyway, I will visit you. I might do a bit of business over there. There must be loads of opportunities for buying and selling cars.'

She laughed aloud. 'I'll find out for you.

Meanwhile,' she produced the envelope which held his Christmas present, 'I want you to have this. With my love.' She kissed his cheek.

He opened the envelope and read the details of the health spa break.

Watching him, she said: 'You see it's for two and it's for any weekend in January. I won't be leaving until February.'

He nodded. 'Yes, I see.' He slipped the envelope into his pocket. 'Well, if you *won't* marry me, I guess I'll have to settle for us being friends. But in January,' he paused, 'can I expect us to enjoy a particularly *warm* friendship?'

'You can bet on it.' She squeezed his hand.

'Good.' He grinned. 'And in our spare time, you might also teach me a few useful French phrases. You know the sort of thing.'

'I do.' She nodded. *'Cela va sans dire*. That goes without saying.'

Twenty-Eight

Ian had to return to London on Boxing Day morning but Helen lingered until after lunch. She would have liked to have stayed longer with her mother but her new life had to be organised. She had a mountain of forms to fill in about her move to France and the flat to put up for sale. Her Christmas had been lovely. She had enjoyed every minute, or almost every minute, but she was also feeling a little disoriented. It was as if she had travelled a long, straight road for ever, searching for a turn-off or a place to stay. Now she had found her haven and she felt more secure but instead of wanting to rest and cherish her security, she realised she wanted to keep travelling. She had found a family and somewhere she could call home but behind that home she now spied roads stretching in different directions. She wanted to explore those roads. She wanted to explore life.

Maybe, she thought, it was Ian's proposal that had sparked off the change in her? She had been shocked. She cared for Ian but she didn't want to marry him. She wasn't ready to settle down. Maybe she never would be.

She had wondered whether she should try and explain how she felt to her mother? But no, she couldn't explain to anyone. How could she explain when truly, she didn't understand her own emotions?

It was when she was packing her suitcase that she thought of Richard. If she could talk to anyone she could talk to him, but it wasn't feasible. The man had done enough for her. Was she to batten on to him for the rest of her life? She would write to him when she was in Paris. She would reassure him she was well and then she would cease their communication. It was for the best, but oh, how she would miss him.

Packing finished, she went round to say goodbye to Stuart. He told her how glad he was that she had come back into Nina's life.

'You've made her so happy.'

He hugged her when she turned to go and told her to be sure to visit again before flying to Paris.

She said she would.

'We'll be over to see you, you know.'

'I'm counting on it.'

Saying goodbye to Nina wasn't too difficult. They had become more easy together. The strain was lessening. Helen realised they were behaving more normally, like most mothers and daughters.

When she took her suitcase out to the car, Nina walked with her and just before saying goodbye, she handed Helen a sealed envelope.

'Open this when you're home, Helen. It came with a covering letter which was addressed to me. It arrived Christmas Eve but in my letter, I was asked not to give you this until after Christmas Day.'

Nina had sounded a little nervous.

'I have an idea what your letter is about. I'm happy about the contents and I hope you'll feel the same way.' She stopped talking and gripped Helen's hand. 'Sorry, I can't say anything else.' She released Helen and smiled. 'You'll ring, won't you? Let me know you got back safely.'

'Of course.' Helen took the envelope and embraced her mother. 'Thank you for a lovely Christmas.'

Nina's eyes filled with tears. 'I can't make up for the lost ones.'

Helen smiled. 'This one helped.'

When she entered the flat, it felt as though she had already moved out. She felt as though she had been away for a month. She took her suitcase through to the bedroom and left it there. She'd unpack later. She kicked off her shoes and slumped in a chair. It was so quiet! The experience of a family Christmas had been exhilarating but now she felt like a survivor from a shipwreck, washed up on a desert island beach. She didn't know whether she welcomed the quiet or hated it. She thought about ringing Val, asking how her Christmas had been, but she decided it was too soon. Instead, she let the quietness flow over her. She began to relax, until she remembered the mysterious letter. She reached for her handbag and took out the envelope. She studied the handwriting. There were only two words on the envelope – her name. The writing looked familiar but she couldn't place it. She ran her thumb beneath the flap and opened the envelope. The letter was quite long. It ran over two pages. She turned to the beginning and read.

My Dear Helen: What I am about to tell you will come as a shock but knowing you as I do, I hope you will read this letter and then quietly consider the implications before jumping to any hasty decisions. We've had our adventures, haven't we?

Helen, still puzzled, turned to the end of the letter and realised it was from Richard. Intrigued, she read on:

Maybe, when you've deliberated over my words, we'll meet up and have more. I'd love that, but the decision is yours. The main thing is, you achieved your objective. You found your mother. But this letter is about you and me.

You must have wondered why I became so involved in your search. I wondered, too. I could tell you that the moment we met I felt some bond between us, but that wouldn't be strictly true. Yes, I was drawn to you but it was when you told me your story and showed me the snapshot of Nina... Well!

You see, I recognised her. The name Nina meant nothing to me but I recognised the girl who had stolen my heart when I was a boy. That sounds so ridiculous. I know it does, but it's the truth. Nina was my first love. The girl I had my first sexual relationship with. It wasn't sordid. Never think that. It wasn't just two kids fumbling each other. It was marvellous. Calf love, perhaps, but none the worse for that. And you were the result of our loving.

Helen gasped. Her gaze raced over the page.

I never knew. I swear it. My parents found out about us and Nina was sacked on the spot. She disappeared from my life. Poor girl, I still can't bear to think about it. But she was strong, she kept you. Bless her for that. And you and I found each other. Wasn't that miraculous? Almost as if fate... But no, I mustn't think like that. At first, I didn't realise and then I looked in the mirror and I saw...

Helen stopped reading. What did he mean? Surely, he didn't...

She dropped Richard's letter on the floor as she stood up. She went to her own mirror and gazed at her reflection. Dear God. He was right. She did look like him. Why hadn't she realised. It was so obvious, Richard was her father.

Richard and June spent Christmas Day at his home. They had a quiet and very happy day. They exchanged presents while still in bed and listened to carols on the radio. Later, they took Reg, who had accompanied June, for a walk. Reg wore his new collar with dignity. Back at the flat he slept while June and Richard shared the tasks of cooking their Christmas meal. Afterwards, they went to bed for an hour and spent their time so pleasurably, they forgot all about Christmas. In the evening they watched a couple of TV programmes. It was what thousands of other couples were doing and they thought it was marvellous.

On Boxing Day, they decided to be a little more ambitious. They talked over ideas.

'Difficult, isn't it?'

'Is it, why?'

'Well, we certainly don't want to go out to eat.' June pulled a face. 'I can't face food until tonight.'

'We could go for a walk along the beach and call in somewhere for a drink.'

'We could, but it's Boxing Day.'

'I know it is.'

June shook her head. 'Don't you remember the Scarborough tradition?'

'What?'

'It's Boxing Day! It's the "revenge of the females" day.'

'Ah!' Richard nodded. 'But you're not going pubbing with friends, are you?'

'Of course not.'

The local tradition had started many years ago. It originated at the bottom end of the town where the fishing community lived. After the hard work of Christmas Day, certain doughty fishermen's wives decided they deserved a day off. So, only cold meats, pickles and pork pies were laid out for their menfolk and the women dressed up and went out on the town with their female friends. Breaking tradition, many of them went into the pubs and ordered drinks. Usually the sole domain of the men, the public houses rang with orders for port and lemon and a nip of gin. Women started enjoying themselves. They roamed the streets, laughed and spoke in loud voices.

The men took fright. They stayed out of the pubs at the bottom of town. Deprived of their usual stamping ground, they devised another way of celebrating Boxing Day.

'We could go down to the beach and watch the Firemen's and Fishermen's Match?'

'Yes, let's do that.'

That was the fishermens' contribution to Boxing Day. An annual football match, played on the South Bay beach and keenly contested between the two teams, the fishermen and a team from the town's firefighters. It was now an established part of Scarborough's Boxing Day celebrations and a considerable amount of money was raised for charity. Over the years added attractions came along. A brass band played. People wore fancy dress. The amusement arcades opened for bingo enthusiasts and there was ice cream for sale if anyone wanted it. No matter what the weather, the Fishermen's and Firemen's match always took place, and this year, the weather was good.

'All right. We'll give it a go.'

June nodded and looked at Reg. 'We'd better leave him at home.'

Her decision was wise. The foreshore teemed with people. The dogs accompanying their owners looked miserable, kept on short leads and jostled by the passers-by. Two wild looking mongrels, obviously strays, were the only ones happy, frolicking around in the sea and fighting over an old fish head that might have been thrown from the fish pier.

Leaning on the iron railings, after the

match had finished, Richard watched them.

'God – they're actually eating it now.' He shuddered.

'Dogs aren't squeamish.' June grinned. 'You wouldn't be so fond of Reg if you knew what he's got up to sometimes.'

'Like what?'

'Well.' She reflected. 'He found a roaming stray chicken one day, at the top of the park where people used to have allotments. Remember?'

Richard nodded.

'It must have escaped from somewhere. Reg grabbed it, snapped its neck and ran all round the top of the park with its corpse flopping from his mouth. Then he sat down and pulled it to pieces. He ate most of it.'

'He didn't?' Richard looked appalled.

'He did. When he'd finished he ran back home with me in hot pursuit. I remember him galloping down the middle of the road, the cars screeching to a halt and him with the chicken's head lolling out of his mouth.'

June bit back a smile at Richard's expression. 'The worst thing was, there was a group of little girls with their teacher having a picnic in the park. They went hysterical. It was like a Hitchcock thriller.'

He shook his head. 'You're making me feel ill. Shall we make a move?'

'OK.' She fell in step with him. 'Let's call in for a drink on the way home. Nothing too fierce. Perhaps a shandy and a sit down.'

'Good idea.' Richard turned his head as the door of a public house opposite to where they were standing flew open and a group of about six females came out. They wore paper hats and were shouting and singing. 'We'll head up the main street though. I don't fancy sitting in the middle of a pack of noisy females.'

June's eyebrows rose. 'I can be noisy sometimes, Richard.'

'Not like them.'

'No.' She thrust her arm through his. 'But they're not doing any harm. They're just enjoying themselves.'

'I know.' He smiled at her. 'But you must admit they're raucous. I prefer women with soft voices, like yours.'

She shook her head. 'Don't put me on a pedestal. I've a temper and I can be loud when I lose it.'

'I won't. In fact,' he hesitated and then continued, 'I think you're just what I need. I am inclined to be a bit of a fuddy-duddy. I'm counting on you to alter that.'

She blushed. 'I'll have to think about it.'

They walked up the main street until June stopped.

'Let's go in here. It's a good pub with a nice atmosphere. I came here with girls from work some time ago for lunch.'

'Oh, I don't know, I...'

'Come on, Richard. It's nice.'

June pushed open the door and went in. Richard followed her, slowly. The pub was the Stafford Inn.

The bar was busy but not crowded. Bill Bretton was behind his counter. He must have spotted their entrance for his voice boomed out above the background chatter.

'Richard Argyle, as I live and breathe. Where've you been keeping yourself?'

Richard turned red.

June looked at him. 'You know him?'

He nodded and walked towards the bar.

As soon as he was close enough, the landlord reached over to shake Richard's hand. 'What happened to you? I've missed your company.'

Richard shrugged. 'Different things. You know how it is.'

Bill Bretton looked from Richard to June and smiled.

'Now I see. Well, it's grand to have you back. What can I get you?'

They ordered their drinks. As he poured them out, Bill asked them if they'd had a good Christmas.

June answered. 'Yes. Lovely.'

Richard was finding it hard to know what to say. He took the glass Bill passed to him and said, a little stiffly, 'How about you?'

'Can't complain.' Bill leaned his elbows on the bar. 'I'm quite pleased Christmas is over. Of course, we have New Year's Eve to contend with but, after that, we can get back to normal. I'll have a bit more time. Talking of which,' he lowered his voice. 'Richard, did you see an article in the *Observer* three days ago, about the latest fiasco in Brussels? Robert Sizer wrote it.'

'No. I did read...'

'Can we get a drink over here?'

Someone was shouting out an order.

'Sod it.'

Bill looked at June and apologised. He turned to serve the customer demanding attention, then he looked back. 'You'll be calling in again, Richard?'

'Yes.' Richard nodded. 'I'll be round in a couple of days' time.'

Bill nodded. 'That's great.'

A few people had left the pub and June spotted two empty chairs. They went to claim them. When she was seated, June asked: 'Are you friends? The landlord was obviously pleased to see you.'

Richard twisted his glass round in his hands.

'Yes. We were.' He looked up, deciding to come clean.

'A while ago, something happened. Bill let me down, quite badly, I thought, although now I come to think about it...'

His voice trailed away.

'What did he do?'

404

'Oh, it was nothing terrible. I just didn't want to call in here any more.'

'But now?'

'I feel differently.'

June sighed. 'No one's perfect, Richard. Don't you think...' she hesitated. 'Don't you think you set too high standards for people, including yourself?'

He stiffened. 'Can standards be too high?'

'Yes, they can.' June took his hand. 'A pub landlord's a busy man; maybe he forgot this particular thing you're talking about. I know I'm sticking my nose in something I know nothing about, but you have to admit, he was delighted to see you walk through that door.'

Richard drank from his glass and considered her words. 'Maybe you're right.' He touched her hand. 'I'll think about it. Now, let's have a change of subject.'

'All right. What?'

'My cleaning lady, Amy, has decided to retire.'

'Oh dear, is that a problem?'

Richard laughed. 'No, it's a blessing. She's a grand old lady but she drives me mad. She thinks she owns me body and soul. I'll want to keep an eye on her though.'

'Why, is she failing in health?'

'Not really. She started a support group to badger the council to give pensioners concessionary rates on the buses and the scheme's snowballed. She's getting involved in all kinds of things and now she's been approached to sit on a pensioners' action group committee. She says she hasn't time to clean for me any more.'

'Good for her.' June's brows drew together. 'But you'll need to find another cleaner.'

'Oh, that's no problem. I'll sort it out.' Richard leaned forward.

'But there's something else I want to discuss with you, and this is important.'

Oh, yes?'

'Yes.'

'What is it?'

'You've been working so hard, June and, as you know, I've had my problems,' Richard paused. 'I think we ought to take a holiday.'

'Really.' June's face lit up. 'That's a lovely idea.'

'I hoped you'd approve. The thing is, where would you like to go?'

'Oh, you pick. I've hardly travelled at all, wherever you choose will be OK with me.'

'Well, I did have one place in mind.'

She looked at him expectantly.

'What about Australia? We could fly to Sydney, stay there for a while and then go off and see more of the country. Maybe we could take a trip to the Barrier Reef? That's supposed to be worth a visit.'

She stared at him. 'Are you serious?'

'Of course.'

'Oh, that would be wonderful. I can't...' She choked.

He took her hands in his. 'There's no need to cry. I've mentioned it before...'

'Yes, but you suggested I went on my own and...'

'Well, now I think we should go together. What do you say?'

'I say yes. Thank you!'

She took a tissue from her bag and dried her eyes.

'Have you a passport?'

'Yes, but it's years old. I'll have to check it's not out of date.'

He nodded, then asked: 'There's one thing. What about Reg?'

'Reg?' She smiled. 'Oh, he'll be OK.'

'You're sure.'

'Yes. He went into kennels years ago and we worried about him, but when I went to collect him, he didn't want to leave. The owner had completely ruined him and it took me ages to take control again.'

They both laughed and then June's eyes refilled with tears.

'Richard, I don't deserve...'

'You do, June. Apart from making me wonderfully happy, you winkle me out of my shell. You make me do things. I need you. Look at today, I wouldn't have come in here without you.' His voice went husky. 'Really, you know, I can never thank you enough for changing my life.'

She gave him a tender look. 'You started doing it yourself, when you began to help your daughter.'

He lowered his head. 'Yes.'

'You're worrying about the letter, aren't you?'

'Not really.'

'You are, I can tell.' June lowered her voice. 'You had to tell her, Richard.'

'I know that.'

'She'll be in touch.'

'Will she? Can you imagine what a shock it will be for her?'

'At first, but then she'll be glad.'

Richard ran his hand over his face. 'I'm not so sure. I've deceived her for months. I can't expect anything, June. I don't deserve anything.'

'You do. You helped her find her mother.'

'Not really. She found Nina herself.' He sighed. 'I don't want to talk about it.'

June became quiet. They finished their drink and then made their way home.

At seven thirty that evening, the telephone rang. Richard was in the kitchen so June took the call.

It was a woman's voice. 'May I speak to Richard Argyle?'

'Of course.' June crossed her fingers. 'Who is it, please?' The caller told her.

'Just one moment.'

June lay down the phone and went to the door. There were tears prickling her eyes.

She shouted. 'Richard, there's a call for you.'

She heard his hurried footsteps. He burst through the kitchen door.

She took a deep breath. 'It's Helen. She said she wanted to speak to her father.'

The publishers hope that this book has given you enjoyable reading. Large Print Books are especially designed to be as easy to see and hold as possible. If you wish a complete list of our books please ask at your local library or write directly to:

Magna Large Print Books
Magna House, Long Preston,
Skipton, North Yorkshire.
BD23 4ND

This Large Print Book for the partially sighted, who cannot read normal print, is published under the auspices of

THE ULVERSCROFT FOUNDATION